RYAN

PART ONE

The Falling Series Book #1

TRACY LORRAINE

Edited by Pinpoint Editing

Proofreading by Luxe Literary Co.

Formatted by Dandelion Cover Designs

Cover design by Dandelion Cover Designs

To,
My biggest fan,
My best supporter,
My biggest inspiration,
My hero,
My best friend,
My mum.

You are missed every day. I wish you were here to see this x

Prologue

Molly

Eight years ago...

"**M**um, I'm going to Becky's sixteenth birthday party tonight, then sleeping at Hannah's," I remind her as I walk into the kitchen where she's sat with her head in an interior design magazine, waving her hands around—presumably trying to dry her nail varnish. I pull out a can of Coke from the fridge before continuing. "I've taken the litre bottle of vodka from the drinks cabinet, and I've got a pack of condoms...you know, just in case." I lean back against the counter and watch for a reaction. *Any* reaction.

"Uh huh."

"I'm pretty sure some of the boys are bringing ecstasy."

"Hmm..." She hums as she turns a page and studies the room pictured.

"Didn't you only have a manicure yesterday? Why are you painting your nails already?"

Now, that gets her attention. Her head snaps up the moment the words 'nails' and 'manicure' leave my mouth. Surprise, surprise; my mother cares more about that than about alcohol, drugs, sex...and me.

"Yes, I did, but I just couldn't find a thing to wear tonight."

I doubt that's actually true, seeing as she's recently turned my eldest brother's old room into her personal wardrobe after already filling her own walk-in. "So, I went to that little boutique in town this morning and found the most perfect dress. Your dad will love it, but it didn't match the colour I chose for my nails yesterday."

"Wow, what a disaster," I mutter as I leave the room. "I'll be going out in about an hour. *Not that you really care.*" I say the last bit quieter, but I'm not sure why; when I look back, Mum is once again too engrossed in her magazine to acknowledge me.

I let out a huge breath and head back up to my room to finish packing for the party. I'm getting ready with my best friend Hannah and her twin Emma, who live next door. We've all been friends for as long as I can remember. Being twins, Hannah and Emma are really close, but Hannah and I are not far behind. The three of us do almost everything together; their parents have often joked that they have triplets, really.

I always laugh along.

Even though they know what my life is like, I don't think any of them really appreciate how much I wish that were true.

I'm just shoving my fourth outfit choice for the night into my bag when I hear my brother downstairs, greeting Mum. She instantly responds to him, which makes me laugh to myself, although it's anything but funny. One of her golden boys has come to visit. I bet if he needed something, she'd ruin that new nail varnish in an instant. God, I can't wait to get out of this hellhole I call home.

"Is Molly still here?" Daniel asks.

Her reply sounds suspiciously like, "I have no idea."

Walking to the other side of the room, I rest my hands on the windowsill and blow out a long breath as I gaze out over the countryside, trying to calm myself down. I keep telling myself not to get worked up by their actions, but sometimes it's easier said than done.

"Hey sis, I'm glad you're still here," Daniel says as he enters my room a few minutes later. My brothers are a lot older than me; I was an unplanned accident fifteen and a half years ago. Daniel is my youngest older brother and, at thirty years old, he's crazy protective of me. Steven is, too, but he now has a serious girlfriend so I'm seeing less of him these days. Daniel is my idol—always has been. He doesn't take life too seriously, does exactly as he pleases, works bloody hard, but always has fun. That's exactly what I want my life to be like, and I plan on making it so—once I get out on my own.

"Hey." I only manage one word because, as soon as I see him, I burst into tears. He pulls me into a tight hug. I hate that Mum and Dad can do this to me. Can make me feel so worthless. It makes me angry every time a tear falls for their actions. I wish I could be stronger.

"What have they done now?" Daniel asks. Both he and Steven know how our parents treat me. Hell, I couldn't count the number of arguments I've overheard about it on both hands and feet, but nothing ever changes. I'm just grateful that I have two amazing older brothers to turn to if I need to. Plus, I have my adopted family next door, who I'm pretty sure would do just about anything for me if I needed it.

"Nothing. I'm fine," I say, pulling away from him and wiping my eyes. I look at him and see the questions in his. "No, really; I'm just being a silly, hormonal teenager."

"Hmm...whatever you say, Molls. You still going to that party tonight?" I don't believe for a second that he buys my lie, but he knows it's easier for me not to

4

discuss it. Nothing he can say is going to make any of it better, anyway.

"Of course, why?"

"I got you something." I watch as he reaches into his coat pocket and pulls out a small bottle of vodka before handing it to me.

"What's this for?" He looks at me and quirks an eyebrow. "I know it's to drink, you fool, but why are you giving it to me?"

"Because I remember what it was like being your age, and I didn't think anyone else would be buying you some. You deserve to act your age, Molly. Let your hair down. You work too damn hard trying to get your grades. But please be sensible. I don't want to be visiting you in the hospital or be an uncle yet. Actually..." He pauses as he reaches into his back pocket and pulls out his wallet.

My eyes widen in embarrassment. "No, no, no...I'm good, you don't need to worry about that."

I hate to admit it, but Daniel is the only one who knows what I've been up to. He let himself into my room one day while I was in my ensuite to find an open box of condoms on the bed and, being the protective brother that he is, counted them and realised two were missing. I'm hoping he doesn't want more of an explanation than that, because I really don't want to sit here and explain to my adult brother that I took myself off to the doctors a while ago and got myself on the pill— you know, just in case. Wouldn't that make Mummy and Daddy proud, to be grandparents while their daughter was still a teenager? Imagine the embarrassment.

"Okay, well, have a good time tonight, and ring me if you have any problems, yeah?"

"I promise."

I know I mentioned drugs and alcohol to my mum downstairs, but my group of friends isn't really into all that. I only said it as a way to provoke her in the hopes of getting some kind of reaction. Yes, there are plenty of kids at school who are at it every weekend, but my group actually cares about getting good grades and good jobs. The bottle of vodka Daniel just handed me will probably be it for us tonight.

"See you later then, kid," he says before kissing my forehead and leaving my room.

"THAT WAS AWESOME," Hannah squeals as the three of us stumble into the twins' bedroom sometime in the early hours of Sunday morning. Emma heads straight over to her side of the room and immediately starts replacing her party clothes with her pyjamas, while Hannah and I sit on her bed and reflect on the evening.

"So...come on, spill it...where did you go with Callum?" Hannah pleads.

"Just for a walk in the garden. I told you earlier!"

"I didn't believe you then, and I still don't now. I

saw you two getting off with each other in the corner before you disappeared."

Callum is the boy at school that every girl dreams of. He's sporty, clever, funny and, of course, seriously hot, which is exactly why no one expected him to show his face tonight. But he did, and let's just say that I got to know him a little better than I did before. I'm yet to decide if that's a good thing or not.

"Will you two keep it down? I want to get up early tomorrow to do some coursework before we go to Grandma's," Emma complains from her bed.

Okay, so I said before that we work hard to get good grades, but Emma takes it to the extreme. I was actually surprised she gave herself tonight off. She's doing A-level maths already and does Spanish lessons after school to get herself an extra GCSE. I think she's putting too much pressure on herself, but she can't seem to stop in her quest to be the best accountant Oxford has ever seen.

"Sorry," we whisper simultaneously.

"So...come on, Molly, tell me," Hannah says, keeping her voice low.

I let out a frustrated breath and go for it. "Okay, so we went outside and found a quiet corner in the garden behind a bush. He pulled me down to the ground and we kissed for a while and let our hands...roam a little." I look up at Hannah and can see her excitement about what might come next.

"Oh my God, did you have sex with him?" she asks,

but says the word *sex* much quieter. I don't know why; it's only Emma who could be listening.

"No, I didn't. I sorta thought we were going to, but by the time I got into his boxers, he was so worked up that he went off like a firework!" I can't help it, I burst out laughing at the memory, earning me another grumble from Emma.

"But I thought Callum's slept with loads of girls?" Hannah asks, confused.

"That's what the rumour mill says...I would be inclined to say that this was his first experience and the rumours are just that: rumours." We fall about giggling like the schoolgirls we are; I guess that vodka hasn't totally worn off yet.

"So, you *were* going to have sex with him, then?"

"Yeah, I guess," I say, shrugging my shoulders.

"But don't you want to wait until you're in love?" she asks innocently.

The only thing I have never told my best friend is that I lost my virginity last year at a party. Hannah has a different outlook on life thanks to her normal, loving family, and I don't want to have to explain my reasons for doing what I did that night—and a few times since. I totally understand her desire to wait until she's in love, and I admire her for it, but what I needed that night— what I *still* need—is to feel wanted by someone. And that first night? That was exactly how I felt.

One

Molly

Present

It's midnight, and I've been sat on Ryan's doorstep for nearly an hour. I've already started on one of the bottles of wine. Although it was a scorching summer's day, the heat has now worn off, the clouds have gathered, and it's lumping it down with rain. I'm trying to tuck myself into his little porch to stop from getting so wet, but with the wind direction, it's not doing much good. I'm soaked through. It was a silly idea to pick white t-shirts when I rebranded the coffee shop; thank God for padded bras!

By the time I'd cleaned and locked up, it was just gone ten. I love working at Cocoa's and have done so since I was sixteen. Hannah and Emma's parents own it. Susan started the business after she finished university. She came into some inheritance and, with the money, Cocoa's was born. The place was a huge part of my childhood. Hannah, Emma, and I would go there after school to do homework or just chat about boys, and it pretty much stayed that way until we finished university. We still have a booth in the back corner dedicated to us.

I will forever be grateful for Susan and her husband, Pete, whom she actually met as a customer in Cocoa's. It was love at first sight for them. Not only did they give me a job, but they took me under their wing when I was much younger.

Megan, who works in the evenings, had a phone call from her boyfriend at eight o'clock saying their little boy was really sick. I let her go home to be with him and finished up the rest of the night on my own.

Once I got in my car, all I could think about was having a nice hot bath and snuggling into bed in my tiny one-bed flat with my boyfriend, Max. We've been together on and off for the past three years, but when Hannah, whom I'd lived with above the coffee shop, decided eight months ago that she wanted her own boyfriend to move into the flat, I decided it was time I moved out and left them to it. Max had suggested I move in with him. I wasn't thrilled by the idea, to be honest, but at the time I didn't have the money to find anywhere decent to live. I hate being alone. I would have had to find someone who was renting out a room anyway, so it seemed like a sensible suggestion and a logical step in our relationship.

A week later, we all moved. Me into Max's flat, and Hannah's boyfriend into the one we'd shared for the past six years.

The ten-minute drive to our home seemed to take forever. I pulled up out the front; it was weird to be parking next to Max's car. He had worked nights the whole time I'd known him.

I dragged my body up the stairs to the third floor and let myself in. I shut the door behind me; the only light was coming from the bedroom. My heart dropped into my stomach when I heard voices and strange noises coming from down the hallway. As quietly as I could, I tiptoed towards them.

When I got to the door, I couldn't believe my eyes. Now, I knew Max was no angel, but I was under the impression that we had put the past behind us when we decided to live together and had become a monogamous couple. Yes, the past few months had been a strain, but still.

What was happening before my eyes on our bed showed me how wrong I was.

I numbly slipped back down the hallway and

grabbed a couple of pairs of knickers that, luckily for me, were drying on the radiator, and left.

I tried to keep myself together as I made a pit stop at the shop on my way to Ryan's house. I didn't want to be one of those emotional women sobbing in the alcohol aisle, trying to decide which bottle would make me forget.

Once I'd paid for two bottles of my favourite wine and a crate of lager for Ryan, I made my way over to his new house. He'd only moved in two weeks ago, although it was months ago that he made the decision to buy the three-story townhouse in the new development on the outskirts of the city. It was basically a pile of bricks when he took me with him to see it for the first time, but I could see why he'd fallen in love with it. It was modern and spacious, with amazing views across fields from the back. From the front, you could see all the lights from the city in the distance. Because it was yet to be finished, it meant Ryan could choose a lot of the interior to suit his taste, and he didn't have to spend his whole summer re-decorating.

Grabbing my phone, I open up my messages to re-read the conversation I'd had with him earlier. He said he was going out tonight to celebrate the end of the school year but that he wasn't expecting to be home late. I guess that didn't really go as planned—not that he'd be expecting me to be sitting here waiting for him.

I'm starting to think I should have gone somewhere

else. It's not that I don't have any other options, but out of all my friends and family, Ryan knows me the best.

What we've been through this year has made us close. I think I can safely say he's turned into my best friend somewhere in the last six months.

As I wait, images of what was happening on my bed flash though my head. I guess I should have seen it coming, really. A leopard never changes it spots, right?

Eventually, the tears come flooding out. To add to my misery, I now have black mascara streaks running down my cheeks and red puffy eyes.

Finally, I see headlights coming my way and Ryan's white Honda Civic pulling into his drive. At first, he looks shocked to see me. That changes to anger as he strides towards me.

Ryan

As I come to a stop, I can see that there's a very wet Molly huddled in my porch. She looks dreadful. I come to a very quick conclusion that it's because of her dick-head of a boyfriend. I knew it was coming; it was just a matter of when.

"Ryan," Molly sobs as I lift her tiny frame off the ground and into a hug. She shakes from both the cold and the sobs wracking her body.

Tucking her into my side, I grab her bags and let us in. On the ground floor, my townhouse has a large room with French doors looking out to the courtyard garden, and a bathroom. I thought it would make an excellent gym. The middle floor is an open-plan kitchen, living, and dining room with a small cloak-room, and the top floor has three bedrooms, one being the master with ensuite and the other a large family bathroom.

I love it.

From the moment I looked at the plans, I just knew it was going to be my little piece of heaven, and I'm still in awe that I was able to buy this place. I'll be forever grateful for the generous gift from Susan and Pete. Nothing will ever make up for what we all lost, but thanks to them, I've been able to attempt to move on with my life.

Currently, there are boxes everywhere. I haven't had much time to unpack with everything I had to do at school to end the year, but my first holiday job is to get this place sorted and looking like a home.

Anger fills my veins as I lead us up to the living room. "It's going to be okay. Let's get you warm and dry and you can tell me what the fucker did." My fists clench. I want to beat the shit out of him for treating her so badly for so long.

"How do you know he's done anything?" Molly asks in a quiet voice.

"I can read you like a book, Molly Carter. Plus, he's

a massive dickhead. I think I've mentioned that before. Only Max can make you feel this bad about yourself."

"Why was I so fucking stupid? I had my doubts, everyone had their doubts, but he convinced me that it was what he wanted. I'm not really surprised, but what does shock me is how much it *hurts*."

"Come on, get your arse upstairs and in the shower. I'll find you a t-shirt to wear."

As I ROOT through a suitcase in one of the spare bedrooms, the door to my ensuite shuts. I pull out my Oxford Brookes polo and leave it on my bed. I hope my choice will make her smile, remembering happier times.

I knock lightly on the door. "Have you got everything you need?"

There's silence for a few seconds, and I can imagine her checking out all the products in the shower, realising they're all for men. Eventually, I hear a quiet "Yes" from the other side of the door.

"Okay, I'll see you downstairs when you're done. Take your time."

I gather up her wet clothes and take them with me. They may be soaked, but I can still smell her vanilla scent on them. It makes me feel oddly warm inside. She's been my rock for the past six months. I don't know what I would have done without her.

As I put everything in the washing machine, I spot her bra poking out of the pile. "What the fuck do I do with this?" I mutter to myself. Something in me wonders if it needs some kind of special cycle in the machine, but fuck if I know. I decide to shove it all in and just put it on a cool, quick wash.

That shouldn't do it much damage, right?

Two

Molly

I stand in the giant, walk-in shower for a good twenty minutes, letting the hot water from the rainfall showerhead soothe my aching muscles.

I could get used to this.

Once I'm finished, I head back into the bedroom and see Ryan's white Oxford Brookes University t-shirt on his bed. I smile for the first time in what feels like forever and pull it over my head. He was wearing this the first night we all met in the student union.

Ryan's also placed my handbag on the bed, obviously knowing from the size of it that there must be something in there I could use, and he would be right. I pull out a hairbrush and try to do something with my hair after not finding any conditioner in the shower. I spritz my favourite perfume and pull on a pair of the knickers I grabbed earlier, feeling very grateful that I don't have to go commando under his t-shirt.

Once I feel almost human again, I head downstairs to where I know there's a big glass of wine waiting for me.

I walk into the open plan living area to find Ryan leaning his hip against the kitchen worktop with his feet crossed, staring closely at his phone. He's changed since he got in and is now wearing long, slouchy navy shorts that hang low on his hips and a fitted white t-shirt that shows off his wide shoulders, slim waist, and muscled chest and arms to perfection. His dirty blonde hair is a mess, as if he's spent the whole time I was in the shower running his hands through it. I've always found Ryan attractive—well, who wouldn't? He's stunning. And his Scouse accent...It's diluted since he first moved to Oxford, but it isn't any less sexy. But he's not my type; I tend to go for slimmer guys with less muscle, although I still remember trying to hit on him the night we met. I kept trying and trying, making a total fool of myself. I was too drunk to realise he was paying no attention to me but was besotted with my best friend. Good times.

His head comes up as I move towards him and his eyes travel slowly from the top of my head to my toes and back again while his teeth attack his bottom lip.

"Everything all right?" I ask, trying not to smirk.

"Um...yeah...sorry, it's just that it's...um...it's been a while, you know," he stutters as his cheeks turn a little pink.

"Yeah, I know what you mean," I mumble to myself more than him. "Plus, I dare any man not to check out my legs." I'm hoping to lighten the mood; I don't want him to be embarrassed. We both know we can never go there, but a harmless bit of looking is fine.

Ryan mutters something under his breath as he turns around to grab my wine.

"What was that?"

"Fuck...uh...the bloody woman next door is staring again. Look." He gestures to the kitchen window and I just see a flash of red hair as she scarpers.

"She's probably just enjoying her few seconds of man-candy."

He shudders before turning back to me. "Your clothes are on a quick wash. They'll be done soon and we can get them drying. I'm guessing they're the only clothes you have with you?"

I follow Ryan into the living room and curl myself up in the middle of his corner sofa with my wine, making myself comfortable.

"All my stuff is in the flat."

"What happened tonight?" Ryan asks. "Fuck, he wasn't with someone else, was he?"

"It's worse than that." My stomach turns over as I picture it again. Watching Ryan's eyebrows rise in question, I continue. "There was one blonde bimbo riding his cock and another sat on his face."

"I'm going to rip his fucking head off. How could he do that to you? And in your fucking bed? He must have known you were going to be home soon. Fuck, I'm going to fucking kill him. I always told you he wasn't good enough for you. I told you this would happen and that you would get hurt."

He paces back and forth in front of me, his hands alternating between running through his hair and clenching into fists at his sides. The muscles in his neck pulse with anger.

I can't help but think Max should be watching his back, because it's going to fucking hurt when Ryan gets his hands on him.

"What did you do?" he asks through gritted teeth.

"I left."

Draining his can of beer, he's silent before going to get a second.

"Can I have a refill, too?" I ask, realising I've drunk my way through my glass telling that story.

Ryan comes back with the bottle and fills me up before placing it on the coffee table and opening his beer. "So, what are you going to do? I guess he doesn't know he's been caught?"

"I have no idea. All I can think about is how stupid I am. Oh, and how when I decide where I'm going to live, I want a shower like yours."

Ryan doesn't look amused by my comment; his eyes urge me to continue.

"You can stop worrying. I'm not going back to him. I never should have moved in with him in the first place."

"You and Max have never had the type of relationship that would end up being something serious, and you knew it; you were just too scared to get out of it. You don't go from fucking about with Max while screwing others to living together and being in a committed relationship."

"All you had to say was 'I told you so'. I don't need a big lecture," I snap, tears pricking my eyes. Ryan pulls me into his chest, rubbing my back.

"Shit, I'm so sorry. I didn't mean to upset you," he whispers in my ear.

My tears eventually cease and I lift my head off Ryan's chest. Looking up into his blue eyes, all I see is compassion. There's no pity at all, which makes my heart a little happier.

I throw my arms around his shoulders and hug him tight. This was why I came here tonight—for my best friend, who will tell me exactly what I need to hear and exactly what I don't want to hear, to pull me out of the rut I have found myself in.

Ryan

"I HATE to break the moment, but I really have to wee," I say into Molly's hair. I feel her shake her head against my neck and it makes me laugh. Standing with her in my arms, I place her back on the sofa before heading out of the room.

When I come back down, I find her pulling her clothes out of the washing machine. "You washed my black jeans with my white top and underwear; how is it possible that you've been living on your own for years, yet you still do that?" She has a deadly serious look on her face, making me laugh.

"Sorry. I was more concerned with what I was meant to do with your bra than about separating the colours. It's like an alien creature to me...is it meant to have its own cycle? Extra special treatment or something?" I comment, trying to sound as serious as she had.

It's her turn to start laughing. It warms my heart to see her happiness after all the misery we've been through. She actually laughs so hard that she has to hold on to the worktop for support.

"You're serious, aren't you?"

I just shrug my shoulder and head back in to the living room, saying over my shoulder, "It's a drier as well, but I'll let you handle that."

"Thank you. It's probably safer; I need something

to wear tomorrow and I'd prefer if it didn't fit a doll," she smiles.

Following me, she helps herself to my iPad and unlocks it.

"What are you doing?" I ask with a laugh as she settles herself at the coffee table.

"I want to start looking for a place to live. I don't want to cramp your style. You've only just moved in; you don't need me in the way."

The thought of her moving somewhere new on her own doesn't sit well with me. I know she hates solitude and would rather live with someone—which is how she ended up living with dickhead Max, after all.

I make a snap decision, but I know it's the right one. "Molly..."

"Yeah," she says without looking up from the screen.

"Molly," I try again to make her look up at me. It works this time, and her eyes eventually meet mine.

"Move in here, with me. You can have the room and bathroom downstairs. You'd have your own space, and your snoring won't keep me awake at night from two floors away." Her eyes widen in shock as she stares at me, processing my words.

"Um..."

I sit and wait. The house is so quiet, I can almost hear the cogs turning in her brain as she contemplates what to say next and whether to take me up on my offer. Eventually, I get bored of waiting.

"This house is too big for me, really. It's so quiet here. The rent will be cheaper than a place of your own, and I'll let you decorate your room however you want." God, I hope she won't take me up on that and paint it Barbie pink or anything crazy. She's still silent. "Molly, tell me what you're thinking."

All of a sudden, she's off the floor and practically running for the stairs.

"Shit!" I get up and run after her. "Molly, come back! You can't leave the house wearing that. Molly!" I shout as I chase her down the stairs.

When I reach the bottom, I realise she has no intention of leaving.

She's stood amongst all the boxes and crap in the downstairs room I've just offered her. She looks back at me, tears in her eyes. Great, I've made her cry again.

"Are you sure? This was going to be your gym. I don't want to take that away from you. You bought this house for peace and quiet. It won't be so peaceful with me around, and definitely not quiet. Do you really mean it?"

"If I wasn't sure, I wouldn't have asked. I have two more spare rooms upstairs that could be my gym. What do *you* want? What would make *you* happy, Molly Carter?"

I watch her closely as she studies her hands and nails, trying to work out what she wants. She opens her mouth to speak and, when it comes out, it's so quiet I almost miss it. "I want this."

"I'm sorry, Molly, you'll have to speak up. What did you say?"

This time, she looks up. The tears are still in her eyes, but I can tell the decision has been made. "I want this. I want to move in." With that, she launches herself at me from across the room with such force that I have to take a step back to stop us toppling over when I catch her.

"Thank you so much, Ry. You have no idea how happy this makes me. I'll be the best housemate ever, I promise. This is it...a new start for me from this day forward. I'm going to do things for me, because I want to, not because anyone else wants or expects me to."

We make our way back upstairs, and I start thinking of all the things we need to do to get us both properly moved in. "When do you want to collect your stuff from the flat?" It should be done as soon as possible so she can put Max behind her.

"Well, he's going out for his mate's birthday tomorrow night. Usually, they're out all night, so I could go then."

"I'm not letting you go alone. Firstly, you'll have to do loads of trips in that roller skate of a car you have, and secondly, just no. I'm coming with you."

"Ryan, you don't have to do that. You've already done more than I could ask of you."

"Okay, how about...Shut up; this isn't up for discussion. What time is he going out, and what time should we head over?"

"You know you're a stubborn arse, right?"

Laughing, I shrug my shoulders at her in response.

"If we go over for seven, he should be well gone by then. That will give us plenty of time to make sure I have everything."

We return to the sofa and Molly pulls the blanket over our legs, settling back into the cushions. "How is it that you've hardly unpacked anything yet, but you have a blanket over the back of your sofa?"

Usually, I would agree with her. It is unusual, but it was the first thing Hannah and I bought after we moved in together. We had many amazing nights together sat under this thing, and it might make me sound like a pussy, but I wanted it here with me in my new house. I wanted a little bit of her with me.

"I can tell by that look on your face. It's Hannah's, isn't it?"

"Yes, it is, but tonight, we're not talking about all that. We're being happy and celebrating you moving in."

"That sounds like a plan, Mr Evans. Chuck the remote over; we need music if we're celebrating."

With that, the sounds of old school hip-hop and R&B fill the room and I groan.

"What?" Molly asks, an innocent look on her face.

"I'd forgotten about your love of this 'music'. Maybe I should have considered that before asking you to move in."

But Molly is already up, dancing around the room with the last of her wine.

In this moment, she looks happy and carefree like all twenty-four-year-olds should. I want her to be like this more. She deserves to be like this more. Hell, we both do after the grief we've been battling for almost six months.

Pain rips through me at the thought of it being that long already. Everything has changed so much and Hannah hasn't been here to experience any of it.

As one song drifts into another, I notice the beat of the songs get more and more sexy—as do Molly's dance moves. She's grinding her hips around and around. I can't help but notice how fucking sexy she is. It's been a long time since I've seen any action and, although my brain knows nothing will ever happen between us, apparently my dick didn't get the message. Thank god for the blanket.

A little bit of guilt washes through me, but I manage to push it to one side.

"Come on, Ry, dance with me," she slurs and gives me her 'come hither' look. *Fuck, don't do that.*

"No, you're okay. I'm fine here, watching."

As the next song comes on, she waves her hands above her head, making my t-shirt rise, revealing the bottom of red lacy knickers that are cut high across her arse—her tight, perky arse.

After another couple of songs with me looking in any direction other than Molly, she starts to stumble around to the point where I think she's going to be on that pretty little arse pretty soon.

"Molly, I think it's time you sat down before you fall down."

"Oooohhhh cooome on...dooon't be a spoil spoort," she slurs as she trips over the coffee table and ends up lying face-down on the sofa.

All of a sudden, she flips herself over with a pout, mumbling about how she can't remember when she last had so much fun, got drunk and danced the night away.

I wasn't going to ruin it by telling her she was only dancing for about thirty minutes, because I can't remember the last time I saw her smile like this.

Eventually, she stops chatting crap and her breathing evens out. I look at the clock and realise it's nearly four in the morning; no wonder she's asleep. I quietly tidy up our mess before scooping her up in my arms and carrying her to my bedroom. Currently, this is the only bed in the house, so until we go shopping, she'll be here with me. I'm not letting her have a bad night's sleep on the sofa.

I tuck her in before stripping down to my boxers and sliding in next to her. I have a super king-sized bed, so it will be easy to sleep together and not even realise there's someone else here.

As soon as my head hits the pillow, I'm out like a light.

Three

Molly

I wake up with a start, trying to work out where the hell I am. It takes a couple of seconds for the fog to lift before I realise I'm in Ryan's bed. "Shit," I mumble as my hands dive under the covers to see what I'm wearing—if anything.

I'm relieved to find I'm still in his t-shirt and I still have underwear on. I know I shouldn't be concerned—this is Ryan I'm talking about, after all. The last thing I remember is dancing around the living room and wondering why he has such a weird look on his face.

I bolt upright in bed when he appears at the door, smiling and saying, "Good morning," way too loudly.

It's then that I realise quite how rough I feel, and I slowly lie back down to try to ease the ache in my head.

"Oh dear, you feeling that good?"

My answer is to glare at him.

"Here, I've brought you water and painkillers. I thought you might need them."

"Thank you," I say in a really croaky voice that makes me laugh to myself. "Why am I in your bed? I don't want you sleeping on the sofa in your own house."

"After you passed out on the sofa, I went to bed, but before I could fall asleep you came in here begging me for sex," he says very seriously.

"Oh God," I say, shaking my head. "You're joking, right? I never did that!" I feel my face get redder and redder and I pull the covers up to hide myself.

"You'll be pleased to know I turned you down. It was tough when you started begging, but I stayed strong."

With that, I totally disappear under the covers, hiding my embarrassment from him. "Oh my God, I'm so sorry. I was really drunk; can you leave the room so I can just sneak out of your house? You'll never have to see me again," I squeak from my hiding place.

"Molly, don't say that."

"Oh, that's fine for you to say. You're not the one mortified by your drunken actions."

"Molly, look at me." He tries to pull the covers from me but I'm clinging to them for dear life. I hear him move to the bottom of the bed and, from there, he peels them back over my head. I immediately cover my face with my hands to hide how embarrassed I am, but I keep my fingers apart enough so I can see him.

After a few seconds of looking at me, he apparently can't contain himself any longer and bursts into laughter. Not just any laughter, but the kind that has him doubling over in pain. Tears fill his eyes, he's laughing so hard, and I make sure to have an unimpressed expression on my face.

Making a grab for a pillow, I launch it at his head, causing him to fall nose-first onto the floor, making his eyes water even more. One hit is not enough for what he just did to me, so I launch a full-on attack.

Eventually, my sense of humour starts to take over, and I'm laughing along with him, and *at* him, seeing as he's now curled up on the carpet, rolling around and holding his nose.

When my side starts hurting, I give up and sit on the end of the bed. He pulls himself up and settles on the floor in front of me. Laughing after everything feels so damn good.

"I'm sorry, it was just too good an opportunity to miss," he says to me, still smirking.

"How long have you been planning that?" I ask him seriously.

"Oh, since I got up about two hours ago."

"You're a dick—you know that, right?"

"I'm sorry." He puts his hands up in surrender. "Now, get your arse in that bathroom and get ready.

We've got a lot to do today. I've already put your dry clothes in there so you can get dressed. Meet me in the kitchen—I'll have breakfast ready."

Ryan leaves the room and I make my way into his ensuite after taking the painkillers he left for me. It takes me a few minutes to realise what he's done, but when I do, I completely forget about his 'joke' this morning. Not only are my dry clothes in a neat pile on the unit, but there's a new toothbrush and a can of women's deodorant next to them. When I look in the shower, I see new bottles of shampoo and conditioner— nice, girly pink ones. There's also a new shower gel, a pink shower puff, and even a pink razor. My eyes start to fill with tears as I take everything in. He may have been up for a couple of hours, planning how to most embarrass me on our first day as housemates, but he's also done this. I don't think anyone has ever done anything so sweet for me before.

While I'm in the shower, I realise what I need to do. This is my first day putting myself first. I need to ring my friend Shane and call in a favour.

Looking at the time on my phone, I realise that it's already nearly midday on his busiest day of the week. I don't expect him to answer, but as I put my phone to my ear, I'm surprised to hear his voice after the first ring.

"Hey, how's our number one groomsmaid?" Shane asks, making me smile. I first met Chris, now Shane's fiancé, at university. He was studying the same graphic design course that Hannah and I were. We all hit it off straight away and he soon became our gay best friend. Then, not long after, he met Shane and fell crazy in love and, well, as they say, the rest is history.

"I need to call in that favour you owe me. Can you fit me in today? I'll explain everything if you can squeeze me in."

"Lucky for you, my last appointment of the day rang in sick, so I'm free after three o'clock this afternoon."

"Thank you so much. I'll see you then. By the way, we're going for a change."

After Shane hangs up, I do that really embarrassing girly clap and jump up and down thing. I'm grateful no one can see me. I'm so excited that I'm going to start the new me off with a bang.

Once I'm ready, I head downstairs. Ryan must have heard me coming because, when I turn the corner, he takes a teabag out of a mug and slides it across the breakfast bar to me. I ignore the tea for now and go straight to Ryan, throwing my arms around his neck.

"Am I forgiven?" he asks cautiously.

"I can't believe you did all that for me. When did you have time?"

"I woke up early and went for a run. I'm still experimenting with routes around here, but I came across a shop on my way back and thought you could do with some girly shit when you woke up. I also got breakfast," he adds, motioning to the fresh croissants and pains au chocolat on the breakfast bar.

"Yum. I think I'm going to enjoy living here," I say as I round the breakfast bar and perch myself on the stool. "So, what's your plan for the day?" I ask Ryan, hoping that whatever he says doesn't involve me, because I already know what I need to do today, and it needs to be on my own.

"Well, we're going to get your stuff tonight at seven, right?"

"Yes. What about the rest of the day?"

"There isn't that much of it left now, really, is there?" he says sarcastically.

"Just because some of us actually need beauty sleep to look good..."

He smiles before he continues. "I need to get your room cleared out so we have somewhere to put your stuff later. What about you?"

"I've got a few things I need to do."

"Do you have any furniture to move in downstairs?"

That makes me realise how little I do have. "No," I answer sadly.

"Okay. Cancel any plans you have for tomorrow. We're going furniture shopping."

"I've never decorated a room before. I can't wait."

"What? Even when you were a kid?" Ryan asks, sounding shocked.

"No, my mum used to get an interior designer to

redo the house every five years or so. It was always the latest fashion at the time. Susan and Pete had the flat above Cocoa's refurbished before we moved in, and Max had been living in his place for a while and liked it the way it was; he didn't want any 'girly shit' around."

"Right, well, here's your chance. You'd better get thinking."

AFTER BREAKFAST, I say goodbye to Ryan and head out, promising I'll be back about six. I'm not looking forward to returning to the flat. Last night already seems like a lifetime ago, but it will be good to close the door on that part of my life and move on.

As I drive down the street I grew up on, I make sure not to slow down in front of my parents' house. It's not like I expect them to be on the look-out. Dad will be working and Mum will be socialising with Oxford's elite somewhere. I have hardly any good memories of that house, and I don't intend on making any now. As I pull into the Morrisons' driveway, however, I begin to smile. I love this house, the people inside, and all the memories I have of growing up here.

"Hello," I shout as I walk in. I'm considered family here, so I haven't knocked on the front door in years.

"In the kitchen," Susan calls back. It's not like I expected them to be anywhere else; they all live in there. They have the homiest house I've ever been in.

It's the total opposite of next door. That was like a show home; I always felt like I was making the place untidy by just being there.

"Hey," I say, smiling as I walk into the room. Susan pulls me into a hug, followed by a kiss on the cheek from Pete. Declan and Lilly are back from university and sitting at the table, finishing their lunch. They both wave and smile around their food. Susan and Pete weren't just lucky enough to have one set of fraternal twins, but two. Apparently, it's genetic. Susan's mum was a twin and so was her grandmother. No one ever expected Susan to carry two sets, though. That was a shocking announcement a little over nineteen years ago. The younger twins are now at university. Lilly is close by in Cheltenham, studying interior design, but Declan decided to go further afield to Exeter to study business. They're both back for the summer, and I can tell by the smile on Susan's face that she loves having her babies home. She had serious empty nest syndrome when they first went; she's such a mother hen.

"Do you want anything to eat, angel?" Susan asks me. She's always called her children 'angel' and, from a young age, that included me. That's why, in the end, Hannah and I decided to name our company Angel Designs. We very quickly decided we were not having any obvious imagery: no halos, wings, or fairy-tale stuff. We went for more of an angels-with-dirty-faces approach. Our logo ended up being black and greys with a splash of magenta. The font we chose was edgy, but it worked for us. We loved it—well, I still do.

"No, I'm fine, thank you. A cup of tea wouldn't go amiss, though," I say with a smile. There's always tea in the pot at this house.

"Of course. You sit down and I'll bring it over."

After a few minutes, all five of us are sat around the table, catching up with each other. I love these moments; I never had them with my family.

"So, Molly, how's Max?" Lilly asks me.

"Ah, well, that's sort of one of the reasons I'm here. It's over, I've left—"

"Thank God for that," Susan butts in.

"Susan," Pete scolds.

"Oh, angel, I'm sorry, but I never liked him. He wasn't good enough for you. He didn't treat you well."

"You're right. I knew it was never going to work. I never loved him, and I know I deserve better. And you know what? I'm going to get it. Today is the first day of the rest of my life."

"Good for you, angel," Susan says, putting her arm around my shoulders.

"So, where are you going to live?" Pete chimes in.

"Well, that's another thing, I—"

"I'll go make up the spare room," Susan butts in again. God, I love her; she doesn't even bat an eyelash about taking care of me like one of her own.

"Thank you, but that won't be necessary. Actually, Ryan has asked me if I'll move into his place."

"I think that's a great idea. We know how much you two have helped each other this year. It will be good to have each other close by," Pete says, nodding his head.

"I'm really excited. He's taking me furniture shopping tomorrow and letting me decorate my room however I want. I've never done that before." I try to ignore the slight twinge in my stomach. Am I betraying Hannah by moving into his house? It's easy to put it to one side when her parents are so encouraging of it.

"Good for you," Susan says, smiling.

"Is Emma around?" I ask. Since the accident, Emma seems to have become the opposite of a recluse. She's never home, but no one knows where she is. She's not always at work, because Susan has rung them before now to speak to her. She's only working part-time, but she won't tell us where she goes or what she does, other than work. I've only seen her a few times, and she rarely replies to messages or answers her phone. I can't imagine how hard losing Hannah must have been for her, but we're all worried.

"She went out earlier this morning," Susan says sadly.

"I'll try to catch up with her to let her know I've moved. Thanks for the tea, but I've got to go and sort out 'new Molly'," I explain.

After we've all said our goodbyes, I jump in my car and head to my next destination. It's now nearly two o'clock, so I don't have much time before I need to be at

Shane's, but lack of time has never stopped me before. I pull into a parking space behind my favourite department store and head inside.

After only fifty minutes, I return to my car with my arms full of bags. Operation: New Molly is well underway.

———

AFTER SPENDING a couple of hours being pampered by one of my closest friends, I'm in a great mood.

Shane wasn't at all surprised by what I wanted done; he said he saw it coming. He had texted Chris to say I was going to be there, so not long after I sat down, he arrived to hear the gossip first-hand and to check that I was okay.

I'm now leaving the salon a new woman. Gone are my long blonde locks in favour of shorter, rich chocolate brown waves with a full fringe. I realised after seeing the blonde bimbos last night that Max had managed to influence my appearance. He was always dropping hints about how hot he thought blondes were and how good I looked with blonde hair. It wasn't until I saw myself in the mirror this morning that I realised how much I actually disliked it, and how bad the shape of my hair was after all the bleach. I decided to return to something more natural, have my fringe back, and cut the length to where the swell of my breasts start.

After Shane had finished blow-drying, I asked him

if he would put on the make-up I'd bought earlier. As well as getting a couple of new outfits, underwear, shoes, and a couple of other bits for my new room, I'd visited my favourite make-up stand and asked for products for my new look. My old gray eye make-up is no longer, and in its place are pallets of purples, teals, and pastels to make my eyes really stand out under my new fringe. I showed Shane what I was going to change into, seeing as I was still wearing my work uniform from the day before, and he decided on the teal eye shadow pallet to go with the flowers in the loose-fitting sleeveless blouse and the bows on the high-heeled court shoes. Team those with new dark blue skinny jeans and I felt like a million pounds.

I said thank you along with my goodbyes to Chris and Shane, promising I'd be around soon to help with all the wedding planning, and I left. I had one more stop to make before going home.

It's early evening when I make my way through the front door, dragging everything I've bought with me to find Ryan topless and about to pick up a box from my room. I let out an involuntary moan at the sight. The muscles in his broad shoulders and down his back ripple as he moves.

My moan must have been louder than I thought. Ryan's attention turns to me, revealing the front of his torso in the process. This time, I manage to control myself, but I can't help but rake my eyes over his pecs and ripped six-pack, and then follow the V that disappears into his loose jogging bottoms. The light sheen of sweat on his body only increases the definition he has.

Oh, fuck me slowly, that's one seriously hot body.

When my eyes make it back up to his face, I see his hair is a mess and falling all over his forehead—but what I really notice is how wide his eyes are as he stares at me.

"Holy shit," I hear him say under his breath as he runs his eyes all over my body. I start to tingle from his attention.

I realise I need to say something to break the atmosphere we've managed to create. "So, I take it you like my new look?" I ask, raising an eyebrow. He shouldn't be looking at me like he is right now. A wave of guilt washes through me as reality hits.

"Holy shit," he says again. He shakes his head like he's trying to get control of himself. "You look...I mean...you look...don't get me wrong, you were gorgeous before, but with the new hair, you look stunning. Shit, seriously hot. I hope that dickhead wakes up one day and realises what he's missing without you, Molls."

I don't really know how to respond to that. Ryan and I have always been very open with each other. My relationship with him hasn't been much different to what I have with Chris and Shane in that we knew we'd never end up in bed with each other, so there has never been any awkwardness or sexual tension between us.

Until now.

"Thank you," I say quietly as I break our eye contact. I feel a weird loss as I look away from him and into the room—*my* room—that's practically empty. "Wow, this is much bigger than I thought when all the boxes were in it. I bet you can rent a flat the size of this in the city for silly money. Talking of money, I'm paying half of everything," I say firmly.

"No fucking way. You can just pay half the bills," he argues.

"I can't do that. I'm living in your home, I need to pay my way. How about half the bills and a third of your mortgage each month?"

"I didn't ask you to move in here for my financial gain, Molly. I asked you because I want you here. I couldn't care less if you stay for free."

"I know that, but it isn't happening. You know me better than that, Ry."

"Half the bills and a quarter of the mortgage," he counters.

"Right, fine. Work out how much it is. Do you want it in cash or transferred into your bank account?"

"You're not going to argue? Cash would be good; I can do the food shopping with it."

"That will be split as well, mister."

"Right, okay. Give me cash, and I'll hide it under

my mattress for a rainy day. Is that better?" he asks, sounding exasperated.

"Yes, much." Thanks to my parents, I have money, and if I can use it to help him out, I will. I will just have to find subtle ways to do it so he doesn't notice.

Ryan then sees all the bags around my feet, where I dropped them when he turned around. "Wow, you've been busy. New hair, and it looks like a new wardrobe in those bags. What are the suitcases for? You going somewhere?" he asks, eyeing the bright pink and purple flowered cases next to me.

"No, I realised I don't have anything to pack my clothes in, and I thought they would come in handy." God, a holiday would go down so well right about now. Sun, sea, relaxing on a beach. Heaven!

Ryan comes towards me, I guess to grab my bags but, as he gets closer, he stops. "Have you been crying? Your eyes are a little red." Wow, it looks like I won't be keeping any secrets from him; he was right last night about being able to read me like a book.

"I stopped at the graveyard to see Hannah on the way home. Told her about everything," I explain, hoping he understands.

"I get it. I actually went earlier myself." With that, he leans in, kisses my forehead, grabs my stuff, and places it in my room. He gets hold of the last box and heads upstairs. "I'll be ready in fifteen," he says as he disappears.

I stand in the middle of my new room, looking

around. I'm so grateful Ryan and I seem to be on the same page for most things. I was dreading him asking me about my visit to Hannah, but he just gets it—so much so that he went as well. I wonder how similar his conversation was to mine.

RYAN FINDS me a little over ten minutes later, sat cross-legged in the middle of my room with a stack of home magazines in my lap. I tried ringing Emma to tell her about leaving Max and moving here, but my call immediately went to voicemail. I shouldn't be surprised, but I hate how she's shut herself off. "What?" I ask when he starts to laugh.

"I just didn't think you'd take this whole decorating thing so seriously."

"I want it to be perfect. I'm thinking shabby chic."

"I'm sorry, shabby what?" he asks, confused.

"Shabby chic. It's a style. Sort of old fashioned, soft pastel colours and really homey. Here, look, like this." I get up and show him the page I was looking at.

"Right, okay. Come on, Miss Molly, get your shoes on and let's get this over and done with."

THIRTY MINUTES LATER, we're pulling up in Ryan's car to the flat I shared with dickhead Max, as he's now seemingly called. His car is here, but all the lights are off. "Oh God, I hope he's not at it again," I muse quietly.

"If he is, by the time I've finished with him, he won't be able to do it again," Ryan growls from the driver's seat.

I love the security of having someone defend me like that.

With a reassuring smile, Ryan jumps out of the car and grabs my suitcases before heading towards the flat. He must be able to sense my hesitation because he reassures me that it will be okay.

We've been at the flat for just over an hour, and we have all the rooms but the kitchen cleared of my things. I'm double-checking everything when I hear a crash in the kitchen. I go running in to find Ryan standing there with a murderous look on his face and a hole in the plasterboard. "What the fuck happened?" I question.

"Sorry, it just made me so fucking mad."

"What did?"

"This..." Ryan points to a used condom on the kitchen worktop.

"Oh." Tears start to well in my eyes. If I ever needed proof that Max wasn't faithful, here it is.

"Molly, come here," Ryan says as he pulls me into his arms. Blowing out a slow breath, I try to keep my emotions in check.

After we finish packing my cooking stuff, we leave the flat. I'm confident that we have everything, although Ryan looks a little unsure, as there are only two suitcases and three boxes.

"I thought you loved shopping?" he asks me as we leave. "How come you only have this much stuff?"

"I had a clear-out when I moved in here. This is all I have."

We drive home in silence, Ryan's anger obvious from his white-knuckle grip on the steering wheel. I feel sick after discovering my entire relationship with Max was a joke. It only adds to the grief and guilt I already feel about moving into Ryan's home.

Four

Ryan

I hear a moan behind me and turn around. I almost can't believe what I'm seeing. It's Molly, but fucking hell, she looks like every man's wet dream. Her dark brown hair rests just on top of her breasts, and she's wearing a blouse unbuttoned enough to give me a cheeky peek of her cleavage. Her legs and arse are shown off nicely in a pair of skin-tight dark jeans. And the shoes...fuck me, the shoes are so sexy. When I eventually meet her eyes, their normal chocolate colour is almost black, and the way she's looking at my half-exposed body makes me think she wants to run her tongue over every line and muscle visible. My cock twitches.

"Molly." My voice comes out as a groan as I make my way to stand in front of her. In her high heels, the top of her head comes in line with my chin, not to the middle of my chest like normal. She's staring straight into my eyes, and I can't help but think that she wants this as much as I do. I watch as she slowly leans her head to the side and moves forward until her lips softly brush mine. My dick hardens in response to her simple touch.

Then, it's as if our control snaps at the same time. All of sudden, our mouths crash together and our tongues touch for the first time. Her hands thread through my hair as mine go to her arse to pull her body against mine. She moans as I run my hands up her sides and gently brush the underside of her breasts, causing her to suck on my tongue. God, how I want her to do that to something else. My mouth leaves hers as I trail kisses across her jaw and down her neck.

"Ryan," I hear her whisper. My hands unbutton her blouse as I suck on her earlobe. I'm dying to get a taste of her nipples.

"Ryan," she groans again as I slip her blouse off and my hands go to her back to release her bra. "Ryan." She's getting louder now, and her chest is rising and falling in excitement.

"Oh, Molly." I slide the straps over her shoulders, preparing myself for what's to come. I'm so turned on, I don't want to cum in my pants like a teenager at just the sight of her perfect tits.

"Ryan." My eyes travel from her eyes down to her exposed...

"Ryan!" She shouts my name this time. I suddenly feel my head snap up and my eyes begrudgingly open.

Fuck, it was a dream.

I look towards my bedroom door and see Molly.

"Having a good dream, were we?" she smirks.

"Shit," I say under my breath, but from the raised eyebrow, I guess she heard.

"Breakfast will be ready in fifteen, so get up," she says as she turns to leave. Just before she disappears from my sight, she looks back and says, "I'd have a cold shower if I were you."

"Ugh," I groan as I look at myself. I'm completely exposed, my boxer briefs barely containing my very obvious excitement, and I'm covered in a sheen of sweat.

"Fuck," I mutter as I drag my body out of bed to follow Molly's advice. I wonder, as I brush my teeth, if I need to buy a lock for my bedroom door, or if it's time I got myself laid? That must be it; I wouldn't be thinking about my best friend like that if I were getting some. The image of Hannah's smiling face filters into my mind and I have to reach out to lean on the counter as grief and guilt hit me so strong that my knees start to buckle. Fuck, it's only been six months. I shouldn't be having these thoughts. Or should I? I've no fucking clue what the right thing to be feeling in a situation like this is, and I don't think there are any rules. All I know is that it's been a long six months and the thought of human contact, a little passion, want, and need sounds so good.

To MY RELIEF, Molly doesn't say anything about my wake-up call when I meet her in the kitchen.

"Smells amazing," I comment as I sit at the breakfast bar next to my waiting coffee. She passes over a plate with toast, scrambled eggs, and bacon.

"Feeling better?" she questions. She focuses on filling her plate, not on me, which I'm relieved about. I'm embarrassed enough; let's move on.

"Much. This is great, thank you. So, I told my mate we would pick his van up sometime before ten," I say, trying to change the topic. It's only now that I take notice of Molly. Her hair is still wet and her face is make-up free. As she steps around the breakfast bar, I notice she's wearing the shortest denim shorts I think I've ever seen, showing off her amazing legs, putting me back into almost as bad a state as I was when I woke up at the sight. She has on a white tank top that's low enough to show the swell of her breasts, and a pale yellow cardigan. It's simple, but seriously fucking hot. I think I've got a problem, and it needs fixing before I do something stupid.

"So, where are we actually going?" Molly questions as we pull away from my mate's drive in his van. It's so big that I'm not hugely confident driving it, but it will fit everything in it that we need to buy.

"Reading."

"Why the hell are we going there? Aren't there enough shops to pick from in Oxford?"

"Yes, I guess there are, but there isn't an IKEA," I reply.

"WHAT?" Molly shouts, scaring the ever-loving shit out of me.

"What? What's wrong?"

"I've always wanted to go to IKEA," she replies. looking at me with a beaming smile that goes all the way to her eyes.

"You've never been?" I ask, laughing at her reaction.

"No. I always hear people talking about it. It sounds awesome. I'm so excited! Eek, it's like an early birthday present for me."

"You never cease to amaze me, Molls." She looks over at me and raises an eyebrow, prompting me to explain. "You've grown up with enough money around you to have anything you could possibly want, but I take you somewhere as everyday as IKEA and you look like I've just made all your dreams come true." And fuck me if I don't love that look on her face right now. I promise myself to put it there as often as possible. I don't really think anyone has bothered to before, and that makes me feel so sad for her.

"Ry, you know I'm not into the whole money thing. I learnt from a young age that I'd rather have no money but loving friends and family around me."

"I do know that. You just take me by surprise with it, sometimes. I used to get dragged around IKEA by my mum and little sisters at least four times a year when I was growing up. It just seems so normal to me." Her bottom lip trembles as she imagines what I've just said. "Molly, don't do that. I want you to be happy. I promise you, you will have a family of your own like that one day. Today is meant to be a happy day." I give her thigh a gentle squeeze to try to break her out of her daydream.

"You're right; today is happy. What was our motto? Live, laugh, love," she says, reminding me of the pact we made together not so long ago.

By one o'clock, we've spent two hours going backwards and forwards around the showroom section while Molly to-and-froed over her choices. At last, we're sat in the café for lunch. I'm stood in the queue, watching Molly sat at a table going through the items on her list against the photos she's taken on her phone.

She eventually decided on pale grey furniture for her bedroom—very shabby chic, apparently.

As I walk over to her with a plate of Swedish meat-balls each, warmth fills me seeing just how happy she is. We still have the marketplace to go. I'm sure her head is going to explode before we get out of here.

"Wow, they were so good. I need the recipe," she comments, having not come up for air once while demolishing her food. I've never known a woman enjoy her food like Molly does but still manage to keep her amazing figure.

"There's a little food hall by the exit. You can buy all the stuff to make them," I explain.

"Really?" she exclaims. I nod in response. "Wow, this place is awesome. Are you done?"

"Yes, come on, let's go," I say as I clear the table.

"Do you think we need a trolley?" Molly asks as we enter the marketplace.

"You're kidding, right?" I ask, laughing. There's no way we're getting out of here without a full trolley.

"I'll take your laughter as a yes, shall I?"

We have a great time looking at everything. I pick up a few things for the house, but I mostly just enjoy watching Molly take it all in. I'm sure the expression on her face is similar to a child's at DisneyLand.

It's almost three by the time I manage to get her away from the candles and into the section to find and pick up all her furniture. Our trolley is overflowing with all sorts of stuff, and I've nearly taken out about five people with the rug Molly chose for her room that's sticking out just at the right height for other shoppers' heads.

"We need to be quick, or we'll end up getting locked in," I say as Molly leads the way with another empty trolley to put all the flat-packs on.

"Ah, that would be awesome. It would be just like that film where they get locked in a department store. I've always wanted to do that! Oh, over here," she says, pointing down an aisle.

"I'm going to go and take the van back."

We've been home for three hours, and we're in flat-pack hell. I've made her bed so at least she can have somewhere comfortable to sleep tonight, and she's just finishing her second bedside table. The two wardrobes, two chests of drawers, and bathroom cabinets are still leaning up against the wall in the hallway. The end is most definitely not in sight.

"Okay, I'll finish this one, then go and make us some sandwiches for when you get back. Are you still set on getting all this done tonight?"

"Yes! You will have a whole bedroom when you eventually get in that bed tonight."

"Okay, well, hurry then, because I can't do this alone."

I do need to get the van back so my mate can go to

work tomorrow, but mostly I need to get away from the sight of Molly leant over a bedside cabinet wearing those shorts with a screwdriver in her hand.

I don't know what's wrong with me. I've never seen Molly in any way but as a platonic friend. Even the first night when we met and she practically threw herself at me, I was just not interested. Maybe it's because that's how she first introduced herself. I've always gone for the quieter girls, the ones who wait to be asked out, not the ones who go after what they want. I guess my type over the years has also been taller, more athletic builds, whereas Molly is shorter and has some seriously sexy curves. We've spent a lot of time together over the past six months, and not once have I had any thoughts that I shouldn't be having about her. I mean, yeah, I did have other things filling my mind, but what's changed so suddenly? She moved in two days ago, and all I can think about is her body, being inside her, and wanting to make her happy.

I think I was right this morning; I seriously need to get laid. *But is it too soon?* a little voice in my head asks, reminding me of everything I've been through.

When I get back an hour later, she has both bedside tables in place and is moving the standing cabinet into the bathroom.

"Wow, you didn't hang around while I was gone," I say, watching her from the doorway.

"I just can't wait to see it all finished. I haven't done the sandwiches, though. I was just going to put this in place, then go make them. I thought you'd be gone longer."

"I did consider staying for a beer and letting you get on with it, but I didn't think that was fair," I explain as I start to open up the packaging for the wardrobes.

I'M TACKING the back of the first wardrobe on when Molly reappears with food and drink.

"Picnic on the bed," she says, nodding towards it.

I finish what I'm doing, then go and sit opposite her with the plate between us. "I need to talk to you about something," I say, grabbing my first sandwich.

"You can't kick me out already; the furniture isn't all made yet."

"Very funny. Actually, we won't be talking about it. I've got to tell you something."

"Okaaay, go on," she's says, starting to look nervous.

"You know what Tuesday is, right?" I ask, but I know the answer. There's no way she'd forget that it's been six months since she lost her best friend. She nods, looking suddenly sad.

"A couple of months ago, I booked to go away so I wouldn't be home and miserable for the anniversary. Since I booked it, thanks to you and that counsellor you found, I feel totally different about it. I no longer want to disappear for a week and be lonely and miserable. I want to go and celebrate her. Does that make sense?"

"Of course it does. I totally get it. I want to celebrate her, too."

"I want you to come with me. I've already—"

"Ryan, no, I can't just tag along because you don't want to leave me alone. Plus, I've got work and shifts at Cocoa's next week."

"Will you listen to me, woman? If you hadn't so rudely interrupted, you would have heard me explain that I've already spoken to Susan, and Lilly and Dec are going to work your shifts at Cocoa's. I've spoken to the company I booked the holiday with, and there's Wi-Fi so you can take your laptop and work on whatever projects you've got at the moment, and they confirmed that although there's only one bed, there is a day bed and plenty of room for two people to stay."

"Well, you really have thought of everything. Where is it?"

"It's a little beach hut right on the sea in Cornwall. Look." I pass her my phone with the details.

"Wow, it's so cute and peaceful."

"It's a private beach, so there won't be any holiday makers on it other than the ones staying in the huts along with us."

"Sounds perfect."

"So, you're in?"

"Do I actually have a choice?" she laughs.

Five

Molly

I was there as soon as the shops opened this morning with a list of what I needed for my week away. I can't wait to get to that little beach hut. I can just see myself sitting in the hot tub overlooking the beach as the sun goes down—complete with a glass of wine. Heaven.

Every time I think about it, butterflies erupt in my stomach, but they never cover the guilt I feel. It shouldn't be *me* excited to go on a holiday with Ryan. I checked the weather forecast when I first woke up this morning. It's going to be amazing all week. Cornwall, here I come.

My full suitcases are on my bed, and I'm double-checking that I have everything. I may have gone a little mad at the shops this morning, which has resulted in me needing both cases, but it's not every day a girl gets taken away.

As well as all the obvious necessities, I ended up with five new bikinis, summer dresses, shorts, vests and t-shirts, a skirt, a pair of flip-flops as well as wedges, new lingerie for the week, and a couple of flowers to go in my hair, Hawaii style.

After crossing off the last items on my list, I zip up my cases and drag them into the hallway. I walk back into my room with a huge smile on my face, just like I have since we finished putting everything together at some ungodly hour this morning. Ryan kept his promise and we didn't stop until everything was together. I knew about it when I got up this morning—every muscle in my body hurt from all the lumping around. I really need to return to my exercise classes once we get back.

Making my way across the room, I grab my laptop and phone and sit on my new chair, putting my feet up on the coffee table that I've set up in front of the French doors leading to the courtyard. I check my emails and to-do lists for the week so I don't fall behind on work. After the accident, I didn't take on as many clients as we had before. Work took a backseat to everything else, but it has started to pick up again—so much so that I'm starting to think I may need to find an office and hire another designer. It's amazing to think that the dream Hannah and I had when we were teenagers might just come true. Dialing on Emma's number, I wait in the hope she'll answer this time. I need to explain all of this to her, but as usual, it rings off and goes to voicemail. Giving up, I shut my laptop down just as I hear Ryan's footsteps down the stairs.

"Two cases? You know we are only going for seven days, right?" He laughs as he pops his head around the door.

"I'm a woman, I can't help it. Don't tell me...you've just got a tiny backpack or something pathetic?" I walk over to the front door, slipping my flip-flops on as I go, and notice I'm not far from wrong; he has a small suit-case which looks miniscule next to mine. I roll my eyes at him. "Whatever," I shrug as I get to him. "I'll carry yours!" I say over my shoulder, as I make my way to his car.

THE JOURNEY HAS BEEN so much fun. I synced my phone to Ryan's car, much to his delight, and we've been singing along with my favourite old-school songs, as well as playing stupid travelling games and taking the piss out of other drivers. We're now driving through the most picturesque little Cornish village, only ten minutes away from our beach hut, according to the SatNav.

"Wow." As we pull up to our allocated parking space on the edge of the small cliff the beach huts are set in, all we can see is the bay in front of us. "Definitely cannot complain about the view," I say, getting out the car and leaning over the fence at the very edge. "Oh my God, look how cute they are!" I can see the tops of five beach huts from here, with their huge balconies overlooking the bay.

"Come on, grab some stuff," Ryan says from behind me as he unloads the suitcases from the car. "We're in number one, so it's this way, by the looks of it," he says, nodding his head over to a sign. We make our way down the winding path to our little home for the week, and I swear the view keeps getting better.

When we get to our hut, I can't believe my eyes. It has to be the nicest of all the ones we've passed. Its balcony wraps around three sides. There's a section for eating with a white bistro set, and at the front there's a giant outside bed for lounging on as well as wooden sun loungers. The final side has the hot tub. The way it's set into the cliff and right at the end of the path makes it completely secluded. We could go the whole week and not see anyone else if we wanted to.

"Don't just stand there staring; let's go check the place out," Ryan says, opening the little gate.

"I think I'm in love," I say when I get inside. The front wall of the beach hut has sliding glass doors so they can be opened. All the furniture in the open-plan kitchen/diner and living room is white, and all the accessories are bright and multi-coloured, bringing the sunshine inside. The bedroom and bathroom are at the back of the hut and follow the same theme. "I want one," I say, spinning around and taking everything in.

"The internet didn't really do it any justice, did it?" Ryan says, putting the suitcases on the stand in the bedroom.

"Ahh," I sigh as I sink into the warm water of the hot tub. As soon as we put our cases in the hut this afternoon, we went in search of a supermarket. When we got back, I made us grilled salmon and asparagus, and Eton mess for dessert with local strawberries. It was so good. I think I may have embarrassed Ryan a little with the appreciative noises I was making while eating it. Ryan washed up and I put on my first bikini of the week—a 1950's style red and white polka dot number—to test out the hot tub.

With a full plastic wine glass in hand, I sit watching the sky change colour as the sun makes its descent for the night, waiting for Ryan to appear. I was going to wait for him so we could get in together, but he was adamant that I should enjoy myself.

Eventually, he comes out of the hut, wearing a pair of pale blue board shorts that hang deliciously low on his hips, showing off all his defined muscles and his sexy V that had me close to drooling the other day. I try my best to keep my eyes on his face, but it's hard to do. We're here to celebrate Hannah. I shouldn't be feeling this way all of a sudden.

I move over so he has enough space to get in, but he seems to have paused at the steps. "Come on, it's so good in here."

This seems to snap him out of his thoughts, and he hops in.

"Is everything okay?" I ask. He hasn't looked at me yet, the muscles in his shoulders pulled tight, his jaw clenched.

"Yeah, fine. You?" he says unconvincingly.

"Yes, amazing. Thank you so much for sharing this with me. It's heaven."

"No problem," he says, opening a can of beer. "When I booked it, I thought the time alone would be good, but as the months have gone on, I couldn't think of anything worse. I actually thought about cancelling it. So, I guess we should be thanking dickhead Max."

I raise my glass. "To Max screwing me over." Then, I touch it to Ryan's can.

"To Max. His loss is my gain." Ryan quickly looks away. I can't help but notice that his cheeks redden slightly.

"So...I hate to ask, but what's the plan for tomorrow? You said you wanted to celebrate, not be miserable, right?" I question gently, not really wanting to bring the subject up.

"Well, as Jo told me for months after the accident,

focus on the good times you had and celebrate what you had together, not on what you've lost. I'm not totally sure how to do that, but I'm sure we'll come up with something," he says, sounding unsure all of a sudden.

Jo was the grief counsellor I found for us after the accident. I cannot believe it's been six months. Six months since I lost my best friend, and Ryan lost his girlfriend. When I think about it, it feels like it could have been last week. Glancing over at him, I feel the weight of whatever's been developing between us press down on my shoulders.

When Ryan phoned me in hysterics in the middle of the night from the hospital and told me to get there as soon as possible, my stomach fell to my feet. When I got there and found out what had actually happened, it felt like my heart left my body. I remember falling into Ryan in floods of tears, and we sobbed together on the floor of the hospital for what felt like hours.

Hannah and Emma had both worked that evening at Cocoa's. When they eventually locked up after a busy night, Emma's car wouldn't start, so Hannah offered to take her back to their parents' house. They weren't far away when Hannah pulled out to cross a junction and a drunk driver flew at them like a bat out of Hell, crashing into the driver's side. According to the medics, Hannah died instantly and wouldn't have been in any pain. Emma, on the other hand, was stuck in the passenger seat with multiple broken bones and bruises. She managed to phone an ambulance and her parents.

Ryan and I seemed to deal with our grief in a similar way. We shut ourselves off from everyone but each other and the Morrisons. Someone recommended Jo to me, and I signed us up for a joint session. We fell in love with her in that first hour. She was straight-talking and didn't do any of the *softly, softly* approach that other people had tried that made my skin crawl. She said it how it was. She would tell us how shitty a situation it was, but that we had to be thankful for the time we did have with her. Celebrate what a wonderful person she was every single day, and relish in the joy she brought to our lives. She told us that we had to continue to live, and we had to find a way to be happy, because that was what Hannah would have wanted for us. We still had lives to live, and they needed to be full of fun and love. Hence our motto: live, laugh, love.

Ryan must have noticed I was taking a trip down memory lane, because at some point he moved next to me and put his arm around my shoulders. I feel his thumb catch a tear I didn't realise had fallen from my eye.

"I'm sorry, we're meant to be celebrating and being happy," I say, leaning my head on his shoulder.

"We are, but that doesn't mean we aren't going to be sad as well sometimes. It's okay, Molls," he whispers in my ear, rubbing his hand up and down my arm in comfort when he feels me crying harder.

Once I pull myself together, I glance over at him and notice his eyes are looking a little wet as well.

"So, the reason I have so much luggage was partly because I overdid the shopping this morning, but also because I brought a few things with me in case we needed them." Ryan raises his eyebrow in question, so I continue. "I brought some of Hannah's favourite DVDs, a couple of photo albums, Twister, and a bottle of Apple Sourz." I can't help but smile at the thought of them and the memories they bring to mind.

"When I said celebrate, I wasn't really thinking I'd have to spend a day watching your favourite girly DVDs, but now that you mention it, I think it's perfect. Thank you for thinking of it, Molly. Why didn't you say anything when I was taking the piss earlier?"

"I didn't want to bring it up before it was necessary. Look what it's done to us!" I laugh, pointing at our smiling yet tear-stained faces. "I don't know how I would have gotten through this without you, Ryan Evans. Thank you," I say, cuddling back into him and looking out to the star-filled sky, hoping Hannah is looking down on us, smiling that we've made it through together.

"You too, Molly," he says, sounding a little choked up.

We spent the rest of the night getting drunk, chatting about everything, and nothing. We did cry some more, but we laughed so much that the happy tears blended with the sad. Ryan was right; we needed to celebrate. She was such an incredible person and filled our lives with so much love and joy that it'll never be possible to forget her.

We eventually turned in in the early hours of Tuesday morning. Somehow, we managed in our drunken states to figure out that there were electronically controlled blinds in the ceiling that came down over the sliding doors, so Ryan wouldn't be awake as soon as the sun rose. I argued that I was okay to sleep on the day bed as I was crashing his holiday, but, ever the gentleman, Ryan point-blank refused and practically pushed me into the bedroom. I showered and changed into my new pyjamas that I thought were a suitable mix between cute and sexy for a holiday with my best friend, and fell fast asleep.

———

I WAKE the next morning to the sound of my mobile ringing. When it stops, I roll over to go back to sleep, but it starts again immediately. Groaning, I open my eyes and try to locate it. By the time I get to it, it stops again. It's Emma, so I ring her back straight away.

"What the fuck do you think you're doing?" Emma shouts down the line. "How could you?"

"Emma, calm down. What's wrong?" Silly question, really—her twin died six months ago today. What *isn't* wrong? My initial anger at her demanding question dies as my sympathy takes over. I can only imagine how's she's feeling today. We all lost so much the day Hannah died, but no one more so than Emma.

"You and Ryan. That didn't take you fucking long, did it? I knew you were after him the whole time he was with Hannah, and as soon as she dies, in you step to take her place. Now you're living with him in the house that Hannah practically paid for, and going away on a holiday with him. How could you Molly, h-how c-c-could you?" She starts to sob uncontrollably. The ball of dread that was sitting heavy in my stomach explodes and I fight to speak around the lump in my throat. I can't help feeling a little guilty even though what she's saying isn't really true, I can't deny the thoughts I've had over the last few days. Her words just confirm how wrong it all is.

"Emma, it's okay. I'm here for you, it's okay." I say in what I hope is a soothing voice as she continues to sob. Eventually, her breathing evens out.

"Molly?"

"Yes, hon?"

"I'm sorry," she says quietly.

"It's okay. You're allowed to be angry, and if that needs to be at me, then that's okay. I'm here for whatever you need." I speak calmly, trying to forget the beginning of our phone call. I know she's only being irrational because she's angry.

"I shouldn't have said that to you. Mum and Dad just said that you came around on Saturday to tell them you've moved in with Ry, and that you were on a holiday with him. I just flipped out, you know? I'm so sorry."

"Em, really, it's fine. I tried to get a hold of you over the weekend to explain everything, but your phone was off. I'll spare you the full details until I see you, but basically, I caught Max cheating, so I went to Ry's. He offered me his downstairs room instead of me finding somewhere of my own. I love it there with him. He's been my rock through this, and I think I've been his. I wasn't expecting to be coming on holiday with him. He booked it for himself months ago, but as he has been dealing with Hannah's death, he realised he didn't want to come here alone like he planned originally. So, he invited me, and we've come to celebrate her. I would never do anything to hurt you, Emma. You know that, don't you? Ryan and I are just friends. He's like my brother, just like he is to you."

"Yeah, I do know that. I'm sorry, I'm just a bit emotional. Hey, he's one seriously hot brother, though, right? How's the beach clothing working out for you?" she says, her normal humour starting to creep in.

"Uh, yeah, not a bad view around here actually, now that you mention it. The bay's pretty nice to look at, too." She laughs.

"Well, I'll let you go and celebrate. Sorry I rang so early, I just needed to shout at you."

"No problem, I'm here for you to abuse anytime you need it. I'll ring you later and make sure you're okay. Keep your bloody phone on."

"Yeah, okay. Talk to you later. Love you."

"Love you too, bye."

I put the phone down and lie back down on the bed. "Wow," I breathe. What a start to the day. That's when the tears come.

Ryan

THE SOUND of Molly's voice wakes me up and I walk over to the door to make sure she's okay. Today is going to be tough for both of us. I put my ear to the door and hear her consoling someone—Emma, I presume.

"Ryan and I are just friends. He's like my brother, just like he is to you," she says, and, for some reason, those words are like a slap to the face.

I walk away from the door and put the blinds up, looking out over the bay, trying to gather my thoughts. I lost my girlfriend six months ago today, the woman I loved more than anything, and here I am, upset because her best friend, now *my* best friend, has just admitted to Emma that I'm like a brother to her. The guilt I've been battling over the past few days hits me once again, but this time it's worse, because I'd told myself she was having similar feelings towards me.

Clearly not.

When my phone also rings and I find my granddad's photo staring back at me, I rush to answer it. Having lost the woman in his life and forced to move on and continue living, he's the only one who really understands what I've been through.

They got together when they were sixteen, were married by the time they were eighteen, and had one kid and another on the way by twenty. They were what most people would probably describe as the perfect couple. They made everything look so easy, and even after all those years together, they were still so in love.

They'd been retired for just over a year when, one morning, my granddad awoke and my gran didn't. She'd suffered a heart attack in her sleep and peacefully drifted off.

My grandad was devastated. He still is.

Their house looks exactly the same as my gran left it before going to bed that night. He hasn't moved a thing.

He's told me how unhealthy it is that he hasn't attempted to move on, but he said that after a lifetime together he's got nothing else to look forward to and that he'd love more than anything to keep her spirit alive.

Since losing Hannah, he's expressed his desire for me not to follow in his footsteps. He's told me time and time again to find the strength to continue with my life. To forge new paths for myself without feeling guilty because it would be what she wanted, too.

Once we hang up, I look out over the sea beyond

and try to pull myself together. Walking back over to the bedroom door, I hear Molly saying goodbye. I stand and listen a little longer to make sure she's okay. It's not long before I hear her start crying. Putting all my feelings aside, I knock on the door. No matter how I feel, she's my best friend, and I need to be here for her like she has been for me.

"Yeah," she replies quietly. I open the door, and she's lying on the bed, sobbing into her pillow.

I lie down in front of her and pull her into my arms so she's against my chest. She throws her right arm and leg over my body and clings on while she cries. I try to comfort her by slowly rubbing my hand up and down her back. Eventually, her breathing evens out.

Six

Molly

I wake up feeling really hot. When I open my eyes, I realise why. My head's on Ryan's naked chest, my arm and leg wrapped tightly around his body. He's holding onto me equally as tight. I spend a few seconds appreciating his sculpted chest before I peer up at his face to see that he's still fast asleep. He looks so young and carefree.

I wish we didn't have to deal with today.

I lie there, looking at him a while longer, before his lips curl up at the corners.

"If you keep staring at me like that, I'll get the wrong idea," he says quietly, his eyes still shut.

I gently smack his chest and lift myself up on my elbow. I hear a thud as my phone slides from the bed, but I don't look away. His eyes open. They're full of love and compassion as he stares back at me. I always know I'm safe when I look into his eyes.

"Thank you for this. I really needed it," I say, looking into his eyes to show him how serious I am. "Emma was on the phone, and she was really upset." "Come on, let's get up and have breakfast on that amazing balcony."

I go to move, but his arm around me tightens slightly. "Thank you for everything, Molly. I really mean it," he says, so sincerely it makes my heart hurt. But then, I see the corner of his lips twitch as he says, "The view from the balcony is pretty good, but I'm not sure it can beat the one I've got right now." He looks down at my chest, a suggestive smirk on his face.

I look down and realise I'm giving him an eyeful. I put my hand over my breasts and jump out of his hold and off the bed, scowling at him.

He puts his hands up in defeat. "I only looked once, I promise," he says, still smiling.

I bend down to pick up my phone. "Oh, come on, you're not playing fair." I look back to see him sat on the edge of the bed, staring at my arse. I can't help but notice the obvious bulge in his boxers. Butterflies erupt in my belly at the thought of being able to affect him so easily.

"Do you want me to ring Emma back and tell her

you've been checking me out?" I ask as I leave the bedroom.

"Oh, come on," he shouts. "Don't even pretend you didn't get a good look this morning, or from the hot tub last night, or when you came in Saturday evening." He chuckles to himself as he starts walking into the living room, but stops to grab a pair of shorts to cover himself up.

"So, about that dream yesterday morning." I deadpan.

"Touché. What's for breakfast?"

WE SPEND what little is left of the morning sat on the balcony eating fresh fruit, granola, and yoghurt. We must have fallen back to sleep for longer than I thought, but I feel better for it.

"Right, today is the only day I'm not going to work, because we're celebrating. So, what's the plan?" I ask Ryan while we tidy up.

"Let's just chill out here, stick on some of that god-awful music Hannah was so obsessed with, and hit the sun loungers."

"Ew, what an awful plan," I say, laughing as I wander through the hut to put on today's bikini—a navy and white striped nautical look. I can't wear the little string bikinis that others do; I need more support than that, so I have to go for the bra-style tops to keep everything in place and under control. Having said that, this one in particular does good things for my cleavage.

"I'll meet you out there. You know the playlist we need on my phone."

I'm just putting my hair up out of the way when the music starts filling the hut. It makes me smile as memories of happier times with Hannah flit through my mind. I grab my Kindle, phone, and suntan lotion before heading out to the balcony.

Ryan's sat on a lounger with his aviators on, sipping a glass of water. I can't help but drop my gaze to check him out; he looks like a bloody model, wearing black shorts with the waistband of his boxers poking out. I'm not sure if it's pleasure or torture, having to look at him.

I can't see his eyes, but I can tell they're roaming over my body. My skin heats under his scrutiny. Grabbing my phone, I open up the camera just in time for his eyes to find mine. There's a wicked glint in them that makes my insides flutter.

"You need to stop doing that," I tell him seriously.

"What? It's not like I'm going to throw you down and have my wicked way with you. I'm merely just appreciating the female form in all its glory." Tingles head south at the image his words create in my head. "Anyway, you're not my type."

And, they're gone.

I don't know why hearing that makes my steps

falter and disappointment flood me. I should be happy about this, right?

"Yeah, I guess not. I've got more curves than all the girls you've been with put together." Hannah was a gorgeous, slim, tall build. She wasn't quite straight up and down—she had a cute, pert arse, and I guess you could say her breasts were a small handful. She also had stunning golden blonde long hair and striking blue eyes. I've seen photos of the girls Ryan dated previously, and they pretty much looked the same. I'm the complete opposite with my rounded arse and hips, tiny waist, and double Ds. Hannah was almost always quiet, polite, and well-spoken, something Ryan often complimented about her. I, on the other hand, say it like it is... and I swear like a trooper.

My shoulders slouch as I stand in front of him. I hand him the bottle I'm holding and turn around. I must look defeated as I do it because he leans into my ear and whispers, "You're gorgeous, Molly. Don't think for a second I was suggesting you're not."

His words and the warmth of his hands lightly skimming down my sides as he massages in the suntan lotion make my knees slightly weak. The tingles return and descend south. A man has never affected me like this. I've never felt this incredible pull before. I used to thrive on the feeling of men wanting me, but I've never desperately wanted them. Sex for me has always been about being wanted, not because I had to have it right then and there.

I clear my throat. "T-thank you." Even to my ears, my voice sounds rough as I quickly scurry away from his hands and onto the outside sofa. I lie down on my stomach and keep my face away from him. Why has it got to be him causing these feelings in me? We've known each other for years and been as close as two friends can get over the last six months without me feeling like this, but a few days of living with him, and he's turned me into a frustrated mess. I squeeze my thighs together to try to dull the ache and chant in my head that he's my friend. I can't imagine Hannah would be too pleased about my feelings towards her boyfriend. The thought causes a giant lump to form in my throat and a tear to run down my cheek. This is so wrong. I shouldn't be feeling like this.

"Molls, are you okay?"

"Yeah, fine. You?" I sound anything but, and he knows me well enough to know that.

"Uh huh, yep, I'm good."

"Hey, do you remember that night we all went bowling?" He laughs, and I turn to look at him.

That did it. We spend the next few hours reminiscing about our memories from university and the following couple of years at work. We had some great times together, and Ryan was right—those times need celebrating. I tell him stories about us growing up and from school, some of which he'd heard before, and some he hadn't.

"Tell me about the first time you met," Ryan says,

after a few minutes of silence between us. He already knows this story, but I humour him anyway, because it's comforting to reflect. It's important that, together, we keep her memory alive.

"My first solid memory is from primary school. We must have been four or five. We went over to get our coats and snacks for break time, and someone had put my lunchbox on a shelf that I couldn't reach. This boy came over and said he would get it down for me if I kissed him. I didn't like that, so I shoved my knee straight between his legs and watched him fall to the ground in pain." Ryan flinches, making me laugh. "When I looked up from him rolling around crying, Hannah was stood behind him and had a big smile on her face. She must have seen the whole thing. She reached up and grabbed my lunchbox easily; she was really tall, even then. After that, we spent every day together."

"What happened to him?"

"Um, well. That didn't put him off. He continued chasing me for that kiss. Eventually, he won, and I lost my virginity to him ten years later at a friend's party. But he turned out to be gay in the end."

"Well, I didn't see that coming." Ryan sounds slightly shocked by my honesty.

"It wasn't worth the long wait."

"You lost your virginity at fourteen?" he asks.

"Yeah, unfortunately. I totally regret it, but to be

honest, if I'd waited until I found someone special like everyone says to, then I'd still be a virgin now."

"That wouldn't be such a bad thing, Molls. It would mean you wouldn't have had to deal with any of the arseholes you've chosen in the past few years."

"True. It's not like I've had years of awesome sex to make up for them, either. They were all as bad in bed as their personalities."

"Please tell me they all had little dicks as well?"

"Um...not all of them, but as the saying goes, it's not about the size, it's what you do with it."

"I never understood why you got with so many different guys when you could have found a nice one to settle down with. I still had the idea in my head that you were having fun doing it, but you've just ruined that for me. So, if you weren't enjoying it, why *were* you doing it?"

"My parents were pretty shitty. They never wanted me. I learnt from a young age that if you take antibiotics whilst on the pill, they stop it working effectively, so here I am. My parents had already had the two boys they wanted. Steven was fourteen and Daniel was twelve by the time I was born.

"It was all planned out; they would take over and expand the family business. They decided that I, on the other hand, would grow up, be just like my mum, and provide them with some grandchildren. They decided not to pay for me to go to private school like my brothers, so I went to the local secondary with

Hannah and Emma. It was a great school, so I can't complain.

"I had different ideas, though. I wanted a career, and I had no intention of ever joining the family business in any capacity. I wanted to be my own person. My parents told me I wasn't going to sixth form and that I would work for them. I told them that wasn't happening, and that I'd move out, if need be, to enable myself to live my own life. Eventually, they came around to the idea of me staying, but they cut me off. The allowance I used to get was put into a trust fund that I couldn't access until I was twenty-one. I'm sure they only did it to try to stop me from going to university.

"So, I spent my two years at sixth form juggling school work and fitting in as many hours as possible. I was desperate to go to university, and I managed to keep my grades up so I would have a good chance of getting in. But the money was an issue. I would never get any loans or anything with my parents' finances as they were."

"How did you manage it?"

"I applied for every kind of funding there was, and I did manage to get a little bit, but not enough. One day, I got a phone call from my gran, my dad's mum, and she asked to see me. She handed me a cheque that was more than enough to cover my three years at university." Tears well in my eyes as I think back to the determination in her eyes that day. She wanted me to have the world. "She died of a heart attack two months later. I was devastated but determined to make her proud."

"Sorry, I think I'm missing the point. What has this got to do with my original question about all the guys?" Ryan looks confused.

"Other than my gran and the Morrisons, I never felt loved. The two people who were meant to love and support me no matter what didn't care about me. When I started going out with boys, they made me feel special... needed and wanted. At first, it was just hand-holding and kissing, but it wasn't long before I was experimenting with more. All I've ever wanted was to find someone to love me and take care of me, like you did with Hannah. I wanted someone to look at me like I am his reason for living. I was so jealous of you guys." I'm a blubbering mess by the time I've finished, and I find myself wrapped in Ryan's arms again.

"I'm so sorry, I keep crying on you. You must be getting fed up of me," I say once I've calmed down.

"Don't be stupid. I've been wanting to know about your parents for years, but Hannah would never tell me. She said it was your story. I'm so sorry your parents were like that. You deserve them to love you, and I know it's not quite the same, but you know you've got me, right? I'll always take care of you. I love you, Molly. You're my best friend."

"I love you too, Ry."

"Your Prince Charming will come when you least expect him, I promise."

His lips press against my head and warmth races through me. He's right; it's not quite the same, but it's bloody good. I squeeze him a little tighter and try my hardest to ignore the tingles that erupt where our naked skin is touching.

Ryan

I'D GUESSED MOST of the things Molly said about her parents from the little bits I'd heard before, but hearing it first-hand still shocks me. I'm so angry they could treat their daughter that way, could try to control her into doing what they wanted. I feel more grateful than ever for my family. Okay, yes, they tried to do something similar, but they accepted my decision in the end and have supported me all the way.

My parents are both very traditional. They always believed that a man should get a 'manly' job like working in construction, find a nice woman, marry her, and make loads of babies together. They believed—a little like Molly's parents, I guess—that the woman should stay home and raise the children while the man worked hard to support his family. This is what they wanted for me: to leave school, get an apprenticeship in a trade, find a job close to home, as well as a nice girlfriend. They never imagined me leaving Liverpool.

I wanted the opposite, just like Molly. I'd wanted to go to college, study sport science, and become a PE teacher from as early as I can remember, and I knew I wanted to leave Liverpool to experience another city. I spent years researching and visiting places I might want to go. I came down to Oxford one weekend with a couple of mates and fell in love with the city. So, Oxford Brookes University it was; all I had to do was get the grades.

My parents have visited me down here a couple of times, but mostly I go up to them. They were not impressed, to say the least, when I decided to stay in Oxford to do my teacher training, and even less impressed when I chose to stay for good. The only bit they liked about it all was Hannah. They loved her.

My parents eased up a little after I moved away. My two younger sisters, Abbi—who is now twenty-one—is about to start her last year of university in Manchester doing primary teaching, and Liv—nineteen—has just finished her first year in Cardiff doing jour-nalism. They didn't seem to get half as much grief as I did when I decided to go away. It always seemed to be the case that I got all the hassle for the decisions I made, but when it came time to make theirs, our parents just seemed to go with it.

"I just wish mine would have come around to the idea like yours did," Molly says quietly.

I've been explaining all about my family to Molly for the last half an hour. It's nice to have someone else who understands what it was like, although my parents were there for me in the end, and still are.

"When was the last time you spoke to your parents?"

"Um...I actually can't remember. I speak to Steven and Daniel quiet often. They tend to keep me updated."

"Have you always got along with your brothers?" I've only met her brothers once, at Hannah's funeral. They came to support Molly, which told me they were nice guys, unlike her parents who couldn't possibly leave their holiday a day early. As you can imagine, I didn't get to talk to them at the time, and she hasn't really mentioned them since.

"Yeah, we speak most weeks. We are as close as we can be with such a big age gap. They've always supported my decision to break away from the family business and have never held it against me. They've both told me on separate occasions that they really wanted to be part of it, and really enjoy taking on the renovations and rental side of the estate agency my dad runs. They've started up a sister company and it's doing really well."

"I'm glad you have them to turn to. Your birthday's soon, so you'll hear from your parents then, right?"

"Oh yeah, I'll hear from them."

AFTER SPENDING THE AFTERNOON REMINISCING, we've somehow managed to drink our way through two pitchers of Pimm's. I don't know about Molly, but I'm starting to feel a little buzzed with the mixture of sun and alcohol.

I watch as she pops the last bit of fruit from her glass into her mouth, and I'm mesmerised by how sexy she looks doing something so simple. When her tongue licks away the juice on her lips, I know I need to get up and do something. "Now that it's cooling down, I think I'll go for a run along the beach." I stand and collect our glasses.

"Okay. I was thinking of heading in for a shower and getting dressed for dinner, anyway. I'm feeling quite cooked."

She's right; she has a lovely glow over her skin, and a bit of a pink nose. I watch as she stands and staggers a little. Yep, it's not just me who's buzzed, then.

I'VE BEEN RUNNING for a long time. My legs burn and sweat's pouring off me. Once I climbed over the rocks we thought were the end of the beach, I found a long sandy stretch that I ran the entire length of, despite it being more touristy than our secluded piece of heaven next door.

I'm now sat on those rocks, looking over the beach and watching a young family building sandcastles. The little girl can't be more than two years old, and her parents are still in their twenties, I'd say. They're having such fun. I know it's stupid to feel it because I am in no way lonely, but that's how I feel in this moment.

Actually, since I lost Hannah, I've felt lonely.

I loved sharing my life with her. It made me feel complete to wake up to her in the morning and hold her in my arms at night before I fell asleep.

That lonely feeling is soon overtaken by guilt. For the past six months, when I've pictured my future, I was alone. All of a sudden, a change in that vision has taken me by surprise and scared the fuck out of me. I now see Molly—and I don't mean living downstairs. I see Molly everywhere.

"Fuck!" I shout as I run my hands through my hair and feel the tears burning behind my eyes. I promised Hannah I would move on one day. Every time I go to her grave, I tell her I will, because I know that's what she would want for me. I was fine with that happening...one day. But how has that one day come so quickly, and why is it Molly? She made it pretty clear this morning that we're just friends, and she sees me as her brother.

What would Hannah think about Molly and me? Molly was her best friend. Would she think it's weird? What would she want me to do?

I sit there for a while longer, trying to get my head together. I come to the decision that I've got to put my new feelings aside—firstly so I can try to make sense of them, and secondly so I can be the friend she needs me to be. If I force anything, I'm likely to push her away, and I need her. If what I'm feeling is meant to happen, then it will.

With that little pep talk over, I head back to the beach hut. What I find when I get there almost makes me forget everything I've just told myself.

Seven

Molly

Ryan's been gone ages. I'm starting to get worried. I called his mobile over half an hour ago, but it rang in the living room. I'm trying to stop myself from worrying by keeping busy. I decided, as we're celebrating tonight, to wear one of the dresses I bought on my holiday shopping trip yesterday. It's a full-length maxi dress with multi-coloured flowers printed all over the thin, sheer fabric. The top is cut low and square across my breasts, showing off my ample cleavage. I've left my hair to dry naturally, tucked a flower behind my ear, and kept my make-up light.

We decided to have Hannah's favourite for dinner.

I've prepped all the ingredients, so when Ryan gets back, it's just the beef that needs cooking. I've also made a pitcher of margaritas to go with the tacos, but in the time I've been waiting, I've already had one too many. Add those to the Pimm's from earlier and I might be having an early night.

I've just finished a pint of water to try to dilute it all when I hear footsteps on the balcony.

"Ryan, is that you? I've been worried sick. You should have taken your—" He appears around the corner. *Oh, holy fucking hell.* "Um...your phone...um...taken it...with you. Shit."

He's standing there in the doorway with the setting sun behind him. His body is tanned and glistening where the light is hitting his sweat, his hair sticking up in all directions, and his eyes...shit, his eyes look like they're asking me to devour him. *Um, yes please,* I think as I stand here, close to drooling. I watch as his tongue darts out to wet his lips. Oh God, I want those lips on me. I squeeze my thighs together to try to relieve the ache, but I swear the pressure makes it worse. I feel like I'm about to melt into a puddle on the floor.

Ryan distracts me from my almost orgasmic state. "Holy motherfucking shit."

My eyes go back up to his after getting my fill of his half-naked body. They're roaming all over me before they come to rest on my breasts.

"Are you trying to kill me?"

When I laugh, his eyes come back up to mine. His

normally bright blues are darker than I've ever seen them.

"I've pretty much got dinner sorted, so if you want to go have a shower, I'll finish it off," I say as a way to distract both of us.

He's sauntering towards me, an intention in his eyes that I don't want to identify.

"I've already laid the table, so you can meet me outside once..."

He's about an inch away from me. My breasts are so close to rubbing up against his chest, I'm worried I'll go off like a rocket if he so much as touches them. His hand rests on my cheek, and he stares into my eyes.

"I don't know what was wrong with all the guys you've been with before, because your body was designed to be worshiped," he growls before swallowing. The muscles in his neck ripple, distracting me. He leans in and whispers, "For hours."

"Ryan...shower," I manage to croak out, when his face moves closer again. I don't think I've ever felt as conflicted as I am in this moment.

"Ryan," I whisper again, breaking the trance. He flinches before kissing my forehead and leaving the room.

I walk out of the hut and lean against the balcony railing, looking over the beach below. What the hell is going on here? Where did all this sexual tension come from?

After Hannah died, we held each other while we

cried. We had nights where we held each other in bed while we slept, but even then, not even a hint of anything sexual was evident. Then, I move in, and suddenly *bam*! He's all I can see and think about.

Nothing can happen between us, though. Just thinking about how Emma reacted when she presumed something was going on is enough to scare me off. How would she react if it actually happened? What about Susan and Pete, or the twins? I could lose them all.

The sudden realisation has me panicking. If something happened between us and it didn't work, I'd lose him as my best friend. There's no way we'd be this close afterwards. The Morrisons might all act like Emma earlier, then I'd not only lose my best friend, but the people I see as my family, too. That cannot happen.

I need to control my feelings where Ryan is concerned. This has to stop. Maybe I need a date, to see someone else. Maybe it's not Ryan I want, but it's my body's way of telling me I'm ready to get out there and find that great guy I've been waiting for.

Instead of going back to dinner, I grab my phone and call Susan to see how she's doing before calling Emma back. I'm glad when she answers. I hope she can start being around a bit more. I really miss her. I also call Lilly and Dec to check up on them. They all sound sad, but they're doing okay.

When Ryan reappears, I've only just started on the beef. "Sorry, I got distracted." I glance over to see him run his hand through his wet hair, leaving it in a sexy mess. I run my eyes over him quickly. He's wearing a black t-shirt stretched across his wide shoulders and chest, paired with tan shorts.

"No problem. We're on holidays, we can do whatever we want."

Dinner was delicious and uneventful, except for the fact that I caught Ryan watching me a number of times. Maybe messy food wasn't a great idea. It felt like every time I licked one of my fingers, his eyes darkened another shade.

As soon as we cleared our plates, I immediately started to clean up—I just couldn't sit there any longer. The tension was killing me.

"I put the DVDs I brought by the TV. Do you want to pick one and put it on? I'm going to get changed." I decided while I was washing up that this situation was somehow the dress's fault, so it's coming off in favour of a tank top and shorts.

When I come out, Ryan is already on the sofa. He's also found the box of chocolate truffles we bought and placed them on the coffee table. As I walk over, I notice which DVD he's chosen. The *Friends with Benefits* box is open with the disc missing. It's like he knows how hot this film makes me. I mean, come on, Justin Timberlake practically naked...who wouldn't get a bit hot?

"Um, why this film?" I try to ask as innocently as possible as I sit on the floor, leaning my back against the sofa in an attempt to keep my distance from him.

"I've never seen it, and you two were always going on about it. Plus, the main actress is fit." He shrugs.

Brilliant, just what we need to add to our sexual tension.

WE'RE ABOUT HALFWAY into the film and I think it's going okay. I mean, yes, it's awkward as fuck, but if I don't look at Ryan at all, it makes it easier. I'm still sat on the floor and it's really un-fucking-comfortable. I can't feel my arse, and I've got pins and needles in my legs, but I'm adamant that I'm not sitting next to him on that small sofa. He continually tells me to come up, but I keep making excuses.

Eventually, it gets so bad that I'm constantly fidgeting. I feel Ryan get up from behind me and come to stand in front of me.

"What are you doing?"

"I could ask you the same thing," he says, as his hands go to my waist and he lifts me up with no effort at all, practically throwing me on the sofa.

"What the fuck was that for?"

"Just get fucking comfortable. I can't cope with the fidgeting any longer."

I curl myself into the far corner from Ryan, and he looks at me with a raised eyebrow. He's right to think this is weird; we've watched loads of films together and we usually sit quite happily next to each other.

"What the fuck now?"

He narrows his eyes. I just need to act normal. I think I've forgotten what normal is with us, though. I just shrug my shoulders in answer to his question.

"Come here." He grabs me and moves me over until I'm up against his side.

I try to relax, I really do, but I know there's a sex scene coming next and I don't know if I can watch and be this close to Ryan without panting or doing something embarrassing. Being pressed up against his hard body and able to smell him is already hard enough.

"What's wrong? You're as tense as a nun at an Ann Summers party."

"Nothing," I mumble.

"Molls, are you uncomfortable watching this with me?" I know he's smirking. Fucking know-it-all. "Fuck, you *are*. Seriously, we've watched worse than this together before now."

I can feel him laughing, and I know he's thinking of the night his mate left the TV on an adult channel and hid the remote. Admittedly, we were pretty drunk and curiosity got the better of us for about thirty minutes, but that was different. The sexual tension between us wasn't as thick as fog on a winter's morning.

"I know, but after earlier it feels a little weird."

"I know, and I'm sorry. You just took me by surprise, standing there looking all hot and sexy. It won't happen again, I promise. Actually, no, I can't promise that. Just relax—it's not like I'm going to jump you any minute. Molly, you might be my best friend, but you're still seriously hot. I can't help appreciating that."

I relax into him a bit more, and he strokes my arm gently. I may have relaxed, but I'm still stupidly aware of my body. I suddenly realise that, the way I'm lying, I'm giving him a great view of my tits again. I try to discreetly pull my top up, but I stop in my tracks when I hear him laugh, "Are you trying to ruin *all* my fun?"

"Fuck off, Ry." I move back to my side of the sofa, grabbing my drink.

When the film finishes, I get up to put the next one in while Ryan gets us fresh drinks. Surely *Bridget Jones' Diary* is a safer choice than the last one.

By THE TIME the credits come up, we're both well past the point of being tipsy. Luckily, the tension has drained, and it's back to being like it always has been. Ish.

"What are you doing?" I ask Ryan as he gets up and starts to move the coffee table.

"Making some space. You said you brought Twister."

"You're kidding. You actually want to play?"

"You bet your sweet arse I do. Come on, Molls, don't be a spoilsport. It's that or strip poker," he says with a smile.

"I'll go get it, then," I say, sounding less than enthusiastic. There is no way this can be a good idea.

I come back with the game for Ryan to set up, the bottle of Apple Sourz, and a couple of glasses. We have a shot each and get started.

We've been playing for twenty minutes, and so far we've avoided any contact and remained on either side of the mat. I'm thinking I might accidently fall over soon to end the game and stop the inevitable. I have my back facing the floor and am looking up at the ceiling, waiting for Ryan to spin and move. He's sort of on his side next to me, with both hands next to each other, but his foot is between mine.

"Right hand, red."

I breathe a sigh of relief, because this means he can just move his hand one spot to the right from where it is now. Unfortunately, Ryan has other ideas. He moves his hand over my body so that he's hovering over me, his face right above mine. His breath caresses my neck, causing goosebumps to appear on my skin. My chest heaves as my breathing intensifies.

"Are you going to spin, Molls?"

"Yeah, sorry." I reach out for the spinner. "Right leg, green."

Fuck.

I move my leg to the other side of his, so that now I'm totally underneath him. This is exactly why I didn't want to play.

I hear a small moan come from the back of Ryan's

throat and I turn to look at him. His eyes are as dark as they were earlier, and he's just less sweaty. His lips are parted where his breathing is coming out in fast pants, and his chest moves dramatically. I look back to his face in time to see his tongue sneak out and wet his bottom lip.

My heart pounds and my temperature is nearly at boiling point. I know that if I don't move, we're going to end up doing something we're going to regret.

I can tell by the determined look in Ryan's eyes that he's not backing down. It's up to me.

I make a snap decision and let my limbs give way so my back hits the floor, and I scramble out from under his body.

Eight

Ryan

It's been three days since our game of Twister. What a stupid fucking idea that was. Yeah, I pretty much knew it would be when I mentioned it, but the thought of being that close to her was too much of a pull. Thank God she didn't come back out to the living area after she ran away, because I would have been caught red-handed jacking off after that little episode.

We've had a great few days. Every morning, Molly has worked on designs for different clients. I love watching her sketch. She gets so engrossed in her thoughts and looks really sexy chewing on her pencil.

All she needs is a pair of glasses to give her that sexy secretary look. I'm trying really hard to curb my feelings for her, but it's not as easy as I initially thought.

We went for a drive yesterday for a look around. It was a typical Cornish town, and all the people were lovely to chat to. Molly dragged me into nearly every shop we came across and we spent longer than I thought possible inside a little art gallery full of paintings of the surrounding countryside. There was one painting in particular that caught her attention, and she spends an inordinate amount of time considering its smallest details. I'm captivated watching her studying the painting and the way she bites down on her bottom lip and moves her finger gently over the paint as if she's experiencing what the very act of painting it might have been like.

I didn't mind following her around, because it made her happy. She couldn't wipe the smile off her face all day. She came back with a number of bags full of bits and bobs for her bedroom at home, and small souvenirs for the Morrisons and Megan's little boy.

Our time here has been amazing, but it's gone so fast. Tomorrow is our last full day. I'm so glad I asked Molly to come with me, even with the odd awkward moment between us. We've done exactly what I wanted us to do. We've celebrated Hannah, and we've relaxed and enjoyed ourselves. I would have been bored here on my own.

We've decided to go out for a meal at the local

pub tonight so we don't have to cook. It's a bit of a walk, but from what the locals have said, it'll be worth it.

Molly is lying on her front on the outdoor sofa, sketching ideas for something on her pad. I walk over with a glass of water and sit next to her.

"What are you working on?" I ask. They look a little suggestive, to say the least.

"A burlesque club—they're doing some bondage-themed nights in a few months and want some promo stuff." I look back down at her sketches, and they start to make sense a bit more now.

"These are amazing, Molls," I tell her honestly. She has hand-drawn a range of bondage items and used the markers to really make them stand out. "I think the whip, blindfold, and the one with the side of a corset on are my favourites."

"I'm going to do one with handcuffs as well, which I think will look quite cool. I'll scan them all in when we get back, edit them further, then add all the text and stuff."

"I can't imagine Hannah working on something like this." Hannah was so sweet; in my head, she and bondage do not go together.

"It would have always been mine to work on, because they liked the hand-drawn elements. Let's be honest, Hannah was a brilliant designer, but she couldn't draw for toffee!" She laughs as she thinks back. "Do you remember when we had to do a life drawing class in our third year? The model was offended by Hannah's sketches."

"Yeah, I remember. She asked me if I would model for her so she could practice, but I didn't want her to knock my self-esteem by drawing some sort of alien thing that was meant to be me."

By the look on her face, Molly's deep in thought.

"What's wrong?"

"Nothing. Just thinking...would you let me draw you?" she asks.

"Um...are you serious? You want to draw me... naked?" I know I've got a pretty good body, but could I really get it all out and lie in front of Molly while she stares at me? All of me?

"I'm serious. I'd love to sketch you and get all these in there." My skin heats as her finger runs over my abs. My dick twitches, ready for action every time her finger touches my skin. "We could put some grapes in front of your manhood if you're worried about how small it is," she deadpans.

"Oh, you'll need more than grapes." I wink at her. "Could you actually take it seriously if I laid out in front of you?"

"It's art—of course I could take it seriously."

"I'll think about it," I mutter, moving back over to my sun lounger. The way she was touching me along with the sweet scent of her perfume is messing with my head as well as my dick. "So, how's work going? I know you took on fewer clients after Hannah died, but it seems it's picking up again,"

"Yeah, it's getting really busy. I'm getting to the point where there's too much for me to do alone, and I need to employ someone else and get an office. But that's such a huge step."

"Molly, you can do anything you set your mind to. If you really think you're at that point, go for it. What's the worst that could happen?"

She smiles and takes a deep breath. "I guess you're right. I'll start looking into stuff when we get back."

"What are we doing for your birthday Saturday night?"

"Megan mentioned us all going out. I just need to text everyone with the details."

"Sounds like a plan; I'm in. Don't make any plans for Friday night, though. You're all mine."

"That sounds a little creepy. What are you going to do with me?"

"Just a little surprise."

I leave Molly looking confused and walk down to the beach with my phone. I've been planning something with Susan and Pete for ages now as a thank you to Molly for everything she's done for all of us these past six months. I wasn't aware up until just now how imminent it could be, but the timing is brilliant for her birthday. Once I've organised everything with Susan, spoken to Emma, and made a few more calls to sort everything out, it's time to get ready for dinner.

"Wow, that food was amazing," Molly says as we walk along the beach after getting back from the pub.

"I don't think I'm going to be able to eat for a week after all that."

"I think I'd drive down here just for a slice of the cheesecake. It was so good."

She's right; the cheesecake was amazing, but she sounded indecent whilst eating it, especially in a packed pub. If people didn't know any better, they'd have thought she was having an orgasm at the dinner table.

We've been walking along slowly for about thirty minutes, carrying our shoes as we step through the shallow seawater. Molly, as always, looks stunning in a strapless white summer dress that's fitted at her waist, then flares out to her knees. The white sets off her new tan well. Her hair is pinned up with a flower in it, exposing her neck. Every time I look at her, all I want to do is put my lips there and taste her skin.

I turn around when I notice she stopped a few seconds ago. She's smiling mischievously. I'm almost scared to ask. Almost. "What?"

"Do you know what we haven't done since we've been here?"

I can think of a number of things we haven't done. "What did you have in mind?" I ask with a smirk.

"We haven't been swimming in the sea. You up for it?"

"Yeah, let's go get changed and come back down," I say as I turn in the direction of the beach hut.

"That's...not exactly what I was thinking." I turn back around to her and find that she's walked up a little from the water and dropped her shoes on the dry sand. She stands so she's facing me and pulls the zip of her dress down. She has a small smile on her face as she watches me watch her.

Shit.

She drops her dress to her feet and stands there, waiting.

Fuck, she's stunning. She's standing there in a white lacy strapless bra and matching tiny knickers that look like they show off most of her arse. I can't move. I'm frozen, staring at her. I'm sure my eyes are bulging out of my head and my mouth is hanging open.

"Ry?"

She walks towards me, slowly, and stops right in front of me.

"Ryan?" she tries again, but it's like I'm dreaming. I'm still immobile as she grasps the top button of my shirt. Agonisingly slowly, it seems, she undoes one at a time, until she's at the bottom. She slips her hands onto my shoulders and pushes my shirt off so it pools on the sand. It's when I feel her hands touch the skin above my waistband that I snap out of my trance. She needs to stop, or she's going to find herself pinned under me in the sand.

"Skinny dipping?" I ask, just to make sure I've understood correctly.

"Well, I don't think going naked is a particularly good idea, so I'm going like this," she laughs.

"You'd be having the same problem if you were stood in my shoes," I say quietly.

She turns and winks at me as she disappears into the sea. "Don't worry, the water's pretty cold. It should sort your problem right out," she says, dropping her gaze to my crotch.

"You're going to regret that, Molly," I say as I drop my shorts and wade into the water in my black boxer briefs as fast as I can, so she can't see exactly how excited I am by this.

She's in up to her neck. I go straight over and pick her up. She wraps her legs around my waist and puts her arms on my shoulders.

"Oh," she says as she wiggles her hips, "I see the cold water didn't work."

"You are in so much trouble, Molly Carter," I scold her, staring straight into her eyes, trying to stare her down and stop her laughing. It doesn't work, but I know what will. I grab her waist and throw her as hard as I can into the water.

"Fuuuuu—" She squeals, but she's cut off as she goes under.

When she resurfaces, she's spluttering and frantically wiping her face. "Do you know how fucking disgusting that tastes, fuckface?" she says, glaring at me.

"No, I wasn't stupid enough to go under like you!" At that, she pushes a wave of water at me, but I see it coming and turn away.

We spend ages messing about in the water like teenagers. It's great to be carefree for a while. Molly is such fun to be around; she doesn't take herself too seriously, and she's quite happy to laugh at herself. I think she's starting to regret winding me up earlier, judging by the number of times she's had to spit out a mouthful of salt water.

I notice that she's started shivering and her teeth are chattering. "I think it's time we got out. You look freezing."

I swim over to where she is and stand close to her.

Time for my revenge.

"Come here," I say as I pull her into my arms and squeeze her tight. "Thanks for this. I like acting like kids again." I kiss her hair, making her look up at me.

"The whole week has been brilliant. Thank you for bringing me. I can't believe it's nearly over, though. I don't feel ready to leave yet."

She makes me laugh as she pouts. "I know, but we still have tomorrow, and then you've got all that new stuff to go in your room when we get back." The thought of that perks her up a little.

I slowly start rubbing my hands up and down her back like I'm warming her up, and I lean forward so I'm whispering in her ear. "Do you know, you're even more gorgeous when you have black makeup running down your face," I tell her softly.

It's completely dark out here but for the light the moon is casting, allowing me to see enough to know I just made goosebumps break out across her skin.

"I don't believe you. No one looks good like that," she replies.

"Believe it."

My hands are still roaming over her back, and I keep pushing them a little closer to her arse or around her sides to her breasts. Her pulse picks up from my touch.

I place a soft kiss under her ear, and I hear her sharp intake of breath at my action. I do it again, and again. Her breaths are coming out fast now, and her pulse pounds against my lips. I move my hands up her back and slip my fingers under the strap of her bra to test the water. She groans and presses her breasts harder into my chest. Her hips slowly start to grind against me, and it takes everything in me not to moan with pleasure. It's now or never, or I'll get carried away. I move my hands around her back one more time as I place another kiss to her neck. This time, I unsnap her bra, pull it away from her, and move towards the shore as quick as I can.

"Ryan, what the fuck?" she squeals from behind me. "Come back, you little fucker!"

I can't help it, I'm crying with laughter as I make

my way to our hut with our clothes.

I stand on our balcony overlooking the beach and Molly, who is still in the sea. She looks seriously lost out there alone. I almost feel bad. Almost.

Eventually, she squares her shoulders as though she's made a decision, and she starts to walk out the water, clutching her breasts in her hands.

When she hits the path to our beach hut, I shout down, "Revenge is sweet, Miss Molly." She looks up at me and growls—yes, actually growls.

As she comes towards me, I hold out the towel I got ready for her. See, I'm not a total dick.

"I cannot believe you did that, you fuckwit. I think I hate you a little bit," she says very seriously as she pulls the towel around her, unfortunately managing not to flash me in the process.

When she's sorted, she bursts out laughing. Thank God. She looked so serious, I thought she was about to castrate me right here. I can't help it, and I laugh along with her.

Once she's calmed down, she walks over to the fridge, pulls out the bottle of Apple Sourz, and pours us both a very large shot. "To embarrassing friends," she says with a laugh. I clink her glass and take a drink.

"To revenge," I say, and we repeat the process.

"I actually cannot believe you did that, Ryan. That took more balls than I gave you credit for."

"Don't you go worrying about my balls, Molly. There is most definitely nothing wrong with them."

Nine

Molly

The last day of our holiday was great. We chilled out by the beach hut, reading and enjoying each other's company.

It's now Friday. I've finished setting up my room, and Ryan's put my shelves and mirror up so I could get everything in place.

Going away wasn't the wisest thing to do, but it was worth all the work I've got to catch up with now. Because I've been in my room, the only time Ryan and I have really seen each other has been at dinner. With his extra time during the school holidays, he's been experimenting in his new kitchen and, I have to say, he's not doing a bad job.

Tonight is the night he's reserved for my birthday surprise. I hate surprises, and Ryan knows this, which is why he's been winding me up about it all week. I now feel like a coiled spring with the pressure of it all. He's told me to dress smart-casual, so I guess we are not going somewhere posh.

I decide to wear the black maxi dress with pink flower print that I didn't wear on the holiday; the jersey material clings in all the right places. I've left my make-up light and just added some eyeliner and mascara to make my eyes stand out a little. I grab my flip-flops out of my wardrobe, my handbag off the bed, and head upstairs to see if he's ready.

I find him sat on the sofa, watching the local news. He notices me straight away, turns the TV off, and comes over to me.

"You look amazing as always, Molly."

"You too." He's wearing light blue jeans that hug his arse and muscular thighs in the most delicious way, and a black fitted t-shirt and black Converse. It's simple, but so hot. He has obviously tried to style his hair but, as usual, his dirty blond locks are falling over his forehead in a sexy mess, and he smells out of this world.

"Right, come on. It's nearly time for your surprise."

I groan in response.

He grabs my hand and pulls me out of the house.

He stops by the passenger door of his car, opens it, and ushers me in.

"Wow, being a gentleman tonight, are we?" I comment.

"Not likely," he says with a huff, making me laugh. That is, until he leans into me, grabs the seatbelt and straps me in. A heated look flickers in his eyes quickly, but it's gone as fast as it appears.

"I am able to do that myself, you know."

"Molls, just be quiet and go with the flow. You're not in control here, I am," he says in his teacher voice.

"Sorry, Mr. Evans," I sing. With that, he pulls something out of his back pocket and moves towards me again. He's so quick that, before I know what's happening, he's tying something around my eyes. Once it's secured, I hear him shut the door and, a couple of seconds later, he gets in the driver's seat and starts the car.

"Is this really necessary?" I growl.

"Just forget that we're going somewhere, and imagine that it's research for that bondage project you were working on last week."

"Um, Ry...I don't think this is quite like that."

"Maybe not, but I thought it might take your mind off it a bit." He smiles. "Have you been to one of the nights you're advertising?" he asks quietly.

"Oh yeah, *all* the time."

He pauses as he considers my words. "You're into all that stuff? You've never talked about it before."

"No, Ry, not really. I've only ever stepped inside for a meeting with the manager."

"Oh um...what about...um..." He clears his throat. "Bondage in general. Have you done that stuff?"

"Ryan, are you getting embarrassed?"

"I just wondered."

"I've never been with anyone I would have trusted enough to do anything like that. What about you?" I ask, but I'm guessing from his hesitation that he hasn't.

He falls silent once again. I can only imagine he's thinking about Hannah.

"Right, we're here. Stay there and I'll help you out."

"Can't I take it off?" I sulk.

"Nope. Hang on."

A couple of minutes later, Ryan is standing behind me with his hands on my waist, steering me in the right direction.

"Right, we're going upstairs. Lift now...okay, up we go."

"Is it much farther?"

"No, we're almost there. Right, stand here." He brings me to a stop and turns me slightly. "Are you ready?"

With that, he unties me.

"What?" I ask as I look around.

I'm in some sort of office. It takes me a few seconds to register that the work hanging on the walls is what Hannah and I had designed since we started the company. I turn around to look at Ryan. He's not standing alone. Next to him are Susan, Pete, and Emma, and all of them have big smiles on their faces.

It's in that moment that it hits me.

"We're in the flat," I say as they all come towards me, wishing me happy birthday and giving me a hug.

"When Ryan moved into his new house, we got some builders in to revamp the place. We were going to rent it out to students again, but none of us wanted anyone living in the place you'd all spent so much time in. We applied to change its use from a flat to an office. Lilly designed the interior, and we asked your brothers to do the work. Then, it was going to sit here, waiting, until you were ready," Susan explains.

"Until I was ready?" Tears sting my eyes.

"When Ryan rang us last week to say that you were talking about hiring, we had to get our arses into gear and get it finished for you."

"You're telling me that all of this is for the business?"

Susan starts laughing. Apparently, the look on my face is priceless.

"Yes, it's for the business. The business that you and our daughter started. We want you to still be able to live out your dream, and this flat is the perfect way for you to do that. Do you like it?"

"You've already done so much for me...this is just too much."

"Angel, we love you like one of our own. We want to do everything we can to help you. Plus, it's for

Hannah as well. She would be so happy to see the business you both dreamed of coming to life."

With that, I throw myself at her and hold her tight as everything she just said settles into my brain. I turn around and give Pete a hug, and then Emma, before I turn and jump into Ryan's arms. I love the Morrisons with all my heart; they're my family, but I never expected them to do something like this for me.

After a few seconds, I realise that no one has said a word. I lift my head out of the crook of Ryan's neck and see Susan, Pete, and Emma staring at us. I suddenly realise how this must look to them and quickly remove myself from Ryan.

"Can I see the rest?" I ask, trying to break the sudden tension.

I'm in awe. The living/dining room is now a large office with two massive desks in it. The bedroom that used to be Hannah's is now a meeting room with a giant table in the center. Susan said they used her room for this because they wanted her to be involved with the decisions. My old room is now a mini living room with a sofa and TV. Emma's old room is currently empty, and the little kitchen and bathroom are the same as before. Everything is black, gray, and pink, to match our branding, and all the furniture is really modern.

Once I've seen everything, we head downstairs and outside. It's then that I get to take in the massive Angel Designs sign hanging between the two front windows. I love it.

As we get back in Ryan's car, Lilly and Dec join us while Emma chooses to go with Susan and Pete. I can't help but think she's pissed off after my display with Ryan upstairs. She's going to have to get used to us being close, because I can't be without him.

I just get settled in my seat when I feel the blindfold coming back around my eyes from behind me.

"For fuck's sake, not again."

"I'm afraid so," Lilly says. "I'm under strict instructions from Ryan."

I hear him and Dec get in the car and join in with Lilly's laughter at my pouting face.

"We aren't going far, Molls, stop sulking," Ryan says. I fold my arms over my chest and huff my annoyance.

RYAN WAS LYING when he said we weren't going far. I've been sat here in the dark for ages. Eventually, the engine turns off and hear the others get out. They've been talking amongst themselves during the journey, but I didn't join in. I was trying to show them how miserable being blindfolded was making me but, apparently, they didn't care.

Once Ryan has successfully guided me to our destination without letting me fall on my arse, he takes the blindfold off.

We're in our favourite pub, and sitting in front of

me are the Morrisons, as well as Steven, his wife Debs, their two little girls, Poppy and Mia, and Daniel.

"Happy birthday, kid," Steven says as comes over to give me a hug.

A wide smile splits my face at seeing everyone I love in one place.

It's been ages since I've spent time with my brothers. I hug Daniel after Steven has put me down, then Debs and the girls, who are very excited to see me. Poppy is six and Mia is four; they're both the spitting image of their mum, with light blonde hair and pale skin. Poppy has her mum's blue eyes, whereas Mia has her dad's green ones. I can just imagine how much stress they're going to cause my big brother when they're teenagers.

"I can't believe you're here!"

"Ryan phoned us at the beginning of the week to invite us. He told us you were going to see the office. What do you think?" Daniel asks.

"I love it. Thank you so much for helping do it."

"Anything for you, Molly-moo," Daniel says, rubbing his hand on my head, messing up my hair as if I were a little kid again.

WE HAD A BRILLIANT EVENING. I was surrounded by my family, and I couldn't be happier. I loved them all, and was grateful to have such amazing people in my life.

It's just past midnight, and I'm sat on the sofa with my laptop. As it's now officially my birthday, I have something to check. Ryan puts some music on and sits next to me with a beer in his hand.

"What are you doing?" he questions.

"I just need to check something."

"What's so important that you dived straight for your laptop as soon as you got in?"

"Nothing much," I say, to try to stop him prying. I hate what I'm about to check, but I need to know what it's going to be this year. I know it will make Ryan mad if I tell him the truth. I get the webpage up and log myself in, opening my account. As usual, it's already there. A lump forms in my throat, and my eyes tear up a bit. Every year, I hope it is going to be different and they'll actually do something to show me they care about me. Even a card would mean more to me than this.

"Molly, what's wrong?"

I knew I should have done this when I was on my own. "Nothing. I'm okay."

I go to shut the lid of my laptop, but Ryan is faster and grabs it from me.

"What is this?" he asks, his eyes running over the page. "Why have you had thirty thousand pounds paid into your account with the reference of 'Love'?"

"It's nothing." I feel myself getting more upset as he turns his head to look at me.

"It's from your parents, isn't it? When you said last week that you would hear from them on your birthday, this is what you meant?"

"Yes. I fucking hate it. Every birthday and Christmas, the only contact I have from them is a bank transfer." Saying it out loud makes the dejection only stronger.

"All I've ever wanted from them is their love, to be actual parents to me, but all they do is palm me off with money. I'm sure it's all a tax fiddle or something, because it's a different amount every time—like they just have some money to lose, so gift it to me. Some years they really 'love' me; others not so much. I would be so happy just to receive a hand-written card from them, because at least they would have gone to the effort of writing it themselves and putting a tiny bit of thought into it."

I take the laptop back and move the money out of my current account and into my savings. I log out, and take a big gulp of wine.

The muscle in Ryan's neck starts to pulse. "Have they always done this?"

"Since I graduated."

"What do you do with it? You don't live like someone who's loaded, and I've seen your bank account before now—it looks like a normal working person's."

I blow out a big breath. "Well, I got big lump when I turned twenty-one. I paid off the debts I'd accumulated as a student, and I gave Susan and Pete the rent I believed I should have been paying for all the years I lived in their flat for free. Then, with my brothers' help, I bought two cheap run-down flats in the city, did them up, and now rent them both out. I wanted to put the money to work, not just blow it on expensive clothes, holidays, and cars, like the other trust fund babies I grew up around. Steven reckons if I sold the flats now, I would easily double my money. I hate that I've used the family business for it, but Steven and Daniel are brilliant at what they do, and I knew I could trust them with it. They're sworn to secrecy. I never want my parents to know.

"I bought my car one year because I needed to meet with clients and taking the bus wasn't cutting it. I paid for the three of us to go to the Caribbean after graduating, too." Hannah and Ryan were together by then, so he would remember that. "I wanted to treat the most important people in my life to an unforgettable holiday. Every year, I give some of it to charity, and I make sure the people I love are looked after—no matter how slyly I have to do it."

Ryan looks thoughtful. "Have you done it to me before?"

"Maybe. I'm not telling you what, though."

"I'm going to let that slide, but I'm watching you, Molly Carter."

I'm woken up Saturday morning by my phone ringing. I begrudgingly open my eyes to see who it is.

"Steven, do you know what time it is?" I grumble. Then, I hear giggling.

"Happy birthday to you, happy birthday to you," my nieces sing to me.

"Aw, thank you, guys. That was lovely. Best birthday present ever."

"Auntie Molly?" Poppy asks.

"Yes, Pops?"

"It's lunchtime. You should be awake by now!" she admonishes me.

"Um, yeah, I guess I should." I hear a commotion in the background as Steven comes on the phone.

"Happy birthday, kid."

We chat for a bit, and I open the present the girls gave me last night. It's my favourite smellies. Debs always picks the best presents. Not long after, I hang up and lie back down, feeling like I could sleep the day away, but my phone goes off again. It's Daniel's turn.

"Happy birthday, Molls."

"Thanks. You sound as bad as I feel," I comment at his sleepy voice.

"I may have gone out after the meal last night," he explains. "Yes, just help yourself," I hear him say away from the phone.

"Got a friend, Daniel?" He's a bit of a player, my youngest big brother.

"Yeah, just some blonde I met last ni—yes, sorry baby, I know you have a name. Is the coffee ready yet?"

"I think I should let you go. If you're up for another night out, we're all going out tonight. Not sure where yet, but I can text you."

"You know me, Molls—can't turn down a night out." My brother may be thirty-seven, but he's still twenty-one at heart. I'm just waiting for the day he meets a woman who knocks him on his arse.

I snuggle back down again into my covers, when I hear a knock at my bedroom door.

"Yeah?" I groan.

"Happy birthday," Ryan chimes as he walks in with a tray of food and a huge bunch of flowers.

"Wow, is that all for me?"

"I thought you could have breakfast in bed." He places the tray down on my bedside table, and I see he's brought me all my favourite pastries, a pot of tea, orange juice, and a huge display of dusky pink flowers of all different types. He stands back and heads to the door.

"Where are you going? I can't eat this all by myself. Come join me."

"I'm just getting your present. Don't worry, I'm not leaving the food!"

He comes back in holding a huge, flat, rectangular giftbox. I feel a huge smile break across my face.

"Can I open it now?" I put my arms out like a little kid.

"Of course, birthday girl." I take it from him and rip into the paper to discover what I suspected.

"When did you go back and get this?"

"I didn't. I rang them and had it delivered to Susan and Pete's house."

Tears well in my eyes as I look down at the canvas in my hands. It's a painting looking out over the bay where we stayed. The roofs of the beach huts are showing, and the sun is going down, just like the night I watched it from the hot tub. When I first saw it in the gallery, I couldn't take my eyes off it. The artist had captured the scene perfectly.

"I can't believe you got it for me. Thank you so much. I love it." I crawl over to him so I can say thank you properly, placing a kiss on his cheek and squeezing him tight. It's when my arms touch his bare skin that I realise he's only in pyjama bottoms. A birthday breakfast can't get any better than this.

"Remind me, what's the plan for later?" Ryan asks around a bite of croissant.

"Megan is coming over later this afternoon to get ready with me, then we're meeting everyone at the Indian at eight before drinks. Chris and Shane have it all planned."

"They'd better not take us to the gay clubs again."

"Are you still grumpy about being hit on repeatedly that night?" I can't help but laugh at his unimpressed face. "Oh, come on, you can't blame them. You're hot." He looks up at me through hooded eyes, and my breath catches. Something sizzles between us and I move away, hoping the distance will take the edge off the connection.

Ten

Ryan

Molly and Megan have been downstairs for a couple of hours, getting ready for tonight. I have no idea what takes so long, but they must be having fun because I can hear them laughing over the music from up here.

I'm stood in the kitchen with a towel wrapped around my waist as I look in the fridge for a beer. A noise startles me and, turning my head, I see Molly heading my way, wearing a little vest top and shorts. Her hair is loosely curled and her makeup done. She walks straight to me; I feel her breasts crush against my back as she leans into the fridge with one hand while resting the other low on my hip. She grabs the bottle of wine and slowly pulls back. Her hand moves from my hip, slides up my abs and wraps around the other side as she hugs me. I can feel her nose against my shoulder as she inhales.

"You smell amazing," she whispers against my skin before she walks out of the room, and down the stairs until I hear her bedroom door shut.

What the fuck was that? Tingles warm my skin and my heart races.

"LADIES, it's half past seven, and the taxi is waiting. Hurry the fuck up," I shout through Molly's bedroom door. I have no idea what they've been doing in there all this time, but I'm expecting something awesome. It took me ten minutes flat to be dressed in dark jeans and a polo shirt. I ran some wax through my hair, and I was ready. I've spent the rest of the evening waiting. I haven't been able to shake the feelings Molly ignited in me earlier, and I can't wait to see her.

Suddenly, the door flies open and Megan walks out, ready to go. She looks good in her black skinny jeans and glittery silver top. Her normally tied up hair is hanging straight around her shoulders, and I notice it's a brighter red than the last time I saw her. She's taller than Molly, which isn't hard, and has more curves thanks to her cute little boy.

"Please tell me she is ready," I say to Megan.

"Yes, she's coming, it'll be worth the wait, I promise."

Shit.

I turn away from Megan when I see movement to my left, and Molly appears from her bathroom. My chin drops to the floor as she sashays towards us. Her hair and make-up is the same as I saw earlier, but now she's wearing a tight, deep purple short dress that shows a small amount of cleavage, making me lick my lips. On her feet are glittery silver heels, which make her exposed legs look extraordinary.

"See what I mean?" Megan says beside me.

Molly turns to grab her bag off her bed, revealing the back of the dress—or lack thereof. I suck in a breath at the amount of exposed skin. I can see almost down to the top of her arse. The desire to run my hands across her back is painful—almost as painful as my dick staining against the fabric of my jeans.

"Ry, you okay?" Molly asks as she moves towards me.

I swallow before nodding my head and saying, "Uh huh," as she walks past me and out the front door. Her scent fills my senses, making my mouth water. I don't think I have ever been as turned on as I am right now, and I haven't even touched her.

"Shit, you've got it bad, haven't you?"

I shake my head. "Sorry, what?"

"Molly. You want her."

What do I say to that?

"She's my best friend, Megan."

With that, I walk out with Megan and lock the door, putting an end to the conversation, but I can tell by the look she's giving me that I haven't convinced her.

THE OTHERS ARE ALREADY SEATED when we arrive, which is no surprise. We quickly say hello to everyone and get sat down. I don't know whether it's a good thing or not that I'm opposite Molly. I'm not close enough to touch her, but every time I look up, she's all I can see. Shane and Chris are busy filling her in on their wedding plans on one side of me, and Megan and Emma are talking about Cocoa's on the other. All I can do is try to concentrate on not just staring at Molly. The guys have tried dragging me into their conversations, but I wasn't really paying attention to anything. They seem to have given up on me now.

As the meal comes to an end, I go over to the bar to settle the bill. If I'm not quick, Molly will beat me to it, and she's not paying for her own birthday meal.

"Can I settle the bill for the table over there?" I ask, pointing in our table's direction.

"Sorry sir, but it's already been paid for. The lady in the purple dress came up here when you first came in, gave me her card details and told me not to let anyone else pay for this meal."

"I should have known." I look back to the table and see Molly grinning at me. Shaking my head at her, I walk off to the men's room.

I'm washing my hands when Shane walks in.

"She looks hot tonight, doesn't she?"

"Who?"

"Don't pretend you haven't noticed. I've watched you watch her the whole time we've been here."

I say nothing.

"Look, Ryan, if you're into her, then go for it. I want to see you both happy. You deserve that after the year you've had. But I should warn you that whilst you've been drooling over Molly, Emma has been shooting daggers from across the table."

"Nothing will happen between us. She's my best friend. She made it quite clear to Emma the other day, I'm like a brother to her." Shane raises an eyebrow at me. "Yes, I was eavesdropping on their conversation. I wanted to make sure she was okay."

"You've got to understand—she's lost her twin, the other half of her, and she suddenly finds out you've moved Molly in. It must have been a shock. But even a blind person could see how much you and Molly care about each other. Emma will be able to see that as well, and if something is destined to happen between the two of you, it will all work out."

"I can't risk it, Shane. I'll see you out there," I say, leaving him to it, but I can't deny that his words ring in my ears as I make my way back to the table.

"Was my fiancé trying to turn you gay in there or something? You've both been gone for ages," Chris laughs as I get back to the table.

"Yeah, we had a quickie in one if the cubicles. Not sure what the fuss is all about; you can keep him," I deadpan, as they all turn to me with shocked looks on their faces. I can't help but laugh.

A COUPLE OF HOURS LATER, we're on the dance floor of one of Oxford's biggest clubs. We're all nicely buzzed, thanks to the shots Shane and Chris ordered for us all.

I've tried my best to stay away from Molly. I don't want to cause any more problems with Emma. I don't want to be the reason they argue.

I watch as a guy who's been eyeing up Molly plucks up the courage to dance with her. I don't like the look of him—he's like the dickheads she would have been with before. He goes up right behind her, puts his hands on her hips, and starts grinding her arse into him. My fists clench at my sides and fire races through my veins as I take in his hands on her body. Looking up, she tries to shrug him off, but he's not having any of it and pulls her tighter to him. I can tell she's getting pissed off, and it makes me want to break the fucker's nose. I move towards them and stand right against her side, removing his hand from her hip.

"Hands off," I growl at him loudly so he can hear me over the music. He looks me up and down and must realise he wouldn't win if he started something with me, then begrudgingly walks off back to his group of mates.

I turn Molly to face me. She puts her arms around my shoulders, leans into me, and whispers in my ear, "Thank you." I grab her hips and pull her against me.

What started out innocent has quite quickly turned into something...not so innocent. Molly turns in my arms so she has her back to my chest and shoves her arse into my groin. She flicks her head around and smiles wickedly at me over her shoulder.

I look up when I feel eyes on me. Shane's smirking in our direction while he dances with Chris, Emma, Megan, and Daniel, who showed up for a drink earlier. He nods at me encouragingly, which catches Emma's attention. She looks our way and her expression hardens. She's really pretty drunk, and she instantly stops moving and looks us up and down. She looks murderous.

She storms over. "What the fuck do you two think you're doing? You promised me nothing was happening," she shouts, waving her arms around in front of us.

"Emma," Molly says, "We're just messing about. Right, Ry?"

Emma turns her attention to me.

"We're just dancing." Listening to myself slur these words to her, I realise just how drunk I actually am.

"You two must think I'm fucking stupid. There's no way you aren't fucking each other."

"Wow, Emma. Chill out. If they say there's nothing going on, then there's nothing going on. Neither Molly nor Ryan would lie to you," Shane shouts above the music.

"But you just saw them! You were *encouraging* it!"

"Emma, they're both drunk. Hell, we all are. We're all just enjoying ourselves."

"You said he was like your brother!" she screams in Molly's direction. "Never in a million years would I dance with Dec like that."

"Emma, if you don't believe us, fine. Go home. We're doing nothing wrong, so get over yourself," Molly growls at her, which shocks me. I've seen her stand her ground with plenty of people before, but I never thought she'd put Emma in her place.

I watch as Emma huffs out a breath and storms off. Daniel comes over, having watched the whole thing, and kisses Molly on the cheek before telling her he's going to make sure Emma gets home okay.

Molly turns to look at me, and I see a single tear fall down her cheek. I know she feels awful about losing her temper. I put my arm around her shoulder. "Do you want to go?" I ask.

"Yes, please."

We say our goodbyes to everyone and apologise for ruining the evening. We're just walking out of the club when Molly's pulled away from me. I look to my right to see the guy who was trying to dance with her.

"What the fuck are you doing?" she shouts.

"Are you ready to dance now?" he snarls, grabbing her and pushing her up against the wall.

"Get the fuck off me!" she screams in his face, forcing me to move.

Slamming my body into his, I watch him stumble to the ground. I turn to make sure Molly's okay before focusing on him.

"He said you'd be a sure thing," he shouts before my fist collides with his jaw.

"Who said that?" I shout at him before taking another shot.

"Me," a familiar voice says from behind me. "I thought maybe she needed a real man for her birthday."

"Max?" Molly whimpers.

I land another punch to the dick on the floor before standing up to face Max. I'm barely at full height when I feel his fist hit my jaw.

"How dare you fucking take her from me," Max growls angrily. "She's mine. You don't get to just move her in with you because you're lonely now your girl-friend's dead." I see red and launch myself at him.

"Ryan, stop!" Molly screams.

Max manages to get a couple more punches in before I have him slumped against the wall, moaning in pain.

"You fucking stay away from her, you cheating

piece of shit. I'll finish you next time. I'll fucking finish you." I'm shaking with anger and I stretch my fingers out, my knuckles aching. How *dare* he treat her this way. Molly comes up to my side and put her arms around me. Still fuelled by too much pent-up anger, I push her away, needing a little space. The look she gives me guts me. Her shoulders drop as she turns and starts walking towards the waiting taxis.

She only makes it a couple of steps before I come to my senses, place my hand on her lower back, and guide her towards a car to take us home.

Molly

RYAN IS silent beside me and hasn't said anything since he threatened Max outside the club, but I can feel his body starting to relax against me.

When the car comes to a stop in front of our house, I throw some cash at the driver and pull Ryan out of the car. He stumbles as we make our way up to the front door.

"Steady, Ry, I'm not going to be able to catch you if you fall."

I open the front door. He trips and crashes into the hallway wall. I grab him around the waist as he starts to slide down, pulling him with me into my room. I sit him on the edge of my bed and place my hands on his cheeks, careful of the bruises and cuts on his face.

"Ryan, are you okay?" I ask gently. He still hasn't said anything.

"I'm just so angry about how you're treated by the people who are meant to care about you."

"It's okay, because I've got you. Thank you for what you did tonight, and I'm sorry you got hurt," I say, gently running my thumb over his lip, causing him to suck in a breath. "Sorry," I whisper.

"I'll always fight for you, Molly. Always."

I really don't know how to reply to that, so I stand and get the first aid kit from upstairs, as well as something cold for his face and hand. I'm stood at the sink filling a sandwich bag with ice when a shiver runs down my spine and a feeling that I'm being watched has me on full alert. When I look up, I see the woman next door staring at me through the window. Grimacing at how nosey she is, I release the blind string and cut her off. When I return, Ryan's exactly as I left him but with his head in his hands. As I move closer, he lifts his head to look at me. His lips quirk up at the corners when I smile at him.

"I'm not even going to attempt to get you upstairs and into bed, so you can stay here. Let's get you comfy, and I'll clean you up and put this ice on you to try to reduce some of the bruising. Arms up." He does as he's told, and I carefully pull his polo shirt over his head, minding his cuts and bruises. Leaning down, I remove his shoes and socks, and then I pull the duvet aside, ready for him.

"Right, lie down with your head on the pillow; you're going to have to help me with your jeans." He follows my orders, undoes his fly, and lifts his hips so I can pull them off. I cover him quickly.

I clean his cuts, making him wince before grabbing the ice bags and placing one on his eye and grabbing his left hand to hold it in place. Then, I turn his right hand over and rest a second bag over his knuckles.

"Are you going to be okay while I get changed?"

He groans, so I take that as a yes, grab a pair of pyjamas, and head to the bathroom.

When I emerge ten minutes later, ready for bed, I'm surprised to see him sat up, drinking the water and looking at me. I was sure he was going to pass out as soon as I left the room.

"Hey. How you doing?"

"I'm fine. Come on, get in."

I walk round to the other side of the bed and follow his instructions. I lie on my back, staring at the ceiling for a few minutes, my heart pounding and my skin tingling with awareness. Goosebumps prickle my skin where Ryan's eyes run over me, so I look over to him and smile.

"I really hate him," Ryan says. "And your parents, and Emma a bit right now." His arm comes around my stomach and pulls me to him until he's spooning me.

"Ry, can we not talk about them, please? I just want

to forget for tonight. Let's go to sleep." He kisses the top of my head and settles in for the night. I fight to keep the small smile from my lips at how right this feels.

I lie awake in Ryan's arms for ages, but it doesn't take long before his breathing slows. My mind's running around all the events that happened this evening. Emma—she's my biggest problem. Do I try to see her and talk to her, or do I let her stew for a while and hope she comes to the conclusion that she overre-acted? What if she tells Susan and Pete, and they're on her side? I don't want to fall out with them, too.

———————

At some point, I must have fallen asleep, because I've just woken up with Ryan still wrapped around me. He makes me feel safe, but at the same time it scares the shit out of me. What I'm not so happy about is his morning erection stabbing me in the bum.

I try to sneak out of his hold, carefully lifting his arm and sliding out from under him, but I'm suddenly pulled back.

"No," he grumbles. I find myself in exactly the same position, and my body tenses.

"Are you awake?" I whisper.

"No," he replies, making me smile.

"Really?"

"Go back to sleep."

"I can't."

"You're not going anywhere, I'm too comfortable."

"Well, I should tell you then that I have a problem."

"What now, Molls?"

"There's something stabbing me in the butt. It's not very comfortable."

He grunts. "I see your problem, and I know a number of ways it can be resolved."

Turning my head, I find a huge grin over his face. I pull myself away from him and turn so I'm facing him squarely.

"Not happening, Evans," I say. "Get yourself under control, please."

"Sorry, my body can't help it, especially while it's cuddled around such a hot one."

"Stop it, Ryan."

"Sorry," he pouts. I smack him gently on his chest. I know he's only teasing—well, I think he is—but that doesn't stop my body from reacting in ways it shouldn't.

"I'm warning you now that we will be having a conversation about what's going on here."

"Molls, do I need to give you a sex ed lesson? It's called an erection; men get them when they're turned on, or first thing in the—"

I put my hand over his mouth. "That's not what I am talking about." I wave my hand between us. "I'm talking about what's been going on between us. I need to get my head together, and so do you, because my guess is that you feel like shit this morning."

"I've felt better, and my face is killing me."

"Well, that's what happens when you get into a fight with two dickheads."

He sucks in a breath as if he's remembering. "Max."

"Don't worry—you left them in a worse state than you're in right now. I don't think they'll be bothering me again."

A FEW HOURS LATER, I find myself sat on a bar stool in Cocoa's, chatting to Megan while she finishes up for the day. I spent a couple of hours upstairs making plans for what I need to do this week and looking at the projects I have at the moment, before coming down to get Megan's opinion on my situation with Ryan. I watch as she locks up and comes to join me where her coffee is waiting. She groans as she sits down.

"Long day?"

"Yes, and it's not helped by the hangover which, by the way, you are totally to blame for." She points at me.

"Tell me if I'm wrong, but I'm pretty sure at some point yesterday you told me you wanted to get wasted because you haven't in so long."

She laughs. "So, I have this weird feeling that you're here because you want to talk about someone." Megan tilts her head and raises her eyebrow.

"No need to be so smug." I tell her about the fight she missed after we left, what happened when we got home, and then this morning. She listens to everything and nods in all the right places.

"I think this conversation is going to take longer than I have. James is going out this evening, so I need to be back for Oscar. Do you want to follow me back? We can order a takeaway."

Twenty minutes later, I'm following Megan into the flat she shares with her boyfriend James and their son.

"Mummy!" Oscar screams when he sees her.

She picks him up and kisses him. "Hey, little man. Have you had a good day with Daddy?"

Oscar is the cutest kid I think I've ever seen. He turned three not so long ago. Like his dad, he's pretty tall, but he has his mum's dark hair and eyes. Megan keeps his hair quite long and scruffs it up with a bit of wax to make him a smaller, dark-haired version of his dad.

"Hey, baby," James says, coming over to Megan and kissing her forehead. I'm so jealous of their easy, yet loving, relationship. They've been together for seven years now, and I'm just waiting for an engagement announcement sometime soon.

"Molly, what did you do to my girlfriend last night? She was up half the night, puking."

"Sorry, but that is not my fault. She's a grown woman and should know when to stop," I laugh.

"Have a good night, ladies," he calls from the hallway.

"I'm not a lady," Oscar shouts from his bedroom.

"No, you're not, little man, sorry. See you later, ladies and Oscar," he chuckles as he leaves the flat.

Megan leaves me to order the dinner while she puts Oscar to bed. I ring and place an order for our favourite Chinese dishes and pour us both glasses of water.

"So, Molly. Million-dollar question. Are you going to get under him or over him?" Megan asks as she comes back into the kitchen, trying not to laugh.

"In the back of my mind, I just see it going tits up and then losing him. I would rather fight to keep him as my friend than do something to remove him from my life completely.

"Then there's Emma. Since the accident, she's distanced herself from everyone. She's made her opinion quite clear. I don't want to trash my friendship with her, and I'm yet to find out if Susan and Pete share her feelings. I cannot lose them; I see them as my parents."

"I understand all that, I do, but what if you make a move with Ryan and it's amazing, and it lasts?" she asks, ever the romantic. "What's the alternative?"

"Putting myself back out there and going on some dates, I guess. Finding out if this attraction to Ryan is because of him, or because I need a bloke in my life."

"Are you sure that's what you want?"

"As sure as I can be."

She pauses. "If you're serious, I have someone I could set you up with."

I nod at her. Megan has good taste in men and is a good judge of character, so I'm as hopeful as I can be. "Okay, who?"

"One of James' friends from work. I think you'd get on great. Should I give him your number?"

"Sure. What's the worst that could happen?"

Eleven

Ryan

I've spent all day lying on the sofa in front of the TV, thoughts of Molly and everything that has happened over the last couple of weeks floating in and out of my mind.

She said before she left this morning that we were going to talk about what's been happening between us. I've been going backwards and forwards over what I want for hours. After the chat I had with Shane last night, what he said keeps coming back to me. What if he's right? What if this is meant to happen?

I eventually give up waiting for her to come home. I haven't heard from her all day, but she said she needed to get her head straight, so I don't want to interrupt her. It's just before midnight when I hear the front door shut. I wait for her to come upstairs, but she doesn't, instead going straight to bed.

After another hour of lying in bed, not sleeping, my need to see her gets the better of me. Knowing she's downstairs is torture. I quietly make my way down to her room. Luckily, her door is slightly open. I peek around the doorframe to see her sound asleep, facing me. A bit of hair has fallen across her face and the rest is lying across her chest. I bite down on my bottom lip and clench my fists. My need to walk over and fix it becomes too much. She's wearing a vest top and tiny shorts, so tiny they don't go anywhere near covering her arse. Her legs are tangled around the duvet at the bottom of the bed. I stand there for a few minutes, just looking at her and listening to her breathing.

It's in that moment that I realise just how much I want her. Just how much I *need* her.

———

Rolling over, I pull my eyelids open. It's already getting on for ten o'clock. Oh, I love the holidays—late nights and even later mornings. Heaven. I jump out of bed and quickly shower and get dressed before heading downstairs, hoping Molly will be there, ready to talk.

When I get to the kitchen, there's no sign of her. I flick the kettle on, then head down to her room to see if she's there. The door is open, but there's still no sign of her. She was obviously up early to get the office set up. I guess my little speech will have to wait.

I end up spending most of the day working out, going for a ridiculously long run, then hitting the weights, trying to keep myself busy.

When I get home, I FaceTime my mum. It's taken me years to get my parents to be able to use it, but I think we've got there at last. I'd totally forgotten about my black eye and busted lip, but one look at me has my mum in a right tizz. It takes me a full ten minutes to calm her down. I explain to her what happened in as little detail I can. She's made it quite clear in the past that she doesn't really like Molly. It didn't bother me before, but now I could throttle Hannah for telling my mum all about her best friend's antics. I always end up having to defend her to my mum, and I hate it.

After we say goodbye, I decide to see if I can get my sisters on a group chat. We were always really close growing up and, I hate to admit it, but I miss them being so far away. To my surprise, they both answer my call. Neither came home from university this summer, much to my parents' disappointment. Abbi has stayed in the flat she shares with her mate and is working with kids at a summer school. Liv has moved out of halls and into a flat with her mates and landed herself a summer job at a local newspaper.

They don't have quite the reaction to my bruised face as Mum did, but they're still concerned. After I finish telling the story again, both of them have soppy looks on their faces as they stare into the camera.

"What's wrong with you two?" I ask them, confused.

"You love her," they say in unison, smiling dopily at me.

"Yeah, of course. She's my best friend," I say, a bit taken aback.

We spend the next hour chatting about our lives— that is, until I hear the front door close, signalling Molly's return. I quickly make my excuses and say my goodbyes to my sisters.

"Hey," I say as she rounds the corner into the room, carrying a couple of shopping bags.

"How are you feeling? Hangover gone now?" she smirks, placing the bags on the counter and pulling out the contents.

"Yeah, fine now, thanks." My brows draw together at the sudden tension between us. I feel like I've missed something.

"Good. I bought ingredients for a carbonara, if that's okay with you?"

"As long as you're cooking, Molls, anything is good with me."

She laughs and turns to get started. "So, what have you been up to?" she asks over her shoulder.

"Not much. Been to the gym and just talked with my family."

"Oh God," she groans. "I bet your mum loved the

look of your face. Please tell me you didn't tell her it was because of me? She already hates me."

"She doesn't hate you, Molly." I'm not sure if that's a lie or not. "I gave her a diluted version of what happened. She understood."

"Yeah, whatever you say, Ry," she says, shaking her head, "How are Abbi and Liv?"

"Both good. They're working hard. I think they're secretly glad they didn't go home this summer. I told them they should come visit. I hope that's okay."

"Of course, it is. It's been ages since I've seen them. And unlike your parents, they actually like me."

Molly continues with dinner while I set the table and pour us both drinks. I sit down and take a sip just as she's plating up.

"Here you go," she says, placing it in front of me.

"Smells amazing, as always. Thank you." Grabbing my knife and fork, I immediately dig in. "So, what have you been doing the last two days?" I ask, curious.

"Well, after I left you yesterday, I went to the office to get a list together for what I need, then I met Megan for coffee. We ended up spending the whole night chatting."

"You spent nearly all day Saturday with her. What the hell did you have to talk about for so long?" Her answer is just to lift her eyebrow at me. I feel my cheeks flush a little, knowing I was their topic of conversation. God, I hope she's come to the same conclusion as me.

"Then, this morning, I got up early to ask my old

lecturer if he could give me any names for a potential new employee."

"Did he have any ideas?"

"He gave me a number for a guy who graduated last year. Apparently, our styles would complement each other well."

"Have you spoken to him?"

"I rang him as soon as I left campus. I'm meeting him at Cocoa's in the morning. "

"That's great. I hope he's as good as your lecturer has made him out to be."

I watch as Molly nervously shifts in her seat, looking at me then back down again, like she's building up to saying something.

"Spit it out, Molls."

"I'vegotadateonfridaynight," she says at such a speed it takes me a few seconds to decipher what she just said. My heart drops and my mouth opens in surprise.

"What?"

"Megan has set me up with one of James' work mates. His name is Adam, and he's taking me to that new Italian place in town."

"That's good, Molly. You need to try to find your Prince Charming," I just about manage to get out through gritted teeth.

Molly chats away to me some more after that little announcement, but I don't hear any of what she says. I just keep replaying what she said in my head.

I've got a date on friday night. *I've got a date on friday night. I've got a date on friday night.*

Molly

RYAN MAKES his excuses after we finish dinner, and he disappears up to his room with disappointment clouding his eyes.

"Shit," I whisper to myself. He looked like a little kid who had just had his new puppy taken away from him. I feel awful. I didn't want to hurt him. I'd convinced myself that he would agree with my decision, but the look on his face has me thinking that wasn't what he wanted at all.

After going through everything I want to talk to Jackson about in the morning, I head to bed, although sleep eludes me for hours. All I can see every time I close my eyes is the look on Ryan's face. I don't want to be the one who puts it there.

It feels like I've only been asleep for two hours when my alarm clock goes off. "Noooo..." I grumble as I lean over and hit the top of it to shut it up. Dragging my exhausted body to sit up, I wipe the sleep from my eyes before I remember why I'm up so early. I'm meeting my possible first employee. The thought of this gives my body the boost it needs.

By NINE O'CLOCK, I'm in our booth at Cocoa's, waiting for Jackson to arrive. I gave him a brief description of myself on the phone yesterday, so he finds me easily when he arrives.

"Molly Carter?" he asks.

I look up and am at a loss for words. The guy stood before me is stunning. The first thing I notice are his eyes; they're bright green. His hair is the colour of dark chocolate, hanging long and shaggy around his face. I think it's probably long enough to tie up. He has strong cheekbones and a square-cut jaw. I pull myself together so I can answer.

"Yep, that's me."

He sticks his arm out towards me, and I can't help but let my eyes travel down the length of his forearm, exposed by his rolled-up shirtsleeve. It's pure muscle with strong veins, packaged in a full sleeve of stunning tattoos. It looks like it could do some serious damage.

I realise I'm ogling my potential employee, so I quickly stick my own hand out. "Nice to meet you, Jackson. Have a seat. What can I get you to drink?"

While he gets comfortable, I quickly nip behind the bar and make his coffee. Lilly is working this morning so doesn't bat an eyelid when I intrude on her.

"Who's that? He is seriously hot," she asks, her eyes roaming over Jackson.

"I'm interviewing him for a job."

"Shit, Molls, you wouldn't get any work done if he was sat opposite you in the office."

"I know, right?"

Jackson must hear us giggling like schoolgirls, because he looks up and smirks at us.

"Fuck," I mutter and make my way back to him with a slightly higher temperature and flushed cheeks.

"Here you go, Jackson," I say, passing his espresso over to him.

"Please, call me Jax. Only my parents call me Jackson. It makes me think I'm in trouble."

"Okay, Jax it is. So, do you want to show me what you've got?" I nod my head towards his portfolio, but instantly flush when he smiles at me and looks down at it on his lap. "I'm dying to see your designs. I've heard great things."

"Wow, these are awesome. You've got some serious talent, Jax. How don't you already have a job?" I ask, thumbing through his work.

"I've had a few interviews over the last year, but my style didn't really suit the companies, I guess," he answers with a shrug of his shoulders.

"Well, I hope their loss is my gain."

"Are you serious?"

I look up and give him a wide smile.

We spend the next hour chatting about the

company and the work we've done so far, and I explain about Cocoa's and the office upstairs when he asks why I keep helping myself to coffee. I talk about Hannah, albeit briefly, and I'm thankful Jax doesn't ask many questions about her. I get the impression that he understands. We talk money, hours, and all the other nitty gritty bits that we need to go through, and generally about ourselves. We're going to be spending quite a bit of time together, so it's important that we can get on.

Eventually, I put our mugs in the dishwasher and take Jax upstairs to see the office and the work I've done recently, so he can get a feel for my style.

"Wow, this place is amazing," he says, walking around.

"I know. After meeting you, I'm going shopping for all the equipment we're going to need."

"We?" he asks, his eyebrows raised.

"Yes, if you're up for it. Correct me if you don't agree, but I think we could have a good thing here. Our design styles complement each other's well, but we have different skills to enable us to do a range of jobs, and we seem to get on well enough. So far, anyway."

"I'm really excited about this, Molly. I think we could have something really good."

"Fantastic. Well...welcome to Angel Designs, Jax Parker." I stick my hand out to him and he grabs it, laughing, then pulls me into a tight hug. It reminds me of a Ryan hug with of all the muscle, but Jax is a smaller build. He doesn't engulf me in quite the same way.

"So, I don't want to intrude on your plans, but I'm free for the rest of the day. Do you want company while you kit this place out? I've got a mate who works in one of the computer stores. He owes me a favour. Hopefully, he can do us a good deal."

"Brilliant. I've got a list." I pull my notebook out of my bag and pass it to him as we head out of the office. "See if you think I've missed anything."

We have a great afternoon picking everything we need and getting it all set up in the office, ready for us to start work. I went down to Cocoa's to grab us some lunch that we ate in our new living room. It was weird to think that this was my bedroom for so many years.

During lunch, Jax tells me all about his girlfriend, Lucy. They've only been together a couple of months, but as far as he's concerned, it was love at first sight. She moved in with him last month. It makes me smile, thinking how at odds his appearance is to his romantic heart.

The more we get to know each other, the more I'm confident that we'll get on really well working together. I was pleased when he started talking about his family to find out that, although they own a chain of restaurants across the country, Jax had no intention of working with them. He wanted to do his own thing, like I did. Luckily for him, his family supported his decision wholeheartedly and have been behind him all the way. I got the impression that he couldn't wait to ring them and tell them about this job.

Jax has to give two weeks' notice at the bar he works at, but he's agreed to come in during the afternoons before he starts his shifts to help me get started here and pick up some of my jobs.

Once we say our goodbyes, I head home. I can't wait to tell Ryan about it all, but, to my disappointment, he isn't at home when I get there. Instead, I ring Susan and tell her everything. I can't say I was surprised that, by the time I rang, she had already heard about Jax from Lilly.

"I hear he's quite the hottie," she says with a laugh.

"He's not bad to look at, and his artwork is stunning. I think we're going to make a really good team. The office looks fantastic—you should pop up when you're next at Cocoa's."

"I'm so glad you found someone so soon that you like so much."

"Thank you so much for what you've done for me. I still can't quite believe it. It does feel like Hannah is part of it."

"You're more than welcome, angel." I can hear her start to well up. We chat for a few more minutes, until she has to go and tend to dinner.

I feel a bit lost for what to do. I was hoping to spend the evening with Ryan, but it doesn't look like that's going to be happening. Instead, I grab my sketchpad, settle on the sofa with the TV on, and coming up with some concepts for my next project.

I AWAKE with a start at three o'clock from a loud banging on the front door. I scramble out of bed to see what's going on, just as Ryan manages to get his key in the door and comes stumbling through into the hallway. When he sees me, he stops and stares at me. The look he gives me sends a shiver down my spine. I've only ever once seen such a cold look in his eyes, and that was Saturday night, right before he punched the guy who pulled me down the street.

He sways on his feet and stumbles back so he's leaning against the wall for support.

"Come on, Ry. Let's get you up to bed." I go to grab him around the waist to help him up the stairs, but he pushes me away.

"I don't need you, Molly," he growls coldly. I'm taken aback by his tone. He's never been anything but nice, so to hear him snap at me is a real shock.

He turns to face the stairs and starts towards them slowly. "I don't need you." He looks totally defeated with his head down and shoulders slumped.

I stand there, shocked, and watch him climb his way up the stairs. Just as he disappears out of my sight, I feel a single tear run down my cheek. Confusion and hurt engulf me as I stand, staring at the empty space where he just was.

I eventually make my way back to my room and lie back on my bed, staring at the ceiling, wondering what the hell just happened. Needless to say, I have another restless night's sleep.

———————

THIS PATTERN with Ryan continues for the next three days. I get up every morning, hoping to see him before I go to the office, but he's still in bed. Then, when I get home in the evenings, he's already gone out.

I've texted him a few times but had no response and, when I ring his phone, it goes straight to voicemail.

By the time I get in from work on Friday night to get ready for my date, I'm surprised to find Ryan sat on the sofa, surrounded by empty beer cans and looking a little worse for wear. I really wish I'd had time to talk to him about what's going on, but I've only got an hour before I need to head out to meet Adam.

Twelve

Ryan

This week has been shit—total shit. Ever since Molly told me about her date, I've been a complete mess, and I can't seem to sort myself out. The only thing that has helped me forget is alcohol. Luckily for me, my mates from school are back and keen to keep up the party lifestyle from their holiday, so we've been out to different bars every night this week. I can't honestly say I remember much of what's happened, but it means I also don't remember thinking or being miserable about Molly.

Tonight is Molly's date, and I made the stupid decision to stay home. I wanted to make sure I was here if she needed me, but at some point during the afternoon, the urge to drown everything out was too strong so I hit the beer—again. Now, I'm not going to be much good if her date goes south.

To say she looked shocked to see me here when she came home would be an understatement. I've missed her so much this week, but the thought of spending time with her at the moment makes my chest hurt. I feel like a complete pussy.

After an amount of time I'm completely unaware of, I hear her coming back up the stairs. When I look up to her, my heart clenches as I see she's wearing the white dress she had on the evening we went out for dinner in Cornwall and ended up in the sea. A giant lump forms in my throat at the memory.

"Well, I'm off. Have a good night, Ryan." The look on her face when she says this is almost as dejected as I feel. She looks at her feet, then turns to walk out. Just before she gets to the door, I find my voice.

"Molly?"

"Yeah?"

"You look gorgeous. I hope he treats you well." I even manage to crack a smile for her.

I MUST HAVE PASSED out on the sofa before she got home, because the next thing I know, the room is really bright, and when I open my eyes, Molly's making a cup of tea in the kitchen.

"Morning," she sings cheerfully, making my head hurt.

I just groan back at her.

"Ry, you're not eighteen anymore. Hangovers from week-long binges are going to last much longer than our university days."

I groan again, roll off the sofa onto my hands and knees, and crawl out of the room and up to my bedroom, where I collapse on my bed and fall back to sleep.

By the time I wake up again, it's the afternoon, and I still feel like death. I drag my arse into the shower in the hope it will wake me up, but it does very little to pull me out of the slump I've found myself in.

I head down to the kitchen, hoping coffee might be more successful. I'm grabbing a mug when a note catches my eye.

Ry,
I've gone out with Megan and Oscar, then I'm having dinner tonight with Jax at The Fat Dog. Maybe lay off the beer today, huh? I'm worried about you.
Love and hugs,
Molly xx

RED HOT ANGER flows through me and the mug in my hand goes flying and smashes against the far wall of the living room.

"Who the fuck is Jax?" I growl.

Leaning back against the kitchen worktop, I shut my eyes and try to calm myself down. Molly swore when she moved in here that she was turning over a new leaf with men, and not using them to make herself feel cared for, but here she is, going out with two different guys on two consecutive nights. She might have ruined me at the moment, but I'm sure as hell not going to let her slip back into her old ways.

Molly

"MOLLY, CAN I ASK YOU SOMETHING?" Megan asks sheepishly, which piques my interest.

"Of course. What's up?" She's looking more and more embarrassed by the second. "Megan, why are you blushing?"

"Um...well, J-James has this um...f-fantasy."

"Megan, I love you both, but I'm not having a three-some with you."

"What? No! Sorry, no, that's not it at all." She laughs once she's recovered from the shock.

"Whatever it is you want to ask me can't be as embarrassing as asking that. Out with it."

"He wants me to pole dance for him. It's his birthday in a couple of months, so I looked up classes and the strip club in town has dance studios at the back where they do lessons. Would you come with me? They're on a Monday night at seven o'clock." She huffs out a breath, as if she's relieved she got the words out.

"Oh my God, yes, of course I'll come. I've always wanted to have a go. I've heard it's hard work, though."

We continue chatting about our new hobby while Oscar wears himself out running around the soft play area.

———

A COUPLE OF HOURS LATER, I'm sat in the pub with Jax. When he mentioned that he was alone tonight, I invited him out to celebrate his now job. I would have invited Ryan to join us, but I assumed he'd be out like every other night this week.

As usual, conversation is easy between us, and we've been chatting about everything and nothing for ages.

"What's the matter, Molly? You don't seem yourself," he asks, looking concerned.

"It's nothing, sorry. I don't want to ruin your evening."

I hadn't realised the situation with Ryan had got to me so much it was obvious. I guess Megan would have noticed if we hadn't spent our time together getting excited about our new class. In order to keep it a secret from James, we agreed to tell people we were just going to a dance class. I really hope Megan is good at it, because she's so excited to give James the best birthday ever.

"You won't ruin my evening, Molly. If you need to get something off your chest, I'm here to listen. I know we haven't actually known each other long, but it doesn't feel like that. I'm here if you need me, is all I'm trying to say."

Staring at him, I blow out a long breath, tears stinging my eyes as I consider where I should start. Jax reaches his hand across the table and squeezes mine in support.

"It's Ryan. He's acting really weird—going out and getting off his face every night, then coming in late. He was really horrible one night, and he's never acted that way to me before. I'm really worried about him."

Jax knows about me living with Ryan and his relationship with Hannah, but I haven't yet mentioned the chemistry between us.

He opens his mouth to speak, but he's suddenly pulled out of his seat and held up against the wall of the pub. My chair crashes to the floor as I jump to my feet.

"Why the fuck is she crying? What have you done to her?" Ryan hollers in Jax's face, holding him up against the wall by his throat.

"Get the fuck off me," Jax growls, making me jump

to action. I start pulling at the arms Ryan has around Jax's throat, pleading for him to let him go.

"Ryan, what the fuck is wrong with you?" I scream in his ear. His hold loosens slightly.

"Wait...you're Ryan?" Jax questions. Ryan just glares at him. "I think you should be asking yourself why Molly's upset," Jax looks Ryan up and down, "Mate," he adds tightly.

At Jax's words, Ryan snaps his head around to me and takes in my tear-stained face. He lets go of Jax and comes to stand in front of me, gently wiping the tears from my face. His features soften and regret fills his eyes.

I spot the manager coming towards us over Ryan's shoulder. "You two go and wait outside whilst I settle the bill—before we have a bigger problem on our hands," I say to them, watching them scurry out of the pub.

Once I've apologised profusely to the manager, paid the bill and left a hefty tip, I make my way out to join Ryan and Jax. They're standing with their backs to the wall, hands in their pockets and staring out over the car park. Both have their jaws set, like they're ready to jump on each other if one of them says the wrong thing. When I see them, I can't help but think what a lucky bitch I am, having two seriously hot men fighting for me. I must have done something right in a previous life.

"Ryan, this is Jax. As in, Jackson Parker, my employee. Jax, this is my idiot best friend, whom I live with." They glance at each other. "I suggest you both make friends, because I'm telling you now that you are both important to me, and I will not have you at each other's throats."

After staring each other down for a few more seconds, Ryan slowly puts his hand out for Jax to shake.

"I'm sorry, mate. I saw red. Molly was upset, and I jumped to conclusions. I'm sure she won't mind me saying she hasn't got the best reputation for picking the good guys."

"Thanks for that, Ry," I say, narrowing my eyes at him.

"It's okay, I understand. I'd probably do the same if she were my girl."

"I'm not his girl," I snap, my frustration at this whole situation growing by the second. "Ryan, I think you've done enough for one night. I suggest you go home."

"Come on, then," he says, and he starts walking away.

"No, I'm not coming with you. I'm way too angry to be anywhere near you right now."

"Where the fuck are you going to go, then?" he asks, looking seriously pissed off.

"Quite honestly, Ryan, it's none of your fucking business. You just go home and calm yourself down before you cause any more damage."

He looks completely deflated by my words. His shoulders slump and he marches to his car. I watch him get in and slam his door, before he punches the steering wheel.

"Wow," Jax says, standing next to me, watching the show and rubbing his neck. "Before I was stopped so abruptly, I was going to say I thought the cause of your problem was that Ryan was into you, but having experienced what I just did, I would say that he's more than just into you, Molly. That guy's got it bad." He turns to look at me with sympathetic eyes.

"Shit."

Twenty minutes later, Jax has dropped me off and I've locked myself into my office for the night. My phone has been going off constantly for the last ten minutes with phone calls and texts from Ryan. I had to put it on silent to save me throwing it at the wall and smashing it to pieces.

I sit down on the edge of the sofa and remove my heels, giving my toes a wiggle to stretch them out after being confined in my shoes for too long. My phone lights up on the coffee table again, displaying Ryan's photo. The one I took when he was sunbathing on the outside sofa at our beach hut. Thinking of that week makes my heart break a little. Look at us now.

Molly: *I'm fine, but I won't be home tonight. I'm too angry with you to be around you at the moment. I will be at the Morrisons' for dinner tomorrow. Maybe I'll see you there.*

Just the thought of going to the Morrisons' tomorrow makes me groan. Not only will I have to see Ryan, but Emma will more than likely be there. It's the only thing Susan and Pete have managed to make her attend since the accident: their monthly family Sunday roasts. I used to love spending the afternoon as part of a real family, but I haven't spoken to Emma since she kicked off last weekend in the club, and I have a feeling I may still be mad at Ryan tomorrow.

After a few moments, my phone lights up again with a reply.

Ryan: *Please forgive me. I was an idiot. x*

Thirteen

Molly

I walk into Susan and Pete's just after one to find everyone already sat around the table. My plan so far has worked: When I got home, Ryan had already left.

Susan looks up from passing the potatoes around. "Ah, angel, we didn't think you were coming."

"I'm sorry I'm late. I've had a bit of a bad morning, but I'm here now." I smile sweetly at her and she accepts my excuse. Ryan's eyes burn into me, and when I look up, there's an empty chair next to him. I also notice that Emma hasn't taken her eyes off her plate since I walked through the door.

I reluctantly take the seat next to Ryan and try to relax, so it's not obvious to everyone that there's an issue between us. As soon as I settle in, I feel Ryan's hand come to rest on my thigh and he leans over to whisper in my ear.

"I was worried you weren't going to come because of me. I'm so sorry, Molly. Please, I hate fighting with you." His voice has a begging quality to it.

I turn towards him. "I came so no one knows there is a problem. Keep your hands off me," I say, removing it from my leg. "Don't piss me off further, and we might just get away with it." I pull back from him to see Emma glaring at us, shaking her head and tutting.

Susan frowns at her but shakes her head and turns my way when her husband speaks up.

"So, Molly, I hear you've employed a designer already. Quite a handsome chap," Pete says, trying the break the tension.

"Oh yeah, he's a catch, all right," Ryan mutters.

"He's lovely, and he's amazing at what he does. I think we're going to work really well together."

Ryan snorts next to me, and I turn my head and glare at him.

"Don't forget how sexy those tattoos are," Lilly adds dreamily from the other side of the table.

"No daughter of mine is going be going out with a tattooed thug, Lilly," Pete chimes in.

"Pete, Jax is most definitely not a thug. He comes from a really nice family. They own that chain of steak and grill restaurants you love. He didn't want to go into the family business."

"How unlucky for us," Ryan whispers beside me.

"And just because he has tattoos, doesn't mean he's a thug. It's art. He designed them himself."

Ryan mutters quietly to himself and my anger at his immature behaviour soars.

"Ryan, would you like to share your thoughts with the table?" I ask him politely.

"No, I'm good, thanks." He smirks at me as he says it.

"Then shut the fuck up," I bark back at him, which makes everyone at the table stop eating and look at us. "Sorry," I mumble, returning my focus back to my plate.

"Oh, a lovers' tiff?" Emma asks sarcastically.

"Children, if you can't be nice to each other, please don't say anything at all," Susan says in a motherly tone.

The rest of the meal goes by in uncomfortable silence. As soon as dessert has been finished, I make the excuse of having loads of work to do and leave as quickly as I can. If I hang around, I'll be interrogated by Susan and the whole mess will just come spilling out of my mouth. I feel bad about not helping clean up, especially as somehow Emma managed to run away even faster than I did, but I'll make sure to do more than my fair share next month.

I head back to the office and drag out the case I

packed earlier to tide me over for a few days. I hate not going home. I love that house and my room, but I know it's just going to end in an argument with Ryan. After lunch today, it was obvious we both need time to calm down.

I get drawn into my work to pass the time and, before I know it, it's evening. I check my phone—twenty-eight missed calls from Ryan and six texts. I open the first text.

Ryan: *Thanks for leaving me to the wrath of Susan. Coward.*

Ryan: *I'm sorry, that was mean. It's just that I was questioned about everything for over an hour.*

Ryan: *I should say, I didn't tell her anything about what is going on. I just fobbed her off.*

Ryan: *Molly, please come home so we can talk. I know I've been a huge dick. I'm sorry.*

Ryan: *Molly, please stop ignoring me. It's killing me, not hearing from you. I hate you being mad at me.*

Ryan: *Molly, I'm so, so sorry. Please talk to me. I was just trying to protect you last night. I shouldn't have jumped to conclusions, and I was stupidly childish today. I'm sorry. Please come home. I hate it here without you.*

Molly: *Ry, it's obvious we both need time to cool off. I'll be home when I don't think the first thing I want to do is shout at you.*

I SEND MY REPLY, put my phone back in my bag, and get back to work. I just sit down when the doorbell rings. I ignore it, presuming it's Ryan trying to talk to me, but it rings again and again. I'm surprised when I hear a woman's voice shouting my name. As I get closer to the door, I realise it's Susan.

"Molly...Angel, I know you're there, your car is here. Open the door."

"Hi, Susan. What are you doing here?" I ask innocently.

"I think we need a chat, don't you?"

I groan loudly. "Come on in. Do you want tea?"

"Yes, please, angel."

I make the tea, then join Susan in the living room.

"I tried talking to Ryan after both you and Emma ran away, but he just kept fobbing me off with rubbish. Emma has been even more distant than usual over the last week, and she won't talk, either. What the hell is going on with you three?" Wow, Susan must mean business. 'Hell' is a swear word in her book.

"I don't know where to start."

"How about the beginning? That usually works best."

I tell her everything about Ryan and me (leaving out the more X-rated parts), Emma and her opinion about us, Ryan and his binge drinking, and the saga with Jax from last night. She sits and listens throughout the whole thing, but she doesn't say anything. She grabs her cup of tea and drinks it, deep in thought.

"Exactly as I thought," she says, putting her mug back on the coffee table.

"Excuse me?"

"Molly, all you kids think we don't see what's happening under our noses, but we do. Most of the time, we just ignore it, so you can all figure it out yourselves. It's obvious how you and Ryan feel about each other. It's in your eyes when you look at each other, or talk about each other. I'm not going to lie; at first, I wasn't too keen on the idea. But the more I see you both together, the more I see how happy you make each other, and that is all I want for both of you. We have all been through a terrible time, and if out of that you two find each other, then I cannot complain.

"As for Emma, well...we all know how much she has struggled—is still struggling—with losing Hannah. She isn't as strong as you and Ryan, but she will get there. When she does, she will see that what's happening between the two of you is okay. She just needs time."

"What about everyone else?" I ask.

"At the end of the day, angel, we all want you both to be happy, and if that means you're together, that's okay."

Ryan

I've been sitting for hours staring at my phone, hoping I would get something else from Molly, but nothing so far. In the end, I decide to go to bed early and try to catch up on some sleep. I just drift off when I'm awakened by banging. I fly out of bed and down the stairs because, in my sleep-induced haze, I think it could be Molly. When I wake up enough to know it's the front door being hammered on, I realise it isn't going to be her because she has a key and would just let herself in.

I must look really disappointed when I open the door and see Susan, because she takes one look at me and pulls me into her arms for a hug.

"Oh, angel, you were hoping it was Molly, weren't you?" she says quietly to me while she comforts me.

"Am I that obvious?"

"You have no idea. Come on, invite me up. I'm dying for a cup of tea. It's been a long day."

"Sorry, yeah, come on in. I'll just go grab a t-shirt."

"That's a shame, I'm starting to understand what my girls see in you," she says with a cheeky smile.

"Um...thanks?" I don't know what to say to that. I can hear her laughing ,though, and it makes me smile.

"You don't need to sound so freaked out, Ryan. I was trying to lighten the mood," she says, still laughing.

When I get back to the living room, I see that Susan has already made a start on the tea.

"So, without meaning to sound rude, what *are* you doing here?"

"I've just been to see Molly." She looks up see my reaction, although I'm not sure why. "She told me everything you were avoiding telling me earlier."

"Right." I should have seen this coming.

"I've given her my advice on the situation between the two of you. Now, I'm here to do the same with you."

Susan stayed for about an hour while we talked

through everything. She refused to tell me what Molly said; that was for her to tell me, really. I admitted something I hadn't realised before. I told Susan that I was in love with Molly. She took this better than I did, especially when I turned into a blubbering mess and apologised to both her and Hannah for falling in love again so soon.

I'm now lying in bed, thinking about everything. "I'm in love with Molly. Shit, when did that happen?" I tell myself I will do everything in my power to show her how serious I am. I fall asleep, happy for the first time in a while, thanks to Susan. She really is an amazing woman.

I WAKE up late the next morning after a long, deep sleep, feeling refreshed, and I head to the gym.

It's when I'm running on the treadmill that I realise what I need to do. I hang around the gym until I know she'll be home from work, and then head over to the Morrisons' house. Someone must be looking down on me and smiling today, because Emma's car is in the drive, which is an unusual sight these days. I let myself in and head for the kitchen, where I know everyone will be. It's just Susan and Emma in the room, and their heads snap up from the tablet they're both staring at aimlessly.

"Hey," I say, walking over to kiss Susan on the

cheek. "I don't know if I said it last night, but thank you."

"My pleasure, angel. I'm glad you're feeling better."

"Emma, could we talk, please?"

Surprise settles on her face.

"I'll leave you both to it," Susan says, scuttling out of the room.

"Um...what's up, Ryan?" she asks suspiciously.

"I need to talk to you, and I need you to listen to me. Can you do that without going off on me?" I say gently.

"I'll do my best."

"Right, here goes, then. I know you're under the impression that there's something going on with Molly and me." She opens her mouth to interrupt me. "Ah, you said you would listen." She closes her mouth and nods. "Well, nothing has actually happened. Yes, we have become really close over the last six months, but it was a completely platonic relationship until she moved in. Something changed. I don't know what it was, and I can't explain it, but there has been this amazing chemistry between us. It scared the shit out of me at first. Molly is my best friend. She's supported me through the worst time of my life, and there I was getting turned on by her doing the simplest things."

Emma screws her face up in disgust. "I said I'd listen, but please spare me the details."

"The thing is, Emma...I want you to know...I'm in love with Molly. No, I didn't ask for it to happen, and I know it's still so soon after Hannah. I do know that, but it just sort of happened. I want you to know that she will never replace Hannah. She will always have a piece of my heart, always, but it's time for me to move on. I know this is hard for you to hear, but I wanted it to be from me."

I look up to see Emma with tears streaming down her cheeks.

"I'm so sorry. I didn't want to upset you, I just wanted you to know everything. You actually know more than Molly does. I haven't told her any of this, and there is a chance that if she doesn't give us a go, then she'll never know, and I'm okay with that, I think. If she doesn't think it's right, then so be it.

"You should know that every time something has nearly happened between us, you're the one who has stopped her. I know you think that we don't care about what you think, but that's not true. Molly misses you terribly."

"Wow," she says, wiping her face with the backs of her hands. "I had no idea you were in love with her."

"Neither did I, until I spoke to your mum yesterday and she made me realise."

"Thank you for being honest with me, Ryan. I really appreciate that. I know I haven't been the easiest person to deal with since the accident, but I'm really trying to move on. It's just so damn hard. I still don't really know how I feel about the two of you, but just know that whatever happens, I'll be there for both of you. You're family to me. Just be warned—if you get together, it may take me some time to come to terms with it. Hannah was my other half, but I know she would want you to move on and be happy, so I need to let that happen."

I pull her into my arms and we sit there holding each other for ages until she calms down.

"Thank you, Emma. If you don't mind, can I suggest something?" She quirks an eyebrow at me. "Could you get in touch with Molly? She really does miss you, and maybe if a conversation about me comes up, you could tell her what you just told me."

"Of course. I don't want to hurt her, and I miss her, too."

After chatting about more general things for a while, the rest of the Morrisons congregate in the kitchen and Susan starts dinner. I end up eating with them again before saying my goodbyes and heading home. The whole drive home, I'm praying that Molly will have come back.

I let out a huge sigh of relief when I turn the corner and see her little Ford outside the house. A wide smile spreads across my face. Unfortunately, it doesn't last long.

I reach into my pocket when my phone starts ringing. I see my mum's name on the screen, press answer, and put it to my ear.

"Mum, what's wrong?" I hear her sobbing into the phone.

"It's your g-grandad. H-he's died," she manages to get out.

Shock envelopes me as I attempt to register what she's just said. "Shit. How's Dad?"

"A mess, Ryan. I'm sorry, but we need you up here."

"Of course. I'll be there as soon as I can. Look after each other, and I'll be there soon. I love you."

"Love you t-too, son. Bye."

I rest my head back on the headrest and process what Mum just told me.

"Fuck!" I shout, slamming my palms down on the steering wheel.

I jump out of the car and run into the house. I head straight for Molly's room; her door is open but she's not there. I turn to leave when I see the bathroom door is shut.

I knock. "Molly, are you in there?"

Fourteen

Molly

"Molly?" his voice comes out as a desperate plea.

"Yes, I'm in here. What do you want? I'm in the bath," I don't mean to sound grumpy, but he's ruining my relaxation. I've spent the last two nights sleeping on the sofa at the office, then I put myself through two hours of flinging my body around a pole with Megan. Whoever said pole dancing was hard work underestimated it massively.

"Molly, please, can I come in?"

"Are you serious?" I ask.

"Molly, it's my grandad. He's...dead. Please." I hear

a thud on the door and can only imagine it was his head.

"Shit." I quickly look down to make sure I'm covered in bubbles before I reply. "Come in."

The door opens and a very distraught Ryan walks in and sits himself on the closed toilet at the end of the bath. He slumps his body forward and puts his head in his hands.

"I'm so sorry, Ry. I know how much your grandad meant to you."

Ryan has told me countless times about how it was his grandad that got him into all sorts of sports. He used to spend all his weekends and holidays with him, watching whatever was on the TV at the time, and his grandad would explain the rules of each sport to him. When he got old enough to start playing them, his grandad was Ryan's biggest supporter. He was always at the side of the football and rugby pitches, in the stands of the cricket ground—just to name a few. I can only imagine how he must be feeling now.

I move myself in the bath so I'm on my stomach with my head at the end, and I reach out for Ryan. He's away with the fairies, so I don't need to worry about flashing him. I place my soggy hand on his forearm, which makes him turn his head to look at me. My breath catches slightly at the pain darkening his eyes. After Hannah died, I hoped I would never see that look in his eyes again.

"I'm so sorry for everything, Molly. I was an idiot. I'm so glad you're back."

"Indeed, you were, and I'm sorry, too. Even if I wasn't back, you could have come to me. I'm always here for you if you need me."

"Please, will you come to Liverpool with me? I promised Mum I'd get up there as soon as I could."

"Er, well, your parents won't be happy. Are you sure you don't just want to go on your own?"

"No, I need you with me. Please, Molly. My parents will be too distracted by what's going on to notice you." His eyes are begging for me to agree.

"Okay, Ryan. I'll do it for you. I'll get out now and pack some stuff. You go and do the same."

A FEW HOURS LATER, we're pulling into Ryan's parents' drive in Liverpool. After a long argument, I eventually persuaded Ryan to let me drive. I didn't really feel like he was in any fit state, so I put my foot down firmly. After hiding his keys.

His mum comes to the door to meet him. I watch as Ryan engulfs her in a hug. I can tell by the movement in her shoulders that she's crying. I stay in the car and give them a moment.

Eventually, she moves away and gestures for him to follow her inside. He puts his hand up to me and waves me in. I hesitantly exit the car and follow behind them into the house. They turn into the living room to join his dad, but I stay in the doorway, slightly out of sight, to give them some space. I hear some banging coming from the kitchen so I head down there in the hope that Abbi and Liv are already here. I'm really pleased when I see both of them stood over the kettle, making a pot of tea.

"How are you both holding up?" I ask when they spot me coming towards them.

"Molly, we didn't know you were coming," they say and give me quick hugs.

"We weren't as close to Grandad as Ryan, being girls and all, but it's still sad," Liv answers.

"I know. He's really upset. He didn't need this after everything else that has happened this year. Your mum seems pretty upset, too, but how's your dad doing?"

Although Ryan's mum and dad have shown their disapproval of me over the years, I actually think they're quite nice people from the stories I've heard, so I do always try to give them the benefit of the doubt.

"Better than we thought. I think he was aware that his dad was getting frail and it wasn't going to be long. Mum seems to be worse than Dad, actually," Abbi explains.

Once everything is on a tray, I follow them to the living room. I hang back by the door again, though. I can't help but feel like I'm intruding on a private family moment. Experiencing their close bond causes as wave of jealousy to wash through me.

They chat for a few minutes while Mrs. Evans pours tea for everyone. I see the moment she notices there is one too many teacups, then watch as her head snaps in my direction and her lips press into a hard line.

I inwardly groan. *Here we go.*

"This is a family matter. I suggest you go home." I feel my eyes pop open and my jaw drops at her words.

A series of voices break me from my shocked state. "Mum!" and "Karen, please!" are shouted by Mr. Evans, Ryan, Abbi, and Liv all at once, mortified by her words.

"No, it's okay. She's right. I don't want to intrude on such a tragic time for you all. Mr. Evans, I'm so sorry to hear about your dad. From what I've heard, he was an amazing guy."

"Thank you, Molly. But please, call me Dave."

"Mum, I asked for Molly to be here. She drove to get me here safely."

"Thank you, Molly," she says unconvincingly.

"You're welcome," I say with my brightest smile.

"But you can go now. Ryan will be fine. He has his family around him." She turns and starts sipping her tea like she's already bored of me.

"Mum, I'm sorry, but Molly's staying. You either need to accept that, or we'll be finding ourselves a hotel for the night."

Mrs. Evans looks like she's been slapped across the face. "Fine, but I suggest she keeps herself scarce. If she were so concerned about family, maybe she should sort her own out."

"Mother, that's enough. I didn't come here to fight. I'll show Molly up to my room so she can get herself settled."

Thank God, I think. *Get me out of here.*

"Ryan, she's not sleeping in your room with you. Have some respect in my house," she scolds.

"Mum, Molly is my friend. She will sleep in my bed—"

"Oh no—" she interrupts.

Ryan throws his mum a death look. "As I was saying, she will sleep in my bed, and I will sleep on the floor. Unless you would prefer we went to that hotel?"

"No, I want *you* here," she says, making it quite clear what she really means.

"Come on, Molly. Let's get our stuff out of the car, and you can get settled upstairs."

A FEW HOURS LATER, I'm lying in Ryan's bed in his childhood room that looks like it hasn't been touched since the day he moved out. There are posters of old indie bands on the walls, all his sport trophies and medals, and a few photos of friends and family. I love looking at old pictures of him. He's always been good-looking, but he used to be tall and lanky. His muscles didn't really come in until he was about eighteen. I look down at the floor where Ryan has laid out some bedding for when he comes up later and sigh.

He tried to convince me to come back down, but I refused point-blank. I'd had enough for one day. I just wanted to curl up in bed. The aches and pains from my earlier activity are getting worse by the minute, so I'm lying here trying to sleep, listening to the rumble of the conversation downstairs, whilst being completely covered in the smell of Ryan.

Eventually, I drift off.

Many hours later, I'm aware of Ryan coming in. After he's stripped out of his clothes, he comes over to me, kisses my forehead, and thanks me for coming before apologising again for his mum. His hand caresses my cheek gently and his soft lips press against my head again before he lies down on his makeshift bed.

A few minutes go by as I try to ignore the tingles from his touch, when I suddenly hear a sob fill the room. Opening my eyes, I look down at Ryan. The moonlight that fills the room allows me to see his back and shoulders shaking. I quickly climb onto the floor with my pillow, get under his covers, and slide myself up behind him. I feel him jump slightly, but he relaxes when he realises it's me. I wrap my arm around his waist and kiss his shoulder before putting my head down next to his. I listen as his sobs eventually fade and his breathing evens out, telling me he's drifted off. After an internal battle, I decide to stay where I am, just in case he wakes up upset. I want to be here for him.

I SPEND most of the next day in Ryan's room, working. Luckily, the IT guy came to the office yesterday morning and networked our laptops so I can access everything. I do make appearances for breakfast and lunch. Everyone is lovely to me apart from Mrs. Evans, not that I'm surprised. Throughout the day, Ryan comes up to check in on me and brings me drinks. I've heard a lot of coming and going downstairs, but I keep out of the way.

I've spoken to Jax a couple of times this afternoon, as he's sent me some final concepts to approve for a new clothing boutique in the city. He sounds crazy happy on the phone, but I put it down to the fact that I'm pretty miserable.

I just hang up when Ryan comes in. "Hey, you okay?" I ask. He's looking a bit dejected.

"Yeah, some of my grandad's friends just left. We've been chatting about him for ages."

"I bet they have some great memories."

"Yeah, they do. I've come to let you know dinner's ready. I've told Mum to be nice, so it's safe."

Yeah, like that will shut her up.

To my surprise, dinner isn't as dramatic as I expect. Mrs. Evans doesn't even look in my direction, which is fine by me. Everyone else is lovely, though, and we spend the meal catching up on each other's lives.

After, I excuse myself and continue working, just to keep busy. I'm once again lying in his bed, staring at the ceiling. I've heard Abbi and Liv come to bed, and I'm pretty sure Dave has as well.

I've been dying for a drink for ages but have been trying to wait until everyone's come up before I venture out. I cave in the end, but I come to a stop halfway down the stairs when I hear my name mentioned. I bend down to look through the balustrade and into the kitchen where the voices are coming from. I can see Ryan sat opposite his mum with his back to me.

"I just don't understand why you're still friends with her. Why is she still clinging to you?"

"Mu—"

"She is the kind of girl you always said you didn't want. You want a nice, sweet girl to settle down with, like Hannah, God rest her soul. Molly has been around the block a few times, to say the least, from what I've heard." My mouth drops open. "You need to be out there finding a nice girl who will make a good wife and mother to your children, not the local bike who will most probably screw you over with someone else."

"I know. I'm struggling with this enough. I don't need you on my case, too."

Tears sting my eyes. How can he say that? How can he not fight for me?

I make a snap decision. I quietly but quickly make

my way back upstairs, shove everything into my bag, and put one of Ryan's hoodies on over my pyjamas. I double-check I've got everything, write a note to leave on his pillow, and sneak back downstairs and out the front door. I throw my stuff in the car, start the engine, and tear out of the drive like a bat out of Hell.

Ryan

I DON'T KNOW how many times I have to defend Molly to my mum. We've been through this shit numerous times over the years, and almost every time I've spoken to her since Hannah died. It's getting to the point that I just agree to get it over with, because I feel like a fucking parrot, constantly repeating the same conversation and answers to her questions.

"Mum, that's it. I've had enough. Every time we talk, you have something to say about her. You're constantly putting her down, and I'm sick to my back teeth of it. Molly is my best friend. Without her, I don't know how I would have got through this year. Quite frankly, I don't care what you think, because you don't have to be her friend. You just have to be nice to her, because she means so much to me. Who I spend time with is up to me, not you. I am an adult, and I can make my own decisions." I slam my palms on the table and force my chair out behind me as I stand to leave.

Mum stares at me like I've grown two heads. I've never lost my temper with her before, and I very rarely swear around her. I look at her for a few more seconds before striding out of the room. All I can think is how much I want to see the person asleep upstairs.

It's dark when I enter the room, so I don't pay much attention to my surroundings. I do as I did last night, taking my clothes off, then walking over to Molly to kiss her goodnight—but, when I get to the bed, it's empty.

"Molly?" I whisper into the room, but nothing. I check the bathroom but it's empty, too. Starting to panic, I walk towards the hall window to look at the driveway. My heart drops. There's an empty space.

"Shit," I mutter as I run my hands through my hair in frustration. I storm back into my room, putting the light on this time. I pull my clothes back on and stuff my things into my bag before turning to leave the room. It's then that I notice a note on my pillow.

You said you would always fight for me.

"FUUUUUCK!" I shout, running down the stairs. Mum is tidying the kitchen when I round the corner.

"Where are your car keys?" I shout, startling her.

"What?" she questions as she spins around.

"Where are your fucking car keys?" I spit at her.

"Ryan, what's happened?"

"You...*you're* what's happened. You, slagging her off...and she's fucking gone because of it. She's packed her stuff, got in her car, and left, all because you can't accept her. Give me your keys," I demand, my hand outstretched.

At that moment, my dad comes around the corner with a set of keys hanging between his fingers. He looks half asleep. I must have woken him up with my shouting.

"Thank you. It's good to know someone cares."

I pat my dad on the shoulder as I turn to leave, jump in Mum's car, and race off. She hardly drives the thing, so it splutters at bit at first. I keep reminding myself to keep my speed in check. I won't be worth much to anyone if I'm dead in a ditch.

I go home first—not because I think she's there, because I know she's not, but because I know I have a spare key to my old flat. There's no way she is going to let me in willingly if she's heard what I think she has.

I almost smile to myself when I see her car behind Cocoa's. I go straight to the door to the flat above and shove the key in the lock. Relief floods me when I realise they haven't changed the locks. I take the stairs three at a time, eager to get to her. The place looks deserted, so I guess she must be in her old room.

My pulse hammers around my body as I walk towards her door. It's shut, so I gently push it open to reveal Molly fast asleep on the sofa, the moonlight casting light across her face where she hasn't shut the curtains. A pile of tissues is next to her head, resting on the armrest. The sight breaks my heart.

I run my fingers down her cheek. I want to wake her up gently, not scare the shit out of her.

"Molly," I whisper, kissing her hair.

She groans lightly, and her eyes flicker as she begins to wake.

"Molly, it's just me. I'm so sorry. I came after you as soon as I realised you'd left," I say in a soothing voice, stroking my hand down her hair.

Her eyelids finally open, but as soon as she realises what's going on, her eyes are wide and she sits bolt upright.

"What the fuck are you doing here? How did you get in?" she asks, looking panicked.

"I knew you'd be here, so I stopped at home and got my key. I had a feeling you wouldn't let me in if I knocked."

"I actually hate you right now. I can't believe you just let her go off on me like that. You didn't even try to defend me—you actually agreed with her. You didn't fight for me. You promised."

"It's not how it looked, Molly. I swear it's not."

"That's what they always say."

She tries pushing me away from where I'm crouched in front of her, but I put my arms on her shoulders to hold her in place.

"Just hear me out, please?" I sit back when I feel her relax under my hands.

"No. I want you to leave." She stands up and strides over to the door. "I don't want you here. I don't even want to look at you."

She turns her face away from me, but not before I see a tear fall onto her cheek.

"I'm not going anywhere until you listen to me," I say, walking over until I'm standing right in front of her. The heat from her body warms mine and my fingers twitch to pull her to me.

Reaching out, I gently take her chin in my hand, and move her head until she's looking at me. Her eyes are red and bloodshot, and she has fresh tears running down her cheeks. "Molly, I do not and will never agree with what my mum thinks of you."

"But you did. I heard you. You said you were *struggling* with it. Struggling with...*with me.*"

"Molly, you were right before when you said my mum hates you. Every time I see her or talk to her, she goes off like she did tonight about you. I've defended you so many times, I couldn't possibly count. I'm constantly repeating myself to her, but she never listens. She's formed her own opinions and refuses to change them, no matter what I say. The last few times she's done it, I've found it easier to let her run out of steam before I say anything. Trust me, it makes the whole thing quicker. If you had hung around, you would have heard me defend you. I think I actually scared her a little because I lost it. She has no right to talk about you the way she does, and it really fucking pisses me off." As I explain, my previous anger starts to flow through my veins.

She looks down at the floor again, but I put my hand on her cheek to pull her back.

"You're shaking,"

"I'm so fucking angry. I thought I'd calmed down on the drive here, but remembering it just makes me mad again. You are the most wonderful person, Molly. I don't know how she can't see that, can't see everything you've done for me this year."

"I'm struggling to understand, Ryan."

"I said I was struggling because I am. I'm struggling with what's been going on between us. I know you spoke to Susan the other night, because she came to see me afterwards. Don't pretend like you don't know what I'm talking about, because I know you do. I don't want to ruin what we've already got either, Molly."

"She told you what I said?"

"No, just that you didn't want to ruin our friendship. She would never break your confidence, you know that."

She stares right into my eyes. "I'm not ruining our friendship because we're both lonely." Her eyes are hard as they stare into mine, as if she's trying to make me believe the words she's saying.

Thinking about my response, I pull my bottom lip into my mouth, but the only thing it achieves is getting

Molly's attention. Her eyes drop and I watch her pupils dilate as I release it and run my tongue along the length. I can almost hear the argument she's having with herself.

"Molly?" I question, trying to bring her back from her daydream. I step a little closer and rub my thumbs under her eyes to wipe away the tears.

Her eyes bore into mine. They're filled with a desire that causes every muscle in my body to clench as I allow myself to imagine what could be about to happen.

Her gaze drops to my lips once again and I slide one hand so that my fingers are tangling in her hair while the other shifts so I can run my thumb along her bottom lip.

She sucks in a breath and her eyes come back to me. The longing I see reflected in them is exactly what I need to close the small amount of space between us.

Dropping my hand to her hip, I take the leap. When our lips meet, fireworks explode within me.

With our lips pressed together, I lean into her, aligning our bodies perfectly. I run my tongue along the join of Molly's lips, asking for her to open up for me. She hesitates and her body freezes. It's just long enough for me to panic. But, a second later, her lips part and I quickly slide my tongue inside. As soon as it touches hers, another round of fireworks erupts through my body and her taste explodes on my tongue. I swear she's the sweetest thing I've ever fucking tasted. Lifting my arm, I cage her in and press her back harder into the wall. I need her to feel exactly what she does to me.

I've kissed a few girls in my time, but none of them were anything like this. It's fucking unbelievable. My pulse races and my temperature soars as our tongues and bodies continue to dance together. I reluctantly pull my mouth away from hers so I can catch my breath. Placing kisses along her jaw and down her neck, I zero in on that sweet spot under her ear. She moans when I caress it with my tongue, and my cock twitches at the thought of running it over the rest of her body.

I'm just about to move back to her lips when her phone starts ringing, snapping us out of our sexual haze. I have to lean back against the wall to stop myself from falling when she slides out from under me. My whole body's weak just from kissing her.

She's breathless and her chest heaves, but it doesn't stop her from answering the phone. "Hello?" I check my watch; it's nearly four o'clock in the morning. Who the hell is calling at this time? "Adam, hi. Are you having a good holiday?"

Hearing his name brings me down from my high. Wanting to hear as much of the conversation as I can, I move over and sit on the sofa next to Molly.

"Yeah, it's great," I hear him say on the other end. "I can't stop thinking about you, though." If I hadn't already come back to earth with a bang, hearing that definitely finished me off.

"Aw, that's sweet, Adam."

"I fly back in early Saturday morning. Will you meet me for breakfast?"

"Um, won't you be tired?"

"Maybe, but I want to see you."

"Uh, okay then. Text me the details."

My heart drops into my stomach.

"Look, Adam, I don't mean to be rude, but you do know what the time is here, don't you?" she questions him.

"The guys just said it should be the middle of the afternoon. Is that not right?"

"Add on about twelve hours and they would be."

"Hang on," I hear him say, followed by, "Oi, you bunch of shits. Don't fucking run, you pussies!" shouted away from the phone. I can't help but grin. "Sorry about that. I think I may have wound them up talking about you to them all week, and they've just got their own back."

"No problem. Let me know where you want to meet Saturday. Enjoy the rest of your holiday." With that, she hangs up and relaxes back on the sofa.

"Look, Ryan..." She turns to me, and I can tell what's coming next just from the look on her face. "What just happened—" She gestures back towards the wall. "Well, it shouldn't have happened. You're my best friend, and I intend on it staying that way. I'm going out with Adam on Saturday, and I suggest you try and find someone to do the same with so we can put whatever's going on between us to bed."

I just stare at her, open-mouthed, completely lost for words. The only thing going around in my head is, 'I love you', but I don't think this is the best time for that little announcement.

And as for me finding someone else? Yeah, I don't think that's going to be happening anytime soon, either.

Fifteen

Molly

I'm staring at my sketchpad the next afternoon. I
should be coming up with a logo for a guy
starting up a new building company in the city,
but all I can think about is last night.

That kiss.

Holy shit, that kiss was like nothing I have ever
experienced before. The moment his lips touched
mine, my entire body was alight. I'm not exactly lacking
experience when it comes to guys, but I can honestly
say I've never felt anything like that before. If Adam
hadn't chosen to ring at that moment, I can only
imagine how far it would have gone, because at the

time, I had no intention of stopping, and I got the idea Ryan didn't either, judging how he was grinding his very obvious excitement against my stomach.

"Molly...Molly...earth calling Molly," I hear Jax saying next to me. I snap my eyes up to him and see his brows drawn down in concern. "You've been away with the fairies all day. Are you sure everything's okay?"

"Uh, yeah, sorry," I say, sounding very unconvincing.

"No, I'm not letting you get away with that. Come on, grab your bag. We're going to that wine bar down the street."

I watch Jax walk back from the bar with our third—or fourth?—glass of wine. We've been chatting about all sorts of things since we've been here. He's told me more about Lucy. I'm so jealous of how goofy he looks when he talks about her. I want someone to look like that when they talk about me.

"Does she not mind you being out getting drunk with me?"

"No, she's fine with it. One of her friends has just broken up with her boyfriend; she's been spending a lot of time with her. Apparently, she's a mess. Lucy's friends are really important to her. She's always doing something with one of them. It's one of the things I love —she's so caring of the people who are important to her." There's that goofy face again that makes my insides twist with jealousy.

I look down at my glass and watch the condensation run down the side. I let out a large breath I didn't realise I was holding.

"So, now you're suitably tipsy...what the hell is wrong?"

"Ryan," I say, looking up at him. I go on to explain everything that has happened over the past few days.

"Let me get this right. You only want to be friends with him, even though you feel so strongly about him?"

"Yes, there's too much at stake."

"So, you're going to torture yourself, and him, by the sounds of it, by keeping up the façade that you just want to be friends?"

"I'm not torturing myself. I love being his friend. And he'll find someone like I've got Adam."

"Hmm, yeah, Molly. You keep telling yourself that." I fix him with the dirtiest look I can manage in my drunken state.

We finish our drinks, then Jax finds us a taxi. I tell him that he should be dropped off first because he lives in the city center, but he refuses and gives the driver my address. He insists that he needs to make sure I'm home safe first. Such a gentleman. I hope Lucy knows just how lucky she is.

I'M at my front door, fumbling around in my giant handbag, trying to find my keys while Jax waits patiently. Eventually, he gives up and rings the doorbell. There are lights on, so Ryan must still be up. I stop hunting and lean against the door, waiting for him to appear and rescue me.

I must have fallen asleep standing up, because the next thing I know, I'm falling into a very naked and slightly damp chest. I open my eyes to find my cheek pressed into Ryan's ripped pec. Looking down at his abs, I see droplets of water running down to soak into the waistband of his boxers. I look lower; it's all he's wearing. My drunken self is very happy with my findings.

I slowly rake my eyes back up his torso until I have my head tipped back so I can look up to his face. I'm shocked by what I see. He's staring straight ahead of him, and his jaw is set like he's about to fight. I turn my head to see he's glaring right at Jax.

"What the fuck have you done to her?" he growls. I feel his hands come around my waist to hold me up.

"What have I done to her? What the fuck, man? We went for a drink after work and got a bit carried away. Molly had some things she needed to get off her chest, and she needed a little Dutch courage to spit it out."

"So, you got her drunk to get what you wanted?"

"What? No! I was being a friend and helping her, listening to her. She's been distracted all day, not been herself at all. Something was obviously seriously both-ering her."

"If she needs a friend because she's got an issue, I'm here. She knows I'm always here for her. You can go now. You've done enough, clearly."

I'm listening to their exchange and want to speak, but my mouth won't connect with my brain and work properly.

"She can't talk to you about everything, Ryan. She is allowed other friends."

"Yes, she is, but not ones who are trying to get in her knickers."

"That's rich," Jax bounces back, making me smile. "I've got a girlfriend; I have no interest in Molly's knickers. I suggest you sort out your attitude ready for when you meet her tomorrow night. I stupidly told Molly to invite you along for dinner with us. I thought it would be good to get to know each other properly, but the more I see of you, the more I'm thinking it's not a good idea. I don't know what she sees in you."

"Likewise."

"Molly, I'll see you at work tomorrow after you've slept off your hangover." I hear Jax walk off, then the car door shutting.

Ryan

Tucking Molly into my side, I push the door closed and gently encourage her towards her bedroom. I should let her sort herself out. It would be the easiest option for me, but her legs are barely holding her upright now.

"Ryan," she moans, as I lower her to the bed. When I stand and look down at her, my breath catches at the determination on her face. "I need you."

I go to step back but I'm not quick enough. Her hands tighten around my waist and she pulls herself back up. Her tits rub against my chest and I have to take a deep breath as I will my body not to react to her. She's drunk off her face and probably won't remember a second of this in the morning. If our time comes, it won't be like this. I want her to remember every single second of it.

Her tiny hands run up over the ridges of my abs and then over my chest before they interlock behind my neck. Even in her shoes, she's not quite tall enough, so she reaches up on her tiptoes. Our lips are barely a breath apart. The scent of the alcohol on her breath hits me and reminds me that I can't allow myself to be swept away like this.

"You shouldn't ever wear clothes, you know? It's even wrong that you're wearing boxers right now," she slurs.

"Molly, you're drunk. Let's get you into bed."

"Umm...good idea. Let's take this to the bed." She releases her hands from behind me, her nails scratching lightly down my back. I can't help the groan that falls from my lips, or the hardening of my cock as she runs her hands over my naked skin.

The moment her fingertips slip under the waistband of my boxers, I know I need to move.

"Come on. Bed," I instruct, gently pushing on her shoulders so she has no choice but to sit back down.

I fall to my knees in front of her and set about undoing her shoes. The clasp is tiny for my giant fingers but, eventually, I drop them both to the floor, ready to get her into bed to sleep off the alcohol coursing through her veins.

"My knight in shining armour," she muses. "Are you sure I can't tempt you?" Her eyes darken and she gives me a salacious smile before her fingers find the bottom of her dress. In one smooth move, she's dropping it to the floor and standing in front of me in the tiniest set of lingerie that I think I've ever laid eyes on. My mouth waters as I run my eyes down the length of her, taking in her dusky pink nipples hiding behind the lace, her tiny waist, and curvaceous legs.

Every muscle in my body is screaming at me to take what I need, but the rational part of me knows that I can't. My cock throbs painfully behind the confines of my boxers, and I breathe a sigh of relief when she takes a step away from me.

"I get it. I get it." Glancing over my shoulder, she winks, her eyes dropping to my crotch. "You just need a little more convincing."

Seeing her hands come up behind her, I panic. The last thing I need is to have any more of her bare skin revealed. Taking a giant step, my fingers encircle her wrists and stop any further movement.

"Molly," I breathe, not quite believing that I'm about to turn her down when she's so clearly willing. "You're drunk, and I know that if you keep going, you're going to regret this in the morning. Believe me when I say that I'd give about anything to have what you're offering, but this isn't the way it's going to happen."

"Just kiss me. Please," she begs, stepping back into me and finding my hands. She brings them around to her smooth stomach and I tense when she tries to encourage them higher.

"This can't happen." Even I can hear the pain in my voice.

"I need you. I need—"

"To sleep this off," I interrupt.

Putting a little more effort in, I manage to lift her and lower her into bed before covering her tempting body with the duvet.

"Come on, Ry. Don't tell me I'm going to have to do it myself." Watching her hand disappear under the duvet is my undoing. I drop a very quick kiss to her forehead and walk out of her room before I'm subjected to more torture.

Closing her bedroom door, I fall back against it and

blow out a long, slow breath as I try to calm my racing heart.

I deserve a fucking medal for doing the right thing.

When I hear movement behind me, I quietly push myself away from the door and start the climb up to my own bedroom. I've no idea what she's doing in there, but the last thing I need is evidence that she's finishing the job she suggested starting.

I walk through my bedroom and directly into the shower. Dropping my boxers, I turn the shower on cold and step inside. It has little effect because all I can see is her covered in that tiny amount of lace, begging me to touch her.

Sixteen

Molly

I wake up to a pounding in my head. It takes me a few seconds to remember why it hurts so much. Flashbacks from last night flit through my mind. Me telling Jax everything about Ryan whilst drinking too much wine. Jax bringing me home and having a stand-off with Ryan at the front door. Me crushed against Ryan's almost naked body. Just the thought of that makes my temperature rise slightly. I don't remember getting in bed, though. I roll over to look at the time to see it's almost midday. God, I need to get to work. I notice a glass of water and packet of painkillers on the bedside table. They're a very welcome sight. I sit up so I can take them, and it's when the covers slide off me that I realise I'm just in my underwear.

Did Ryan strip me off last night and get me into bed? Oh God, I hope I didn't do anything stupid.

Thirty minutes later, I'm dressed and ready for work. Thankfully, my head is starting to clear, thanks to the tablets Ryan left for me. I head upstairs for breakfast—or lunch, I guess. When I enter the living area, Ryan's sat at the breakfast bar in front of his laptop with a cup of coffee halfway to his mouth. When he hears me coming, he puts it back down and looks over at me with a smirk on his face.

"What's that look for?" I watch him laugh at me. "What?"

"If you don't know, Molly, then I'm not telling you."

"Shit, what did I do last night? The last thing I remember is Jax leaving."

"That's a good thing. You probably wouldn't be facing me right now."

"Speaking of Jax, the four of us are going out for dinner tonight, and you will be nice."

"Why are you dragging me along? I don't want to spend a Friday night with him."

"Because it's important to me. You, Ryan, are my best friend, and Jax is my friend. I want you both to get along because you're both in my life, and neither of you are going anywhere anytime soon. Plus, I'm dying to meet Lucy, but I don't want to be a gooseberry."

"Brilliant," he replies sarcastically.

WE MEET Jax and Lucy outside The Fat Dog. The second Ryan sees him, he tenses beside me.

"Just chill out, yeah?"

"I'll do my best," he says unconvincingly.

Molly, Ryan, this is Lucy," Jax says excitedly.

"Hi," is all Lucy says as she runs her eyes down the length of me. She soon dismisses us and turns back into Jax's side.

Ryan and I follow behind them as the waiter directs us to our table. His eyes burn into me, and as I look over, I'm not surprised to find the same confused look on his face as is probably on mine.

If I thought Jax looked like a lovesick puppy at work, it's nothing to what he's like with Lucy.

As we take our seats and grab the menus, Lucy fusses about rearranging the table and constantly reaches out to touch Jax. It's as if she's staking her claim.

"You can order for me, baby," Lucy says, smiling up at Jax like he'd just hung the moon.

He nods, and looks at the options while she turns her gaze on me. Her eyes run over my face once again, as if she's sizing me up.

"So Jax said you work as a receptionist?" I ask,

trying to break the tension, hoping to find some common ground.

"At the moment, but I'm hoping to give that up soon. Isn't that right, baby?"

"Yep," Jax mutters, still too focused on filling his stomach.

"Can I show them?" He nods, and I narrow my eyes at the two of them. "Isn't it beautiful? It's almost two carats." She swoons, staring down at the giant rock on her finger. "We're going to have a Christmas wedding, aren't we, baby?" She looks up at Jax with huge puppy dog eyes. I roll my eyes the second I glance at Ryan, who's also noticed her over-the-top behaviour.

"You can have whatever you want. I told you, money's no object." Her eyes light up as she turns and places a kiss to his cheek. "I love you."

"Well, I guess congratulations are in order."

"Thank you," she says sweetly, before suggesting Jax buy a bottle of champagne to celebrate.

Ryan's eyes burn into me. He looks about as confused by the couple in front of us as I am.

We have a nice enough night. Ryan and Jax do a decent job of pretending to get along, but I'm pretty convinced that I never see the real Lucy. I'd like to think that Jax is a better judge of character, so I try to push my concerns to the back of my mind and attempt to start up a friendship with her.

THE SECOND RYAN and I are alone, the words tumble from my lips. "I can't believe the size of that engagement ring. It must have cost Jax thousands. I wasn't in a million years expecting him to announce he had asked Lucy to marry him. I mean, they've only been together a couple of months. They barely know each other."

"Yeah, it's fast, but if it's right, it's right, and you just know."

"I guess so. What did you think of Lucy?" I ask. I'm driving us back home after our meal with the happy couple.

"She was...okay," he says, shrugging his shoulders.

"There was something strange about her. She seemed...fake. Like she was constantly trying too hard."

"Yeah. It was like she was doing anything she could to keep Jax happy. It was a bit too much of 'yes, Jax', 'no, Jax', 'whatever you say, Jax' and batting her eyelashes."

"She was not what I imagined at all from the way he talks about her. He loves her and wants to marry her, though, so I guess that's all that matters."

"As long as he isn't trying to get at you, I'm happy."

"Seriously, Ryan, what is your issue with him? He was nothing but nice to you tonight."

"I just don't like him. He was only nice to me because you were there."

"You're talking shit, Ry," I say, pulling up in the drive and getting out. "I'm going to get changed. If you're going to the kitchen, pour me a glass of wine, please."

"Thank you," I say to Ryan as I settle myself on the sofa in front of a glass of wine he's left for me on the coffee table.

I feel his eyes on me as I take a sip and relax back on the sofa. Looking over, I find I'm right. "What?"

"You could wear a little more, you know."

"Fine, I'll go change. I didn't mean to offend you," I say sarcastically. I can tell by his face that isn't what he meant, but he still refuses to tell me what I did last night, so I think a little payback is in order.

"It...it doesn't offend me, Molly."

I'm stood right in front of him, so I have to tip my head up to look at him. I try to keep an innocent look on my face. It's hard, because I just want to laugh at his embarrassment. "So, what's the issue?" I can't help my face breaking into a smile. I know that what I'm wearing probably isn't all that appropriate, but I'm desperate to know the truth about last night. My white vest is a little on the thin side and my shorts show off the bottom of my arse, but it's summer, and the humidity, even at night, is through the roof right now. Plus, I'm at home. I should be able to dress how I like.

"You're such a fucking tease, you know that?" he says as the corners of his lips start to twitch. "Seeing you like that doesn't offend me one bit," he advises, then moves his head next to mine and whispers in my ear. "It makes me want to rip off what's still covering you and fuck you against the wall." He turns and walks out of the room.

Ryan

BEFORE I KNOW IT, it's Tuesday and I'm packing, ready for my much needed break from Molly. After the night in her bedroom and then that damn near see-through vest, I think a little space is just what I need. I'm heading to Liverpool for my Grandad's funeral and then to spend some time with my sisters in both Manchester and Cardiff. I hate the idea of being away from Molly for so long, but I do think it's the right thing to do. The more time I spend with her, the more I'm struggling with my feelings, and it's killing me to watch her go out with Adam. Every time she comes home from being with him, I can tell she likes him more and more. She's been her usual flirty self with me, but she's becoming more distant and we haven't had any more awkward moments since Friday night. She spent practically all weekend with him, and when she's been home, she's been constantly texting him.

"Ry, you up there?"

"Yeah." I hear her walk up the stairs and, in a few seconds, she appears in my doorway.

"You nearly ready to go?"

"Almost. You got much planned while I'm gone?" I don't know why I ask this, because I really don't want to know what she's planning with Adam. I continue folding my clothes as she gets comfortable in the middle of my bed.

"Work, mostly. Adam's coming over for dinner tomorrow night, and I'm going out with Jax and Lucy again on Friday evening. Not sure other than that, but I'd like to see Emma. I thought she might have been in contact by now."

Yeah, I'd hoped that, too. She promised me when I spilled my guts to her that she would get in touch with Molly.

We continue chatting about our plans until I'm totally packed and ready to head out. "Right, I think I'm done and ready to go." I look up and see Molly wince as she goes to move. "You still hurting from your dance class last night?"

"Yes, I didn't realise how unfit I was. Pull me up." She puts her hand out for me and I give her a tug. She moans as she gets to her feet.

"It's only a dance class. How strenuous can it be?"

"You'd be surprised. Come on, let's get you on your way. The sooner you go, the sooner you'll be back. I'm going to miss you."

"I'll miss you, too. Come here." I pull her in for a

hug and kiss the top of her head while she's in my arms. She smells so good. Oh how I want to walk back over to the bed and throw her down on it.

Ten minutes later, we've said our goodbyes, and I'm on my way to Liverpool. I hated seeing the tears in Molly's eyes as I pulled away from the house, but my desire to go back and comfort her was just another reminder of why I need this time. I have to sort out my feelings for her so that when I come back, we can be the great friends we were before all this weirdness happened. Surely, I can fall out of love as fast as I fell in it, right?

Seventeen

Molly

"Pull yourself together, woman; he'll be back in just over a week. Get a grip," I say to myself as I walk back into the house, having watched Ryan drive away. I didn't think I would get so upset at the thought of him not being here. I hate the idea of spending the night alone, so I walk over to my bed and grab my phone.

"Molly, how are you doing?" Shane asks when he answers the phone.

"Ryan's just left for a week with his family. I don't want to be alone. Have you two got any plans tonight?"

"No, we're staying in and ordering a takeaway. We were going to plan our stag do—you want to join us?"

The second I hang up, I slip my shoes on, grab my bag, and head out the door.

I love spending time with Shane and Chris. They always make me laugh so much. They don't take life too seriously, and they're constantly taking the piss out of each other. They've told me everything I could possibly need to know about their wedding. It's the last Saturday in November in a hotel on the outskirts of the city.

They have a black, white, and red theme. Apparently, as groomsmaid, I have to wear a little black dress, bow tie, and little top hat. To my surprise, it looks much cuter than the image I had in my mind—thank God.

They've decided to have a joint stag do as nearly all their friends are mutual. They've hired out a VIP section of one of the clubs in the city and are having a 'pimps and hos' theme. We're going to have a meal, then drink and dance the night away. I can't wait. It sounds like it will be a lot of fun—plus, we get to dress up like idiots.

I end up sleeping in their guest room. I miss my bed, but I know the house is going to feel horribly empty without Ryan.

I'm stood in my kitchen, piping the lemon meringue

pie I've made for dinner tonight with Adam. He should be here in thirty minutes. I really like him—he's a nice guy, but he isn't really doing it for me. He's fun and makes me laugh. I originally thought, with him being a banker, he'd be boring, but he isn't at all. He's a bit of an adrenaline junkie and has done all sorts of crazy things. When I'm with him, it's great, but I can't help wondering what it would be like if it was Ryan sat opposite me instead. I think what's between us is just friendship, but I'm willing to give it a little longer to see if anything sparks.

I put the pie in the oven just as the doorbell rings. I jog downstairs and open the door to let him in.

"Hi," I say, smiling at him. He's wearing light blue jeans and a white t-shirt. He hasn't shaved for a couple of days, making his stubble almost as long as his short, almost-black hair. When I invited him over, I said it was a casual thing, and I'm glad he took that seriously. I'm wearing my boyfriend jeans and a tank top. My hair is in a messy bun on my head, and I've only got a little make-up on.

"Hey, you look good, Molly." He reaches his hand up to my cheek. "You've got flour on your face," he says, wiping it off.

I can't help but feel disappointed. If Ryan did that to me, it would make my pulse rate increase. But I feel nothing.

"Thanks. I always end up covered—I'm a messy cook."

"As long as you're a good cook, that's fine by me." He shuts the door behind him and follows me up the stairs. "Wow, you were right—nice house," he says as we enter the living area.

"I know, I love it here. Can I get you a drink?"

We have a nice evening eating, drinking, and chatting. He's so easy to talk to. The conversation just flows. We never have any awkward silences. He was impressed with my cooking, and he actually went to the extreme of trying to find the packaging I could have hidden because he thought I'd bought it all and was passing it off as mine.

As the night draws to an end, Adam is a perfect gentleman. We have a little kiss at the front door before he leaves, but he doesn't push for anything further.

After tidying upstairs, I get myself settled in bed with my Kindle. I end up reading for hours and, when I eventually decide to go to sleep, it's not my date I drift off thinking about—it's Ryan. This time apart was meant to sort out my head, but I can't stop thinking about him.

⸻

WHEN I GET HOME from our dance class Monday night, I immediately run myself a bath and pour in loads of my favourite relaxing bubble bath in the hope that it will make me ache less in the morning. I just get in and comfortable when my phone rings. I lean over to dry my hands and grab it, groaning when I see it's actually Ryan FaceTiming me. I move myself so I'm on my front and balance my phone on the towel on the toilet. I make sure I'm covered in bubbles before I answer.

"You've got to be fucking kidding me," Ryan says as soon as I answer. "I don't see you for almost a week, and when I do, you're naked in the bath."

"Nice to see you, too. How's Cardiff?"

"It's not bad. They talk funny, though. Liv showed us around the place yesterday, but she's to work this week so Abbi and I just chilled out at her place today, then had a takeaway when she got home. What about you?"

"Just worked, really. We've had so much come in. I went out with Adam again on Saturday night. He took me for a meal and to the cinema, which was nice. Megan and I went to our dance class tonight, hence the bath. Anything to stop it hurting so much in the morning."

"You know I did a massage course when I was at university? I'm sure I could work wonders on your body," Ryan suggests. I watch his eyes darken as he thinks about it. I guess his time away from me has been as effective as mine away from him. The idea of having his hands all over my body has me squeezing my thighs together to try to stop my clit throbbing.

"Uh...I think the bath should do it. Thanks, though."

"Well, if you change your mind, I'm more than willing."

We chat for a few more minutes about what we've been up to, as I try to drag my mind out of the gutter.

"Do you know what day you're going to be home yet?"

"No, we haven't made any decisions. I'm thinking Friday."

"Okay, well, let me know. Enjoy the rest of your week."

"Yeah, you too. Speak soon. Love you, Molls," he says, then hangs up.

"Love you, too," I mutter to myself.

I lie back in the bath and get comfortable again. Between my legs is still pounding, and thinking about that massage only makes it worse. It's been too long since I had an orgasm, I think to myself, while sliding my hand down my stomach to the place that's causing me grief. I rest my head back while my fingers get to work. I can't help my mind going back to that kiss in the office and letting my imagination run wild. I come with his name rolling off my tongue.

I PUT my phone back down on my desk. I've been trying to get a hold of Emma all week, but my calls just go straight to voicemail. It's really starting to piss me off.

The front door slams just after one o'clock, announcing Jax's arrival. His feet pound up the stairs. When he appears at the top, he looks livid.

"Jax, what's wrong?" I ask, rushing over to him.

"She was fucking playing me. She never fucking loved me, she just wanted to screw me over and take as much money as she could."

"Wait, what?" I ask, a little confused, as I grab his hand and drag him to the living room so we can sit.

"When I got home yesterday, I found her handbag on the side with a load of paperwork spilling out of it. I wouldn't usually look, but a few things haven't added up recently. They were addressed to a Charlotte Smith. I didn't think much of it until I saw a passport, so I grabbed it and opened it to the photo page. There was her picture, next to the name 'Charlotte Smith'. She was fucking playing me."

"What did you do?"

"I waited for her. The look on her face was priceless as I confronted her. She just broke down in tears, telling me how sorry she was. It took a while, but eventually she admitted that her name was Charlotte. She made Lucy up so I couldn't find anything out about her. It turns out everything she'd told me was one big lie. The times I thought she was with her friends, she was actually with her boyfriend, her partner in crime. They had targeted me because of my family's money. She made herself the perfect girlfriend so I would fall for her, and got me to buy her a stupidly expensive ring just so she could pawn it and take the cash. God knows what else they would have done if I hadn't figured it out."

"Fuck, I'm so sorry, Jax."

"I was blinded by how perfect she seemed. I pulled the ring off her finger, made sure I still had the wedding band in my room, and threw her out of the flat, swiftly followed by her stuff. I then called a locksmith to change the locks. I never want to lay eyes on her again. I can't fucking believe how stupid I was. It was all an act." He puts his elbows on his knees and his head in his hands. I pull him into my side and put both my arms around him in comfort.

"I'm so sorry, Jax," I repeat.

We sit, silent for a few minutes while he gets himself together.

"Right. Come on, we've got work to do. I'm not sitting here letting her make me miserable. She can fuck off if she thinks I'm going to waste any more of my time on her from now on."

"Good for you. But we're not working. Come on, we're going for lunch, then I've got something I want you to help me with."

A COUPLE OF HOURS LATER, Jax is pulling up outside my house, having followed me here after lunch. I give him a quick tour before letting him get comfortable in the living room with a beer. I quickly go downstairs to change and grab my sketchpad.

"After Hannah died, I decided I wanted a tattoo. I wanted something to remind me how short life is, so I've been sketching. I've done loads based on the forget-me-not, different patterns and words...But I think I've got my final design."

"That's so exciting. Your first tattoo. Let me see."

"I was also hoping you could recommend someone —you know, seeing as you have one or two yourself."

He flicks through my sketches. "These are really good, Molly."

"Thanks. It's that one," I say, pointing at one of the designs. "Jax?"

"Yeah."

"What made you get yours? Can I see them?"

"Is that your way of asking me to get naked?" he laughs.

"No, Jackson, it's me asking to see your tats! Now, kit off!"

I watch as he pulls his t-shirt over his head, revealing his toned torso and the tattoos that continue up his chest, ribs, and over his stomach.

"Wow. They're awesome," I say, running my finger over the one on his ribs. Jax goes on to point out each one and why he got it. I'm totally mesmerised by the ink.

"So, where do you want yours?" I stand and run my finger down my side from my bra strap to my waist.

"Yeah, that should look good. Have you got any grease-proof paper?"

"Yeah, why?"

"I'm going to trace your design, then we can place it on your skin so we can get an idea of what it'll be like."

"That makes sense," I say, heading over to the kitchen.

I watch as Jax makes quick work of tracing my design with a sharpie. I pass him some scissors when he's done so he can cut it to size.

"Right, ready?" he asks me. I nod and lift the side of my vest.

"You're going to need to take your top off, Molly."

I quirk my eyebrow at him. "Now who's the one trying to get who naked?"

"You won't get the full impact if your top and bra are in the way." My eyes widen and my chin drops at his suggestion. "You can cover your front up still. You haven't got to stand there totally naked, flashing me. Not that I'd complain, of course."

"Shut up, Jax. I'm your boss!"

I turn my back to him and lift my top over my head. I remove my bra and throw it on to the sofa before gathering my top up and holding it in front of the girls, hiding them from view. "Better?" I ask, turning back to him.

"Yes." He grabs the sketch and holds it against my side. "What do you think?"

"I think I love it. You're the only one that I've told about this. I haven't even told Ryan."

"Your secret is safe with me. Can you hold it? I'll take a picture with your phone."

"What the fuck are you doing? Get your fucking hands off her, arsehole!" Ryan's shouting scares the shit out of me. I turn towards the door to see him storming our way, looking murderous. Jax is still holding the paper to my side but he quickly screws it up and puts it in his pocket. Just as he pulls his hand out, Ryan grabs his arm and throws him across the room.

"Ryan, what the fuck? Chill out. Jax wasn't doing anything."

"Then why the fuck are you both stood here half-naked? I fucking told you he wanted in your knickers."

"Dude, that is not what's going on here. Molly's my boss, and like I said before, I want nothing to do with her knickers. I was just helping her out with something."

"What the fuck could you be helping her with that involves both of you being topless?"

Jax looks at me for help. I only just told him Ryan didn't know, but it looks like I'm going to have to tell him now.

"Ryan," I say, walking over to him. "I want to get a tattoo, and I was asking Jax to help me with the design. He's topless because I asked to look at his ink, and I am because he was showing me what my design could look like. That's it."

"You're getting a tattoo? Since when?" Ryan's voice has softened, and his body has visibly relaxed.

"I've been thinking about it for a while. I'll explain later. Right now, I'd like to put my top back on, if you don't mind. Turn around, both of you," I demand, and watch them both do as they're told.

I'm just doing my bra up when I look to my left and see Ryan watching me in the mirror. His eyes meet mine and he quickly turns away, looking embarrassed. I put my top on and turn around just as Abbi walks into the room.

"Abbi, I wasn't expecting you," I say, walking over to her, but she doesn't even look at me. Her focus is solely on Jax. I glance at him and see he's just as transfixed with her. I look back to Abbi to see her cheeks redden and her usually bright blue eyes darken.

I put my arms around Abbi and pull her in to a hug. "Close your mouth, Abbi. You'll start drooling in a minute," I whisper in her ear. This seems to snap her out of it.

"Sorry. Who is he? He's seriously hot," she whispers back.

"So, how come you came back early?" I ask Ryan, changing the subject before he blows a fuse at the way his sister's eyeing up Jax.

"Liv had loads of work to do so we decided to come here. Abbi is staying until Saturday, if it's okay with you."

"Of course, it is. Have you guys eaten?"

"No, not yet. We were going to see what you wanted to do. Takeaway?"

"Yes, perfect. Jax, are you staying to eat? If you want to drink, you're more than welcome to stay the night." I see Abbi's eyes light up at this suggestion.

"Uh, as long as Ryan doesn't mind. It's his home, after all," Jax says politely, but I can tell he's dying for him to say yes. I fix Ryan with a glare.

"Of course, no problem with me," he says through gritted teeth.

"Awesome, I'll get the menus."

We decide on Chinese, order a shit load of dishes, and put them in the middle of the table for everyone to have a bit of. I watch Abbi and Jax chat between themselves while we eat. Apart from looking at their plates, they don't take their eyes off each other.

I can feel the tension coming off Ryan in waves. He's clearly unhappy about this. I place my hand on his thigh, making him jump. When I've finished eating, I lean in to whisper in his ear. "Chill out, Ryan. It's not that bad." He just turns and stares at me in total disbelief.

I wait until he's finished eating before I say loudly, "Ryan, could you come downstairs with me a minute? I need you to look at something." I don't know why I said it aloud —Abbi and Jax are so lost in their own world, they wouldn't hear a bomb go off. Ryan doesn't move, so I have to pull him from his seat and out of the room.

"For fuck's sake, Ryan, get a grip."

"Get a grip. Are you fucking serious? Did you not see them?" He gestures above our heads with his hand. "I do not want him lusting after my little sister. He's not good enough for her, and forgive me if I'm wrong, but he's fucking engaged."

"Oh, come on, Ryan. Your little sister is an adult, and Jax is actually a really decent guy. Actually, he is no longer engaged since-"

"They only got engaged two weeks ago! What the fuck happened?" Ryan interrupts me.

"It turns out we were right not to like her. She was playing him for his money. Completely screwed him over."

"I still don't like him." Ryan is actually pouting. I lift my hand and flick his bottom lip, "Hey. Stop being such a pansy about this. Jax is a great guy, and your sister is a great girl. If they get on as well as it looks like they're going to—I mean, sexual tension, *hello*—then we should be happy for them."

"Please do not say the words 'sexual tension' and my sister in the same sentence again."

"Ryan?"

"Yeah?"

"Welcome home. I've missed you," I say, then throw my arms around him and squeeze him tight.

Ryan

HAVING her body against mine has my dick hardening instantly. I put my arms around her and nuzzle my nose in her hair. God, I've missed her. I breathe in through my nose and take in her usual scent. Her hair smells of toffee from her shampoo, and her skin like sweet vanilla. She smells like home to me. It might be ridiculous, but I'm a little jealous that Molly told Jax about the tattoo before me. I thought I knew everything about her, so it hurts a little. I'm yet to find out what this tattoo is, but I'm dying to know.

If it wasn't clear from my reaction when I first arrived home, it's now really obvious that my time away from her hasn't dampened my feelings at all. I really don't know what to do about it. I want her so bad, but she's still pulling the 'just friends' card. I'm pretty sure she's lying to herself, but I don't know what I have to do to make her throw caution to the wind and give us a go. I just need to be patient.

"Ryan, you need to chill out and let them enjoy this. Imagine if it was the other way around and you found someone you had that kind of chemistry with," Molly says, dragging me back to what's happening upstairs.

I have to bite my tongue to stop me from saying something I could regret.

"Would you want your sister ruining it for you?"

I just look down at my feet.

"No. I didn't think so," she finishes for me. "Let's go to bed and leave them to figure out what *is* between them. Alone."

"Yeah, I guess you're right. I don't like it, but you're right. Let's go to bed. Yours or mine?" I ask cheekily, flashing her a cocky smile.

"How about you go to yours, and I go to mine?" she says with a raised eyebrow.

"If you insist."

"I do. Night, Ryan. I'm glad you're back."

She gives me a kiss on the cheek and I begrudgingly walk away from her once again.

I WAKE up with the sun streaming through the crack in the curtains and a raging hard-on from the dream I was in the middle of about Molly. I can't help but feel total disappointment that it was just a dream. The thought of me coming home yesterday and being ravaged by her as I stepped through the door was much better than the reality.

I drag my sorry arse out of bed, jump in the shower, and set about relieving myself with thoughts of my very vivid dream still in my head. It doesn't take very long before I'm shooting my load over the tiles. I don't feel any better for it, though. My hand just isn't doing it for me these days.

I throw on some clothes after drying off, and I'm

making my way downstairs when I stop at the sound of Molly's voice. "You two might want to move before Ryan gets down here. He's having a hard enough time already with what's going on with you two. He doesn't need to see it first-hand."

I groan to myself and scrub my hands across my face. What the fuck am I about to walk into?

I take a deep breath, then finish my descent and enter the living area. When I look up, I see Jax pulling up his jeans and Abbi doing up her shirt. They both look guilty as sin.

"Ugh, my eyes." I grumble as I walk past them towards Molly, who instantly distracts me from the half-dressed couple in my living room. She has on skin-tight white jeans and a black crop top, showing off her toned stomach.

"Wow, Molly. Those dance classes are doing wonders for your curves." I have to say something. She looks too hot not to.

I hear Jax laugh, then cough to try and hide it. I don't think anything of it because my sister is probably doing something inappropriate behind my back. I run my eyes up and down Molly's body again. My temperature rises and my heartbeat picks up.

"Ryan," she warns in a low voice. "Don't."

I can't help feeling disappointed, like I did when I woke up.

"So," she announces loudly to everyone. "We're all going out tonight. I've text Megan and James, Shane and Chris, and they're all up for it. Oh, and Adam, of course."

Oh, fucking brilliant. I get to meet Adam and potentially watch Molly be all over him.

"I'm not sure I'm up for it, what with school starting next week and all." I try to sound convincing.

"Shut up, old man," Abbi says from behind me. "You're coming; no excuses." I turn around and see Abbi's puppy dog eyes looking back at me.

"Yes, come on, *old man,* it's the last chance you'll get for a while," Molly joins in.

I look back at her to see a similar look on her face that I've just seen on Abbi's. They both know I can't say no to them.

JUST OVER TEN HOURS LATER, I find myself in a bar in the city, being introduced to Adam.

"It's so good to finally meet you. Molly's always talking about you," he says to me as we shake hands. I don't like him. He could be the nicest guy in the world, but he has what I want.

"Really? Well, I haven't heard much about you."

I know I shouldn't have said it, but I couldn't help myself. Luckily, Megan and James join us and distract him.

"Ryan, if you're anything but nice to him, Molly will never forgive you," Abbi whispers in my ear.

After a good number of drinks, we head down the street to a nightclub. We all go straight onto the dance floor and I instantly feel left out as I watch the couples pair off. I swallow my pride and walk towards the bar to drown my sorrows, but a hand on my arm stops me. I turn to look at who it is; a tall, slender blonde smiles back at me. She was just the type I used to go for before I fell hard for Molly.

She leans in towards me so I can hear her. "You look lonely. Dance with me?"

I glance to where my friends are dancing and see Molly's eyes on me over Adam's shoulder. She quickly diverts them when she sees me looking back. I can't help but think that her watching me dance with another woman might make her realise that it should be her.

"Sure," I say to the blonde. "Come on."

Eighteen

Molly

I've been watching some blonde bimbo grind herself against Ryan's body for the last four songs, and I hate it. She has her hands all over him, and all I can think about is how he would feel, how soft his skin is, how hard his muscles are.

Completely lost in my imagination, I feel myself start dancing with Adam how I would like to dance with Ryan. I shut my eyes and let my body take over. I move so that his leg is between mine and I grind against him to the beat of the music. I run my hands over his body, ignoring the little voice in my mind that says he isn't muscular enough. When he speaks into my ear, I can't help but think his voice isn't deep enough. But the images in my head are turning me on so much that I drown out those thoughts.

Tilting my head up, I capture Adam's lips with my own. His hands slide down to my arse and he pulls me tight against his very obvious erection. His tongue teases the seam of my lips until I open up for him. As soon as I do, he invades my mouth and tangles with mine. That little voice starts again, telling me how he doesn't taste right, how he doesn't set my whole body on fire with his kiss. But again, I try to push those thoughts away and continue.

Adam's chest is rising and falling at such a rate that he has to pull away from my lips so he can catch his breath. He trails kisses across my jaw and down my neck, so I chance a look in Ryan's direction. What I see almost has me pushing Adam off me. He's completely still while the blonde continues to rub herself against him, staring right at me with an empty look in his eyes.

I watch as realisation hits him. He looks me right in the eyes before grabbing the blonde behind her head and crashing her lips to his. She instantly closes her eyes and lets him in. Ryan, on the other hand, still has his eyes locked on me as he practically devours her before my eyes. I feel like someone has just kicked me in the stomach, knocking all the wind out of me.

Adam places a kiss on my lips and continues along the side of my face. "Take me to your place," I say against his ear.

"Are you sure?" he asks with his eyebrows drawn together.

"Yes."

I grab his hand and begin to pull him from the dance floor, but not before looking back at Ryan. He's still watching me with the blonde's lips attached to his neck. I smirk at him as we move and see his eyebrows rise and his head shake from side to side slightly, like he can't believe what I'm doing.

Adam quickly finds us a taxi, and we're soon heading to his flat.

As soon as we're through the front door, he's on me. He carefully guides us into his living room and, in seconds, I feel the sofa hit the backs of my knees. He gently lays me down and kneels between my legs so he can continue kissing me. His hand runs from my ankle up to my waist before slipping under my top and coming to a stop when he's cupping my breast. He lies down harder on top of me and grinds his hard dick against my core.

Trailing his lips across my cheek and down my neck, he breathes me in. "You're so sexy, Molly," he moans as he runs his tongue around the edge of my ear. "I can't wait to feel your skin against mine."

My heart's racing, but it's not for the reason it should be. None of this is right. I shouldn't be here. I shouldn't be with him. My hands tremble as I try to figure out the right thing to do. My arms move of their own accord and run up his back, but it's a slender body, not the ripped, muscular one I desire.

Fuck, what am I doing?

"Adam, I'm sorry. I can't do this." I push at his shoulders, trying desperately to get his weight off me.

I watch as he pulls his head back from my neck, removes his hand from my breast and places it on my cheek.

"It's okay. We don't have to do more than you're happy with. I just thought you were turned on and wanted this."

"I thought I did, but I'm not ready." I close my eyes so he can't see the tears in them or the real reason I called a halt on things. He's just all wrong.

"Come on, let's go to bed." My eyes fly open in shock. "To sleep, Molly. I meant what I said. I really like you. I'm more than happy to take this slow." He stands up and pulls me with him. I bite my lips to stop myself from admitting the truth.

I slip my jeans off while Adam is in the bathroom, then slide into his bed. When he comes back in, he's wearing his boxers and a t-shirt. I roll over so I'm facing the edge of the bed when he climbs in. I can feel him peering down at me, but I keep my eyes shut and stay still.

"Molly?" he whispers.

"Hmm?"

"Can I hold you?" he asks nervously.

"Mmhmm." It wasn't until my head hit the pillow

that I realised just how exhausted I was. Adam releases a breath as he slides his front to my back and gently wraps his arm around my waist.

"Goodnight, Molly," he says next to my ear, then places a kiss to my head.

I drift off to sleep. The last time I was cuddling in bed, it was with Ryan.

"Morning, sleepyhead," Adam says as I appear in his living room, probably looking as bad as I feel.

I grunt in response.

"Oh, that good?" he says with a laugh. "Do you want tea or coffee?

"Tea, please," I manage to get out.

"Okay, sit down. I'll be right back."

I sit on the sofa and put my head back on the cushion. I must have had more to drink last night than I realised. I think back over the night's events and instantly feel awful for how I treated Ryan, but he was giving as good as he got with that blonde. I wonder if he took her home. The thought makes me want to empty my stomach right here.

This is crazy. What are we doing to each other? Why can't I be brave enough to just take the jump with him?

I spend the rest of the morning with Adam, and once I'm feeling like I can make the journey without being ill, I ask him to drive me home. When we pull up outside my house, I lean over and give him a quick kiss on the cheek.

"Thank you. I'll speak to you soon."

"No problem. Enjoy the rest of your weekend," he says, before I get out and walk over to the front door to let myself in.

I let myself in and stand and listen to see if I can hear any voices, but it's silent. I go into my room to dump my bag and take my shoes off before I head upstairs to make myself another cup of tea to have with the bath I'm running.

Walking into the living area, the first thing I see is glass smashed all over the kitchen, along with what could be a couple of mugs or a plate; I can't tell with the mess. I scan the rest of the room and see Ryan on the sofa. I'm presuming he's asleep, but I can see worry lines on his face and the tightness of his shoulders. I step a little closer to him. There's dried blood on his fists.

Shit, did he get in a fight last night?

I walk over to the kitchen, trying not to stand on any of the shards while grabbing the dustpan and brush to start cleaning it up. I just bend down to start when I hear shuffling behind me.

"Leave it," Ryan snarls in a harsh voice.

I turn to look at him, and the expression on his face is the same one from the club last night. His eyes are completely empty. His eyebrows are drawn together, a deep line formed between them, and his lips are turned down in what I can only describe as disgust. He hasn't moved, though. He's still on the sofa. Once I've had enough time to study him, he turns away from me to stare ahead.

"I want a cup of tea, and I'm not standing on all of this to get it." I turn back around to start cleaning it up.

"You always get what you want," he says patronisingly behind me.

I'm gobsmacked. I can't find any words to answer that remark, so I choose to ignore it. "What happened here?"

"You ha—"

Just as he starts to spit his answer back at me, the blonde from last night appears in the doorway. She's in the same clothes, but obviously fresh from the shower. I stare at her with wide eyes.

Holy fuck, he did bring her back. A lump climbs up into my throat and tears sting my eyes. I turn around and continue cleaning the mess up so neither of them can see how upset I am.

"You all set, Holly?" Ryan says as he gets up and walks over to her.

"Yes, thank you for letting me have a shower. How are you feeling?"

My back tingles like they're looking at me after that comment, but I'm too scared to turn around and find out.

"Like shit, but you really helped. Thank you."

"My pleasure. You have my number. If you need anything, please call," she says, making me want to be sick again. "My taxi's outside."

"Seriously, thank you. I don't know what I would have done without you," he says quieter, but I still catch it.

After a few more moments, I hear her walking down the stairs, and Ryan flops back on the sofa.

I finish cleaning up and put the kettle on when I can safely reach it.

"So, you were going to tell me what happened. Go on," I prompt.

"It was an accident," he says, shrugging.

"An accident," I repeat. "Multiple smashed glasses and mugs was an accident?"

"Yes. I was drunk."

"Not drunk enough not to spend the night with Holly, though, evidently." I can't help my acidic tone.

"Evidently," he repeats sarcastically before turning away and putting the TV on.

"Okay. Do you want coffee?"

"No," he answers abruptly, so I make my tea and get the hell out of there.

I stay in the bath until it's too cold to sit in any longer, trying to process my thoughts. Ryan brought the blonde home. The thought makes me feel sick to my stomach, but wasn't that what I suggested to him a couple of weeks ago? Except I never really meant it. I didn't want it to happen. I was—still am—too scared to admit my feelings for Ryan.

What if I'm too late?

Ryan

I can't believe Molly pulled him out of the club. She promised me she was going to change, that she was going to wait to make sure the guy was worthy of her. But there she goes—after what, a handful of dates?—home with him. I feel sick just thinking about it.

The woman rubbing herself up against me whispers in my ear, "So, trying to make her jealous didn't work, then?"

I look down to the blonde, confused. "What?"

"I said, trying to make her jealous didn't work, then? That was what you were trying to do, right?" She looks at me, dead serious.

"Uh, I guess, yeah. But why would you...?"

"I came with my friends, like you. Also like you, they're all paired up. I wanted someone to dance with who wouldn't want in my knickers, so when I saw you pining over her, I thought you'd get me what I wanted: a dance with a hot guy. And I might actually help you out in the long run. I'm sorry I didn't." I just stare back at her in disbelief.

"I can't believe you would do that. You don't even know me."

"I'm a good judge of character, and it's telling me you're a good one. I just saw an opportunity to help, so..."

Wow. "Do you want a drink, um..."

"Holly," she adds. "Yes, that would be good."

"I'm Ryan. Come on." I place my hand at the small of her back and guide her to a quiet section of the bar. Once we have drinks, Holly points over to a booth in the corner.

"So, I...uh...sorry, you've just taken me totally by surprise," I say to Holly. "I can't believe you did that."

She shrugs her shoulders in response and has a sip of her drink.

"But you let me kiss you?" I'm still completely baffled by her.

"Was her face as good as I pictured?"

"Uh, yeah, actually, it was pretty good, apart from it made her whisper in her bloke's ear and then drag him out of the club. Didn't quite have the desired effect." I put my elbows on the table and drop my head into my hands.

I end up getting so drunk I can barely walk, so Holly has to escort me home after telling her mates where she's going.

There's a small part of me that's hopeful I'll find Molly asleep in her bed when I get home, so as soon as I stumble into the hallway, I go straight for her room and fling the door open. Nothing.

The image of Molly dancing with Adam won't leave me. I end up pacing the living room, but every time I close my eyes, all I can see is her grinding against him and kissing him.

"Argh!" I growl, before planting my fist into the wall of the living room, then the other one for good measure. The pain takes away my thoughts of them for all of five seconds. I walk over to the kitchen and sweep the glasses and mugs off the draining board, watching them crash to the floor, breaking into shards—just like my heart.

"I fucking love her. Why can't she see that? Why?" I cry.

After showing Holly up to my bed, I get myself settled on the sofa with the blanket Hannah and I bought together. I really don't need those memories, too.

I must have fallen asleep at some point because, the next thing I know, I'm looking up to see Molly's arse as she's bent over, about to sweep up the mess in the kitchen.

"Leave it," I growl at her, a little harsher than I intended.

She turns to look at me and it feels like a knife is pushed right though my heart. She looks like she had a late night. I try my very best not to think about what that entailed.

Nineteen

Molly

Seven Weeks Later...

The last few weeks since Ryan went back to work have been bloody awful. Ryan's done his best to avoid me at all cost and seems to spend way more time at school than he needs to. I miss him terribly; the house is so empty and quiet without him.

Everything else has pretty much continued as normal, and although I've pretty much decided my relationship with Adam isn't going to go anywhere romantically, we've still been hanging out. He's a good guy, and I like spending time with him.

Megan and I are still loving our pole dancing lessons, so much so that we've signed up to a slightly more advanced class. Tonight is the first one, and I'm a little apprehensive. I've also taken up a life drawing class on a Wednesdays at the local college. It's an eight-week course, and next week is the last one. I'm really going to miss it. Ever since talking about it with Ryan when we were on holiday, I kept thinking about giving it a go again. We've had a range of models we sketch throughout the classes, and it's been exhilarating to do something I always loved so much. We can submit any of the sketches we've done in class, or one we've done outside, if we wish, to an end-of-course competition. I know exactly what—or who—I want to submit, but it's just a case of convincing him.

"Oh, come on, please," I beg with my best puppy dog eyes and pouty lips.

"Molly, stop it with the face." He laughs at me.

"I'll buy you anything you want. Well, within reason. I'll ply you with alcohol if it will help, and I'll feed you. Please. You've seen my work; you said your-self that it was good. I promise I won't make you look hideous!"

"I know you're good at it. That's not the point!" he argues, shaking his head.

"Well, what is the point, then? I've spoken to Abbi, and she's totally fine with it as long as she can have a copy!" The connection Abbi and Jax had that very first night is still going strong. He's been spending most of his weekends up in Manchester with her.

"Ugh," Jax groans.

"Why me? Why not Ryan? His body is better than mine."

"Because I'm desperate to sketch those tattoos, and Ryan's still avoiding me. Man up and get naked for me. It's art; you've done it before."

"Let me ask you something. Would you do it for me?"

I answer without hesitation. "Yes. Come on, I've promised already, you can cover up your junk."

"I knew taking this job was a bad idea," he groans, shaking his head.

"Stop being a pussy, Jax."

"Right, fine, but you seriously owe me one."

"Yay!" I say, jumping up and running over to hug him. "Thank you, thank you!"

"You knew I'd cave eventually. I couldn't listen to you anymore. It's all you've spoken about for days."

"Okay, so you're busy tomorrow, right? But can you do Sunday?"

"Yeah, I guess so."

"Brilliant. So, come over to mine in the morning. I'll have everything set up and ready to go, so we can get straight to it."

"At yours? Won't Ryan be about? I don't want him watching. It's bad enough you'll be staring at me."

"He's still keeping out of my way. Plus, he won't want to look at your naked arse. He's still unconvinced about your relationship with his sister. He doesn't need to see what she sees during your dirty weekends."

"He needs to chill out."

"You don't need to tell me that."

I CLIMB my aching body up the stairs in search of a glass of wine after pole dancing. I was right to be apprehensive about it. It was so much harder than our Monday night class. It doesn't help that I landed on my arse a good couple of times, much to Megan's delight.

To my surprise, Ryan's sat in the living room, watching telly. "Are you okay?" he asks, looking concerned.

"Yeah. Megan and I started a more advanced dance class tonight. It was *definitely* more advanced. I need wine and a hot bath. I'm sure I'm not going to be able to move tomorrow."

"Make sure you drink enough water first."

"Yes, Dad!"

"Hey, just looking out for you. I wouldn't want to have to come down and pull your passed out, naked arse from the bath."

"Yeah, you're probably right. If you need me, you know where I'll be." I grab a glass of wine—and water—and head downstairs.

Thirty minutes later, my glass is empty, and I'm overheating. I wrap myself up in my huge fluffy towel and head into my room.

"Shit!" My heart pounds as I find Ryan sitting on the edge of my bed, waiting for me. "Fucking hell, Ry. You could have warned me you'd be there." I place my hand over my racing heart and take a couple of deep breaths to try to calm it whilst pulling my towel tighter around my body.

I look from him to my bedside table that has my bottle of wine, a can of beer, and a bottle of something I don't recognise on it. I place my glass next to the wine bottle and pick up the other bottle. Massage oil.

Oh, fuck no. No, no, no.

"Uh, Ry?" I turn back to him with the oil in my hand.

"Molly, don't look so worried. I'm going to make it better for you. You'll thank me in the morning,"

I really doubt that. Having Ryan's hands all over me is going to be torture. I can feel myself getting worked up at the mere thought of it. "I don't think it's a good idea, Ry."

"Oh, shut up. Put a dry towel on the bed, then lie face down on it," he says, like it's the most normal thing in the world.

"I'm not lying naked on my bed for you."

"Okay, put your pyjama shorts on, but you'll need to be topless so I can do your back."

"I can't believe you're making me do this."

"I'm not making you do anything. If you really don't want me to, I won't."

I stand and look at him as I weigh up my options: get seriously turned on by Ryan, or not be able to move in the morning.

"Right, turn around," I demand. I grab a pair of knickers and shorts from my drawers and slide them on under my towel. I go into the bathroom to grab a dry towel and do as he says after pouring myself a large glass of wine and taking a massive gulp.

"Okay, ready," I say, after I've made myself as comfortable as possible in this situation. I hear Ryan's sharp intake of breath as he turns around. I crane my neck to see him but instantly regret it as I his eyes darken, running over my body.

"Ryan, get on with it before I change my mind," I say, hoping to snap him out of his perusal.

I watch him grab the oil and pour some in his hands before rubbing them together to warm them up. He goes to the bottom of the bed and starts with my left leg.

"Holy fuck," I moan. "That's so good."

"Told you. Now, just relax."

I try to do just that as he works his way up both of my legs, digging his fingers into my sore muscles, but the higher he gets, the harder it is to relax...and the harder my clit is pounding. I'm trying my best not to make it obvious that I'm turned on, but I'm sure my heavy breathing is a major giveaway. I'm also trying desperately hard not to make any noises, because the couple of times I have, they sounded very suggestive even to my own ears.

"Molly?"

"Uh huh?"

"I just wanted to apologise for acting like a stroppy teenager since I've gone back to work. I've been stuck in my own head, I'm sorry."

"It's okay...ahh, Ry. I know you've been...ahh, busy." I can't help the appreciative noises that escape as I speak.

"That wasn't really what I meant, but thanks."

I'm just about to ask more, but he moves to my back and totally distracts me.

"Your tattoo is looking good. Does it still hurt?" Ryan asks, running his finger over it.

"No, it's fine now."

Jax went with me and held my hand because it hurt like a bitch, but now the scabs have cleared and the slight swelling and pinkness has gone, I'm really pleased with it. The artist Jax suggested was pure genius; it looks better than I ever could have imagined.

I hadn't told Ryan I was getting it done, and we hadn't spoken about it since the night he found Jax and I planning it and he flew off the handle. When he eventually appeared after work that evening, he found me sitting at the coffee table, leaning over my sketchpad, doing some work. I was so engrossed in what I was doing, I didn't hear him come into the room until he cleared his throat. I looked up at him to see him staring back with desire in his eyes.

"Is everything okay, Ry?" I asked suspiciously.

"I...um...yeah. Molly?"

"Yeah?"

"You need to go and put some more clothes on."

It was only then that I looked down at myself and realised the way I was leaning over the coffee table in my loose top meant that Ryan could practically see everything. Suddenly, the look in his eyes made more sense to me. I put my pencil down and pulled my top up as I stood.

"I had my tattoo done today," I said, pulling up the bottom of my top to show him the giant plaster. "I can't have anything rub against it for a few days." He swallowed hard as he looked at my side.

"Right, but you can wear something bigger than that, right? You can have one of my t-shirts, if you want."

"No, it's okay."

I went to leave the room to change, but not before I caught Ryan adjusting himself as he walked into the kitchen. Even after weeks of barely talking, the effect we have on each other is still the same.

I'm brought back from my daydream with a gasp as Ryan's fingers gently brush the sides of my breasts.

"Sorry," he mutters behind me.

He's sitting across the backs of my thighs, and I can feel the unmistakable shape of his erection pressing into my arse. I really need to put a stop to this, but it feels so good.

"Ry?"

"Yeah?" God, his voice sounds so sexy when he's turned on. It gets gravelly and even deeper than normal.

"I think I'm done," I say regretfully.

"Shit, I'm sorry. I can't help it."

"It's okay, I just think it's time to stop."

"Let me just finish your shoulders."

"Okay."

I lay my head back down and let him continue. After a couple of minutes, I feel his hands come to a stop, but they rest on my lower back as he sits back on his heels and lets out a huge sigh.

Lifting myself up slightly, I turn my head to look at him. His eyes are shut and his head's tipped back towards the ceiling.

"Ry," I whisper. This brings his head down and his eyes open, making me gasp. They're so dark, they're almost black.

After staring at me for a couple of seconds, he moves to get off me. I shift slightly to my other side, and the first thing I see is the huge bulge in his jeans. My mouth waters instantly. How easy would it be to reach out to him? He's only a foot away from me. I raise my eyes until I meet his, and I watch as he runs them over my half-naked body once more before he announces he's going for a shower.

"I've probably used all the hot water."

"I won't need any," he says over his shoulder.

Ryan

I LET the cold water run over me, but it does very little to calm me down. The last hour has been both heaven and hell mixed into one. Having my hands all over Molly is something I've dreamt about for so long now, but the reality of it was so much better than I could have ever imagined. Her skin is silky soft and perfect. I love every mole and freckle that I committed to memory during her massage, but having her laid half-naked under me, so close yet so far away at the same time, was pure torture. All I wanted to do was flip her over and kiss her as if my life depended on it.

I've missed her so much over the last few weeks, and I know it's my own fault. I distanced myself from her after the night she stayed at Adam's. I just couldn't take it, watching her get close to him and their relationship develop. She's still seeing him, but she hasn't stayed out all night since.

I've been seeing Holly regularly, but only as friends. Neither of us is interested in anything happening. I'm sure Molly thinks we're dating, and I know I should have said something to correct her, but I just can't bring myself to do it when I know she's seeing Adam.

I take my painfully hard dick in my hand and start stroking it up and down. With thoughts of a half-naked Molly under me and the noises she was making ringing in my ears, it's not long before I feel the familiar warming sensation in my lower back before my balls draw up to my body and my dick twitches in my hand as I come. The relief is welcome, but it only takes the edge off. What I really need is Molly.

"I WAS JUST GOING to come and wake you. I've made breakfast," Molly says as I enter the living area the next morning.

I take in what she's wearing. My life is a little easier now that it's colder. Gone are the little shorts and vest tops in favour of jeans, long sleeved t-shirts, and jumpers. She still looks hot as fuck, though. This morning, she's wearing baggy jeans and a white, long sleeved t-shirt. It's simple but sexy. Her curves are more toned since she's been going to the dance classes, making my hands itch to touch her again. I shove them in my pockets to stop them moving of their own accord.

"How are you feeling?"

"Great—only a little sore. You've got magic fingers."

"You have no idea what I can do with these," I say suggestively, pulling my hands back out and wiggling my fingers at her. I watch her cheeks redden before she turns her attention back to the breakfast.

We spend the day together like we used to. Last night might have been all kinds of painful, but it seems we've had a breakthrough in our relationship, and we're almost back to normal. When I say normal, I don't mean pre-Molly-moving-in platonic friends. I mean post-Molly-moving-in, awkward and full of sexual tension and chemistry. Every time we touch, tingles shoot through my body. Every time she's close and I smell her, my dick twitches. Every time I look at her, I have an internal fight not to reach out and touch her.

Next Saturday is Shane and Chris' stag do, so we spend the day out shopping, trying to decide what the hell we wear to a 'pimps and hos' party. Normally, I hate shopping with women, but today is a different story. Molly's been trying on teeny tiny, slutty outfits. I tried to convince her she needed photographic evidence of each so she could make an informed decision but, for some reason, she didn't want me taking photos. Every time she came out of the dressing room, my dick got a little harder. She went through the entire range of outfits: schoolgirl, French maid, nurse, police officer, soldier. You name it, she tried it on. I was in my fucking element.

I knew my favourite as soon as she came out in it, but I refused to tell her which one it was. She reckons she could tell by my reaction, but is refusing to tell me which one she chose. She made me leave the shop before she bought it. I'm not sure if it will be a good thing or not if she gets the right one. Yes, she will look sexy as hell, and I'll enjoy it immensely, but she's going to the damn party with Adam, so it won't be me who gets to have my hands all over her. It's going to be a torturous night no matter what she's picked.

After getting a lot of stick from Molly for copping out, I decide to just wear my suit with a tank top under it. She did convince me to buy some ghastly chain to wear around my neck, and some god-awful, shiny shoes. God, this party's going to suck. I've got to dress like a dick while she walks around like sex on legs.

Once we have everything we need, we head to the supermarket. Molly insisted on cooking a meal for us, so I'm just letting her get on with it while I push the trolley around behind her, trying not to just stare at her arse.

We have a really good night together, chatting and laughing like we used to. It was almost like the last few weeks of awkwardness never happened. Molly talks about work and how busy they are. She tries to tell me about Jax and Abbi, but I put my fingers in my ears and make her stop. I'm still not totally sure about Jax, but I've come to realise over the past few weeks that he's a really good guy, and I think my problem with him is that I'm jealous of how much time he spends with Molly and how well they get on. If anything good can come out of him and my sister, it's that I know he isn't after Molly, which was my initial concern about him.

She only ever has good stuff to say about him, so I think I just need to get over myself and be nice.

Once we've eaten, we sit and watch a couple of films together. It doesn't escape my notice that the whole evening, Molly has tried to keep a bit of distance between us. She doesn't come and sit next to me like she used to. Whenever she needs something in the kitchen, she won't lean around me and just grab it; she asks me to move or get it for her. I'm undecided whether her keeping space between us is a good thing or not, but I guess she doesn't want a repeat of last night. As the credits roll up on the second film, Molly announces she's off to bed.

"I've got loads of marking to do tomorrow, so you probably won't see much of me," I say.

"Okay, I've got Jax coming over to work on something, anyway. I'll see you tomorrow. Night." She leans over and kisses my cheek.

"Goodnight, gorgeous." I don't know where it comes from, but I feel as shocked as Molly looks.

I wait for her to leave before tidying up and heading up to bed myself. I can't help but look to the other half of my bed and wish that she were there, not downstairs in her own.

Twenty

Molly

I quickly check my phone as I sit on the edge of the bed and notice a message from Emma. I still haven't heard from her since my birthday. I've been to two more Morrison Sunday dinners, but she didn't come to either. Ryan keeps asking if I've heard from her like he knows something I don't, but every time I question him, he just shrugs and passes it off.

Emma: *I'm sorry I haven't been around, but I'm ready to talk if you are.*

I just stare at my phone in shock.

Molly: *I can only do Thursday night, unless you just want to pop into the office when you're free?*

Emma: *I'll meet you in our usual seat at 5. See you there.*

What's she going to say? Come to think of it, what I am going to say to her? I'd be lying if I told her nothing has happened, or that I hadn't thought about something happening with Ryan. I have loved every minute of today with him, spending time together like we used to. I'm starting to wonder if maybe us giving something a go wouldn't be such a bad idea. I mean, I pushed so hard for us to just be friends that I basically lost him for the last few weeks. What if we were always meant to be together? Everything happens for a reason, right?

I WAKE up the next morning to my phone ringing. Picking it up, I see Jax's face smiling back at me.

"Morning," I croak out.

"Okay, that answers my question. I was going to see if you were up and wanted me already?"

I quickly glance at the time. "Jax, it's seven-thirty on a Sunday morning. Why on earth would you think I'd be up? And why are you up, for that matter?"

"Uh...I'm...sortofabitnervous," he says, so fast I almost miss it.

"Hang on—confident and cocky Jackson Parker is so nervous about posing for me that he couldn't sleep?"

"Don't rub it in or I'll cancel and you'll have to find some other mug to get naked."

"Fine, yeah, sorry. Well, I'm awake now if you want to head over. I'll get the garden set up."

"The garden?" he asks nervously. "It's freezing outside. You cannot be serious?" I can't help but laugh.

"You'll be on my bed, don't worry. Hey, I'll even put the heating up for you. Don't want you getting cold while you're naked!"

"Molly, I'm warning you."

"Sorry, you're just making it too easy. Get your arse over here now. I'll be ready."

I can't help but smile to myself as I hang up the phone.

Dragging my sleepy body from bed, I get myself dressed and ready for the day. I go for comfortable and grab a pair of lounge trousers and a tank top. I've just told Jax I'll put the heating up, and I don't want to melt. I pull my hair on top of my head in a messy bun and leave my face clear of make-up. I make my bed and grab the silk fabric I bought for this. I wanted something soft and feminine to contradict Jax's bad boy looks. I've cut a bit off the end so I can drape it over him to cover him up. Then, I shove some cushions under the fabric to give it some definition. I can scrunch it up where it's needed once he arrives and gets in place.

I'm just coming back down the stairs with a tray filled with tea, coffee, and pastries when I hear a quiet knock on the door.

When I open it, I'm shocked by what I see. Jax is standing there, looking back at me, but his face is a little green. He has his hands twisting around each other in front of him, and his foot is bouncing on the ground.

I open the door wider for him to enter before closing it behind him. He turns to look at me with the same scared, deer-in-headlights look. I move over to him and wrap my arms around his shoulders.

"Jax, don't look so scared. It's only me." I rub my hands up and down his back in comfort.

"I know, I just can't stop the nerves. I feel like I'm going to be sick."

"Yeah, you kind of look it. Come on, I've made coffee and breakfast. We don't have to get started straight away. Let's chill for a bit first."

"Yeah, sure...okay."

I grab his hand and pull him into my room. He sits on the side of the bed and sips his coffee. I can see how tense he is, but I don't really know what to do to help him other than get started so he can see it's really not that scary.

THIRTY MINUTES LATER, Jax is stood in front of me in his boxers. I've just finished faffing about with the silk sheet, and I'm ready for him to get into place.

"Right, you take this." I hand him the smaller bit of fabric. "I'll go in the bathroom while you get yourself sorted, then give me a shout."

"Do I really have to get naked? Can't I just chuck this fabric over me so it covers my boxers?" He looks at me with pleading eyes.

"No, I want as much on show as possible. Come on, Jax, it will be fine." I walk away from him into my bathroom and wait.

"You seriously owe me one for this," Jax mutters before I hear the bed move, but he doesn't say anything else.

"Are you done?"

"Ugh, yes. Let's get this over with, then never speak of it again."

I walk out and look over to him. His face is now bright red with embarrassment.

"Stop looking so worried. You look hot. Abbi is

going to love it, and I'm sure her reaction will make this worthwhile for you."

"You'd better be right." I go over to him to adjust the sheet around him. "Careful, pull that any lower and it may as well not be there."

"Chill out. Trust me when I say that I have no intention of seeing your dick, Jax." He still doesn't look convinced. "Trust me," I say again, hoping it might make him relax.

"You know, you could be wearing less," he teases, and I'm pleased when I see his usual cocky grin.

"Uh, no. If you ever take up life drawing, I'll repay the favour, but I need to focus on this."

"Spoil sport."

I just stick my tongue out at him.

The time seems to fly, and before I know it, hours have passed. After drifting off to sleep, Jax is starting to complain he's uncomfortable. I keep telling him to suck it up, but I know I'm being mean. I'm going to have to let him move soon.

I'm so engrossed in my sketch that I don't hear the footsteps coming towards my room. Jax obviously doesn't either, because both our heads shoot to the door when it opens.

"What the fuck?" Ryan asks, taking in the scene before him. "Dude, what the fuck are you doing?" I look over to Jax and see a mixture of shock and embarrassment wash over him.

"You said he was busy upstairs and wouldn't come down," Jax growls at me.

"I said he was busy. I didn't promise anything else." I shrug.

"Molly, why is Jax naked on your bed?"

"I've been doing a life drawing class. I've got to do a final piece, and Jax agreed to be my model."

"I got bullied into it. I didn't agree easily," Jax mutters under his breath.

"How did I not know you were doing a life drawing class?"

"You haven't really been about much. It wasn't a secret. I actually signed up because of that conversation we had on our holiday."

"I'll leave you to it, then," he says, walking away.

"Well, he looked royally pissed off," Jax says once Ryan is upstairs.

"He's trying to like you, Jax, but we do get caught in some compromising positions."

I sketch for another hour before I think I've finished. I've done it in charcoal so it's all black and white. I've managed to capture Jax's ink as I wanted it, and I'm really pleased with the result.

"Right, I'm done." I turn my sketch around to show him.

"Holy fuck, that's good."

"See, I told you to trust me. Right, I'm going to head upstairs so you can get dressed. Thank you so much for doing this for me."

"No problem. It wasn't as bad as I thought it would be, actually."

"Told you so."

The moment I open my bedroom door, the scent of home cooking fills my nose. My stomach rumbles, but when I get upstairs, I head straight for the kettle. I'm dying for a cup of tea. Ryan's sitting at the table, surrounded by folders he's marking, with a deep frown on his face.

"Hey, do you want a coffee?"

"No thanks," he says stroppily.

"Molly, I'm going to head off. I've taken a picture of your drawing and sent it to Abbi. She says she wants it framed," Jax says, shaking his head, a goofy smile appearing at the mention of her.

"No problem, I'll get it sorted for her after I've handed it in. Thanks again, Jax, I really appreciate you doing that for me. I'll see you in the morning."

"Yeah, bye. Bye, Ryan," he adds before he leaves the room, but Ryan just grunts in response.

I make my tea before heading over to him and leaning my hip against the table next to him. "What's wrong?"

"Nothing," he snaps.

"It doesn't look like nothing. Tell me."

"Him," he spits, gesturing to where Jax was just stood.

"What's he done now?"

"You asked him to model for you."

"Are you jealous? Did you want me to ask you?"

Ryan lowers his head as if embarrassed. "You know what? Yes, I am," he says, raising his determined eyes back to mine. "I thought I was your best friend. Not only did I not know you were taking this class, but you also didn't ask me. I hate that we've drifted apart. I miss you."

"You didn't seem too up for modelling when we spoke about it in the summer, so I didn't think you would do it, anyway."

"We were just messing about in the summer. I'd do anything for you, and you know that." He reaches his hand out and grabs my free one, caressing the back with his thumb and sending tingles up my arm—so much so that I have to put my tea down so I don't drop it. "I hate that you've been staring at him practically naked all morning."

Shit, he really is jealous. "It was art, Ry. I was looking at him like I would a bowl of fruit."

"That may be true, but it doesn't help me." He stands in front of me and cups my cheek with his other hand. "I don't want you having some other guy's body in your mind," he says quietly. "How would you feel if the situation was reversed?"

I don't even have to think about it; the thought alone makes me feel sick. "Uh..."

"Exactly." His hand slides around to the back of my head, his fingers thread into my hair, and he pulls me towards him. For a second, I think he's going to kiss me, but at the last minute, he presses his lips to my forehead.

His breath caresses my face and I can't help but close my eyes as I revel in his touch, his closeness.

We both stay still for a few seconds longer before he places his lips against mine for the briefest kiss, before stepping away and walking towards the kitchen.

I stand there and stare, completely confused. I snap myself out of it just in time to see him adjust himself as he comes to a stop in front of the fridge. He pulls out a bottle of wine and pours me a glass. I watch, mesmerised, as he slides it over the counter so it's in front of one of the stools at the breakfast bar, before placing his palms flat on the counter and leaning his hips forward to rest against the worktop.

"Come on, dinner will be ten minutes...I think," he says, nodding to my glass of wine.

I slowly walk over, taking my hoodie off as I go. After that little interaction, I most definitely don't need it on to keep me warm. I throw it on the sofa as I pass and sit myself up on the stool before taking a sip of my wine.

I look up when my skin begins to tingle under his stare. His eyes are glued to the bit of cleavage I've just revealed. His tongue sneaks out and runs over his bottom lip before he swallows, making the muscles in his neck ripple.

"Come and sit down."

"I...uh...I think I need to stay on this side of the

counter for a while." His eyes drop to his crotch briefly and I follow them, suddenly realising why he's over there.

"Oh. So, did you get all your work done?" I try to come up with something that might help break the tension surrounding us, but it has little effect.

We chat for a few more minutes before the buzzer goes off on the oven and Ryan dishes up our dinner. I hop off the stool and join him.

The lasagne is delicious, especially for a first attempt, but standing side by side as we clean up from dinner is torture. Every time I brush against him, sparks fly, and I know he's feeling the same because, every time it happens, his eyes snap to mine.

Once we've finished, I excuse myself so I can go downstairs and get changed into something more comfortable. I decide to have a quick shower before getting my PJs on and heading back upstairs.

Ryan is watching some nature programme when I join him on the sofa. He's sat in the middle seat of his corner sofa with his legs stretched out on one side, so I go to sit at the end closest to the kitchen.

"What are you doing?"

"Uh, sitting down?"

"Not over there, you're not. Come here."

I've just placed my glass on the coffee table when his hands firmly grip my hips and pull me backward until I'm sat right up against his side. He settles himself and puts his legs back up on the cushions before pulling me into him so my front is against his side. With one arm around my shoulder, he uses the other one to pull mine around his waist. I tense.

"Relax, Molls. Put your legs up, your head down, and just chill."

I do as he says, placing my legs alongside his and putting my head on his still naked chest. I try to relax but it's hard, pressed up against his smoking hot body. His hand strokes up and down my arm, trying to relax me, and it actually works. I let out a huge sigh and snuggle into him.

"That's it," he says, kissing the top of my head. "I've missed this." He holds me tighter and pulls the blanket over us.

Ryan

"Shit." It's still dark, so it can't be too late. We must have fallen asleep on the sofa after we got comfortable last night.

Molly's lying completely on top of me. How can I be that comfortable? Her arms are on my shoulders, her body flush against mine, and her legs are on either side of me. I shift slightly and realise that my dick is throbbing—not only because I've got Molly cuddled around me, but because her hot centre is right on top of it. The friction is so good that I want to keep moving against her, but I don't think she'll appreciate that wake-up call at the moment.

I stretch my arm out and grab my phone—it's nearly six o'clock—just before my alarm goes off. Putting it back down, I turn my attention to the beauty still fast asleep on top of me.

Leaning down, I press my lips against her hair. "Molly," I whisper. "It's time to wake up." I watch as her eyelids start to flutter. I continue running my hands up and down her back and I'm aware of the moment she's awake and realises what's happening because goosebumps cover her skin. I kiss her head again before I feel her move. Sitting up all of a sudden, my hands slip around so they're on her waist, and I manage to contain the growl that creeps up my throat as she moves against my dick.

"Shit, did we fall asleep? What time is it?" she asks sleepily, looking really cute. Her hair's a mess, her cheeks are pink, and her eyes look like she could be still asleep.

"Yeah, we did, but it's okay. It's not even six yet. Come lie back down. You looked pretty comfy."

She smiles at me, looking embarrassed, but I don't miss her checking out my chest and stomach. She suddenly tenses as she realises what she's straddling. "I...uh...should probably move."

I reach my hand up to her cheek to make her look at me. "Why? Come on, lie down." I give her waist a tug and, after a couple of seconds, she moves herself forward and lies back on my chest with her face turned to look at me.

She must notice me grimace as she moves over me again. "What's wrong? she asks, concerned.

"Nothing. It just, uh, felt good when you moved."

Her eyes widen slightly at this, but to my surprise she stays put. To my utter shock, she actually wiggles her arse, causing a moan to escape my mouth. She just looks at me and laughs.

"Someone's a little horny this morning, are they?"

"You've no idea."

Her arse moves slightly again, as her lips twitch teasingly. Leaning towards her, I whisper in her ear, "If you keep doing that, you could find yourself in a dangerous position." She just shrugs and holds me tighter. She shoves her face into my neck where I feel her breathe me in. It causes a huge smile to break across my face.

We continue to lie like that, just holding each other, until my phone alarm goes off. I move my arms from around Molly's back and place them on her waist to gently push her up.

"Nooooo," she complains as I move her. "Ring in sick and we can stay like this all day."

"As much as I'd love to do that, I really can't." She pouts at me and gives me her puppy dog eyes. "Trust me when I say there is nowhere in the entire world I'd rather be than under you right now, but I have to go to work."

I join her in sitting up, making us chest to chest again. I wrap my arms around her for one last squeeze and kiss her forehead, looking back at her as she stares into my eyes. My heart skips a beat when her eyes drop to focus on my mouth. My chest heaves as my heart rate picks up. She looks back up to my eyes before leaning forward and pressing her lips to mine.

Neither of us moves. We just sit there, enjoying the closeness. After a few more seconds, she pulls away and opens her eyes. I don't think I've ever seen them so full of hunger. I'm close to throwing caution to the wind and carrying her to my bed for the day so I can have my lips on every part of her body.

To my disappointment, she gets herself up and stretches before heading to the kitchen. "Coffee?"

"Please," I say, following her lead. I may have had the best night's sleep I've had for a long time, but the sofa wasn't the most comfortable of places.

After putting the kettle on, Molly turns around and leans back against the counter. "Ry?"

"Yeah?" I say on a yawn.

"Um...you might want to do something about that," she nods her head towards my very tented trousers, "before you go to school." She can't help herself and bursts into giggles.

The kettle whistles, and she turns around to make

our drinks. Walking up behind her, I cage her in with my arms and shove my crotch against her lower back.

"You could offer to help, you know," I say in a low voice, brushing my lips against the smooth skin of her neck.

She shoves her arse back into me. "Not this time, big boy. Go get ready, or you'll be late."

I'M TOTALLY DISTRACTED all day. All I can think about is how Molly's body lined up perfectly with mine. How she smelled when I held her close. How soft her lips were when they were on mine, and every other tiny thing that happened last night and this morning. We had a meeting after school, but I couldn't tell anyone what it was about.

I drive home with a smile on my face, thinking about what could be in store for us. Molly has a dance class tonight and I'm seriously hoping I get to give her another massage. I'm desperate to have my hands on her again.

I'm on the sofa watching TV when she comes in. She still looks a little hot and sweaty from her class, which has my dick twitching in my jeans. She shrugs her jacket off, revealing a tiny crop top sports bra thing that gives her awesome cleavage and shows off her toned stomach. She's also got skin-tight leggings on that coordinate with the top.

"Fucking hell, Molly. Are you trying to kill me?" I say, running my eyes up and down her curves.

"I'm hot, sweaty, and minging. Seriously?"

Does she have no idea what she looks like? My eyes are fixed on her as she walks over to the sink and pours a glass of water, giving me a great show of her arse. I can't help but groan at the sight. I walk up behind her and put my hands on her bare waist. She flinches slightly and stops drinking when I touch her.

"You really have no idea how fucking sexy you are, do you?" I can't help running my nose around the edge of her ear. When I breathe out, tiny goosebumps prick her skin. Good, she's just as affected as I am. Placing her glass on the worktop, she turns to look up at me.

"I'm going to have a bath, then I'll be up to make dinner, okay?"

"Sure," I say, following her out of the room.

"What are you doing?"

"Thought you might need a hand." I grin.

"No, I'm all good." She turns and playfully pushes my chest to send me back into the living room, but she's so small, I don't move at all. "I won't be long."

I kiss her forehead before she turns around, and I slap her arse as she walks away. She shakes her head as she descends the stairs.

It feels like the longest thirty minutes of my life before she comes back up. Knowing she's down there in a nice, hot, bubbly bath, naked, is pure hell.

When she appears, she is in her standard lounge

trousers, tank top, and zip-up hoodie. Molly looks hot all the time, but I think I prefer her like she is now: relaxed, comfortable, with her hair un-styled in a mess on top of her head, and no make-up on. She's just Molly like this.

My Molly.

She quickly whips up a chicken salad for us before bringing it over to me. She sits on the floor, her plate on the coffee table, and tucks in.

"Was your class good? You don't look to be in as much pain tonight."

"It actually felt easier after doing the more advanced class on Friday. We're thinking about stopping the Monday night one and just doing the harder one from now on."

"So, you're not going to be needing a massage tonight, then? I was looking forward to that."

"I bet you were, you dirty dog."

I just shrug at her and continue eating.

After we've cleared our plates, we stay where we are, chatting about our day and what we have planned this week. Molly has just explained that she's meeting Emma for the first time since her birthday on Thursday. I can't believe it's taken her this long to get in touch with Molly. She really did need some thinking time—I just hope she's come to the right conclusions. Molly tells me about having dinner with Adam tomorrow after work. I can't lie, I feel a little sick knowing she'll be spending the evening with him. After what's gone on between us the last couple of days, I sort of hoped he'd get the boot.

I notice Molly start to roll her shoulders while we're chatting. "You seizing up?" I ask, ever hopeful.

"Yeah, a little. It'll be okay, though."

She must be crazy if she thinks I'm going to pass on a chance to touch her. "Scoot over and come sit in between my legs."

I throw a cushion down for her to sit on and tap the edge of the sofa to encourage her over. It doesn't take much, because she's soon taking off her hoodie and moving towards me. My hands instantly go to her shoulders to try to relieve her discomfort.

"Ahh, that's good," she moans, turning me on more than I wish to admit.

I continue working her shoulders and the top of her back. But it's not long before I start to push my luck, and I slide the straps of her top to the edges of her shoulders. Molly doesn't seem fazed, so I continue. I move down the tops of her arms and then back up again. I keep repeating this, each time pushing her top a little farther down. I can't see the front of her, but it can't be covering too much right now.

Eventually, the pull of her body and her vanilla scent is too much, and I can't stop myself leaning forward and placing a soft kiss just beneath her ear. Her entire body shudders. She tilts her head to the side and I take that as permission to continue. I trail kisses down the side of her neck before following her hairline and working my way up the other side when she moves. Needing more, I sneak my tongue out and caress her skin with each kiss. She tastes incredible. My dick presses painfully against my jeans.

I need to focus. This is about Molly, not me. I need to take this slowly. If she's open to the idea of us, I don't want to rush her and scare her off.

My hands gently brush over her skin while my lips continue exploring her neck and ears. I slide them up her arms, down her back, and up again to her shoulders. When I bring my fingers to the top of her chest, she moans quietly, giving me the confidence to continue. I move them lower towards her breasts. I can feel how heavily she's breathing under my fingertips. As much as I want to continue, I know I can't. I move them back down her arms and follow their movement over her shoulders with my lips.

I feel her head move and, when I open my eyes, she's leaning it right back and is looking at me upside down. The passion in her eyes makes my already ragged breath catch in my throat.

Staring right down at her, I move my eyes from hers down to her mouth, then continue over her neck and down her chest. I was right; her top is barely covering her pebbled nipples. Her chest moves dramatically as her heart races beneath.

I lower my head and rub our noses together, making her lips twitch up at the sides. I need my lips on hers now. I move myself forward and press my mouth to hers. Fireworks fly through my body at the contact. Neither of us moves for a few seconds, but then I feel her tongue run across my lips. I open my them and touch my tongue against hers. Our kiss only lasts a short couple of seconds before she moves to the side.

Disappointment floods my body as she stands up, but, to my utter surprise, she turns around and straddles my lap. She stares deep into my eyes like they hold all the secrets in the world, and she places her hands on my cheeks before bringing her mouth back to mine. It takes me a couple of seconds to get into it because I'm so surprised, but when I do, I put my hands on her lower back and pull her flush against me while I tangle my tongue with hers, exploring her mouth.

It's a slow but passionate kiss, and it feels like it goes on forever, but when she eventually pulls back, I realise it wasn't long enough at all. I could live the rest of my life just kissing her and be happy. I look into her brown eyes. They're sparkling with happiness, excitement, and pure lust. She has a small, seductive smile on her lips that makes me want to have them on me again.

"Goodnight, Ryan," she whispers, kissing me quickly one last time and grabbing her top to stop it from completely falling. She stops at the doorway, turns, and gives me a heart-stopping smile before disappearing.

Twenty-one

Molly

I've been in bed for forty minutes and still can't wipe the smile off my face. That was, well, just wow. I don't even know how to describe it other than 'completely-out of-this-world-amazing'. The electric shocks are still going off around my body at the memory of his tongue moving against mine.

When Ryan's lips are on mine, I feel things I never have before. I feel beautiful, sexy, wanted, needed, safe, loved.

Loved.

Holy shit, I'm in love with Ryan. It hits me like an articulated lorry. Fuck.

My heart pounds in my chest as the realisation settles in. I'm in love with Ryan Evans. Not just a little in love—full-blown, earth-shatteringly in love with him.

Needless to say, I don't get much sleep. I spend most of the time tossing and turning, wondering what to do about my situation. Do I tell Ryan how I feel? Will he feel the same? What will everyone think? Will his parents accept me?

"Morning, gorgeous," Ryan says with a huge smile on his face as he walks over to me in the kitchen and wraps his arms around me, pulling me into a bone-crushing hug.

"Morning," I say, muffled by his chest.

"I've got to go. I've got a meeting before school." He presses a quick kiss on my lips before leaving the room. "I'll see you later."

Oh shit, I'd forgotten about my date with Adam. Fuck it, I can't just cancel last minute. He's been really good to me; he deserves better than that. "I, uh...I'm out tonight, remember?"

His face drops. "Oh, you're still going?" he asks, shaking his head. "Sorry, I just thought..." He runs his hands through his hair and turns away from me. "Have a good time." With that, he leaves.

"Fuck." I didn't mean to hurt him, but I need to

deal with Adam the right way. He's been a good friend to me.

———

"MOLLY, are you okay? You've been really distracted all night." Adam looks concerned.

"I've just got a headache. It's been a long day." It's not a lie. I've spent all day worrying about Ryan. I've texted him a couple of times but have only had short replies. He's really not happy with me.

I give Adam my apologies and make my way home not long after that conversation. He says goodbye but still has a concerned look on his face.

The house is in darkness when I get home, so I presume Ryan has already gone to bed—that, or he doesn't want to talk to me and is hiding in his room. I grab myself a glass of water and a couple of painkillers before getting myself ready for bed.

I'm lying in bed, feeling sorry for Adam and trying to figure out the best way to deal with this whole situation, when I hear my bedroom door open. I'm not surprised. I've noticed Ryan always comes down to check on me after I've been out with Adam.

I keep my eyes shut and stay still, but he doesn't leave. After a few seconds, I feel the bed dip as he sits behind me. He gently sweeps a piece of my hair out of my face and tucks it behind my ear. I have to really focus on my breathing not to allow my heart rate pick up, giving away that I'm awake.

He sits there a while longer, obviously watching me. I'm dying to open my eyes, but I have a pretty good idea of what will happen if I do, and I'm not in the right frame of mind to be doing anything right now.

The bed dips again and Ryan's lips touch my shoulder with a gentle kiss.

"Goodnight, sweet Molly. I love you," he whispers before getting up, walking out the door and up the stairs.

My eyes are as wide as they can be as soon as I know he can't see me.

***

"Hi, angel. How are you?" Susan asks as I sit myself on a bar stool in Cocoa's.

It's Thursday night, and I'm meant to be meeting Emma in ten minutes. I'm feeling really apprehensive.

I didn't see Ryan last night because I did a late shift here for Susan. He was already in bed when I got in. I didn't need to go and check because I could hear him snoring from the living room.

"I'm good. You?"

"Looking forward to Christmas and having Lilly and Dec back. Emma is still out of the house all the time, and we have no idea where she is or what she's doing."

"I'm meant to be meeting her here in a few minutes."

I watch Susan's eyebrows rise. She knows what's happened between us in the last few months, and she looks as worried as I feel.

"Oh, well, I hope it goes okay. I know you miss her." Just as she says that, Emma walks around the front of the shop and enters. "I'll get your coffees and bring them over," Susan says as she spots her daughter.

"Thank you." I head off towards our usual booth.

She sits down opposite me and we just stare at each other for a few seconds, as if we're both trying to form what we want to say.

"Emma, I..." I try to break the silence, but I still have no idea where to start. I'm more than grateful when she interrupts me.

"Molly, no. Please let me speak, I need to get this out." She lets out a big breath before looking down at her hands, rested on the table. She composes herself before she looks back up at me. "Molly, I'm really sorry. I've been completely out of order. I know it's not an excuse, but this year has been so hard for me. I feel like I've lost the other half of me, and my head's been a total mess. I mean, it still is, but I've been working through things and trying to get everything sorted. I know that I jumped off the deep end with my reaction to thinking there was something going on between you and Ryan, but I just felt like you'd forgotten about Hannah."

I go to say something, but she stops me.

"I know that's not true. I know that some of my feelings have been completely irrational. I know that you both loved her and have spent this year dealing with losing her in your own ways, the same as me. You both seemed to have dealt with it so well. I've been so jealous that, while you two got on with your lives, I've completely fallen apart.

"Molly, I miss you so much, and I'm sorry it's taken me this long to get everything together, but if you'll have me, I want to try to go back to how we used to be. Friends?"

I scoot out from my side of the booth to join Emma on her side. When I get there, I throw my arms around her shoulders, pulling her in for a hug.

"I'm sorry, too. I said some awful things I didn't mean. I know I should have come to talk to you about the situation with Ryan, but you've been so damn hard to get a hold of."

I feel her nod against my shoulder. When I pull back and look at her, tears are shining in her eyes, just like they are in mine.

"I'm in love with him, Emma," I blurt out. "Shit, I wasn't going to say that. It just fell out. I only figured this out the other night, and it's confusing the fuck out of me."

"Have you told him?"

"No, not yet."

"I think you should," she says with a knowing smile.

I go on to explain everything she's missed out on. I tell her about Adam, Holly, Jax, and Abbi. About Ryan avoiding me for what felt like forever, and then about this last week—leaving out any details she won't want to hear.

"Molly, I never in a million years thought I would ever say this, but I think you should go for it. Put the poor boy out of his misery, Molls."

We end up sitting there chatting for so long that Susan brings us some food over. It's almost nine before we say our goodbyes and head home.

***

RYAN'S CAR isn't outside the house when I arrive home. I'm really disappointed. After having my talk with Emma, I was ready to sit down with him and sort this out once and for all.

I put my stuff in my room before heading upstairs to get a drink and slob in front of the TV for a bit. As soon as I enter the kitchen area, I spot a piece of paper on the worktop.

Molly,
I've gone out with Holly. Don't worry about doing me any dinner.
See you later.
Ryan x

I JUST STAND THERE, staring at his handwriting. I feel like I've just been kicked in the stomach. Now, I understand his reaction to me saying that I was going out with Adam on Tuesday night. I'm sure the look on my face right now is similar to his that morning.

Deciding against sitting in front of the TV and waiting for him to come home, I take myself back downstairs for an early night—not that I'm going to be sleeping anytime soon.

I hear the front door open just before midnight, and his head pops around my door.

"Hey Molls, you awake?"

"Yeah, the front door woke me up," I lie. In reality, I was still thinking about him.

"Sorry, I'll leave you to sleep. Goodnight."

"Night."

I listen to him climb the stairs before going back to not sleeping.

AFTER A LONG DAY meeting with clients and many bad nights' sleep this week, I'm feeling ready to go home and spend my Friday evening snuggled down on the sofa with a glass of wine and a good chick flick. But I've just arrived for my pole dancing class with Megan to find out that tonight's class is a two-hour session because the instructor is on holiday next week. Everyone else looks excited by the prospect. I, on the other hand, want to find a corner to hide in and sleep.

"Come on, Molly, look at least a little enthusiastic."

I plaster a smile on my face and do my best to look like I'm enjoying myself for the next two hours.

By the time our instructor does our cooldown routine, I'm really ready to have a hot bath and hit my bed. Megan has to practically drag me from the club to my car. When we usually leave this place on a Monday night, it's pretty dead—in complete contrast to what is going on now. There are drunken men in all directions. Many are shouting and hollering our way. Clearly, they think we're dancers from the club, finishing our shift for the night. We put our heads down, along with the other ladies who leave at the same time as us, and head straight for our cars. I say goodbye to Megan and make quick work of getting home.

I have my music on, hot bath running with bubbles so high they're spilling down the sides, and a glass of wine on the side waiting for me.

I just slip my weary body into the hot, soothing water when a loud bang rattles the house. I sit up so fast the water sloshes all over the floor. My heart thunders in my chest as I wait for something else to happen.

"Molly!" Ryan hollers from the hallway.

"In here," I shout back, but not at the same crazy volume.

The bathroom door flies open with such force, I

think it's going to come off the hinges. Ryan looks seriously pissed off. I stare at him in shock.

"What the fuck do you think you're doing, Molly? Why the fuck did you ever think that was a good idea? I mean, for fuck's sake, all those slime balls looking at you. You promised me you'd changed, that you weren't going to be like that anymore. First, you go off and sleep with Adam, and now I find out you've been doing this. What the fuck, Molly? You'd better have some good fucking reasons."

I watch as he rants and throws random questions at me. His hands have been through his hair so many times I've lost count.

"Ryan, calm the fuck down. You're going to have to explain what you're going on about. I'm a little confused."

"I'm fucking livid. I'm so motherfucking angry that you would put yourself in that position."

"I don't know what you are talking about." Then, the penny drops. "Wait. You saw me tonight, didn't you?"

"Yes, I fucking saw you. Care to explain why I saw you leaving a sleazy strip club in your skimpy clothes, looking exhausted? Why the fuck would you want to do that? It's not like you need the money."

"You think I was working at the strip club?" I can't help but laugh at this, but the murderous look on Ryan's face soon stops me.

"Well, what the fuck else would you be doing there

on a Friday night? Is that what you've been doing when you said you were going to dance classes? Dancing for arseholes for money?"

"Ry, seriously, calm down. It's not what it looks like. Come here." I put my hand out for him. He steps forward begrudgingly and takes my hand in his. "I am not dancing for scumbags for money, and I do not work at the strip club."

"What have you been doing, then?" he asks, looking thoroughly confused. It's only now he's calmed down a bit that I can tell he's been drinking.

"The club has dance studios at the back. I guess the dancers train there and stuff, but they also rent them out. Megan and I have been going to pole dancing lessons."

"Pole dancing lessons? Why the hell didn't you tell me?" Now, he just looks hurt.

"It was Megan's idea. Apparently, it's one of James' fantasies for her to pole dance for him. She swore me to secrecy because she didn't want him finding out and ruining the surprise."

I watch Ryan as he takes this on board. He drops to his knees in front of me and grabs my other hand.

"I'm sorry, Molly. I just jumped to conclusions. I saw you leaving and there were guys shouting stuff, and I just thought... I just saw red, the thought of guys staring at your body like that. I'm so sorry."

I pull my hand from his and cup his cheek, stroking my thumb gently over his cheekbone. "It's okay. I never thought someone would see us and think that. I should have told you. I'm sorry, too."

I move my hand to the back of his head and pull his lips to mine. He only stays there for a couple of seconds before he pulls away and stands up. "What are you do —" My eyes widen in shock. "Oh."

He pulls his t-shirt over his head before making quick work of the button and zip at his waist. He takes his shoes and socks off, then steps out of his jeans. I can't help my eyes roaming over his perfect body. He's barely touched me but still, his boxers are tented. His hands go to the waistband and I suddenly don't know where to look. He bends slightly and his boxers slide down his legs before he steps out of them. He snaps his eyes to mine. "It's okay, Molls. It's all yours."

I can't help the blush that floods my cheeks at his words. He moves towards me and I break my eye contact and run them down his fine body. My breath catches in my throat as I follow his happy trail to his fully erect cock. I swallow hard and lick my lips. I don't realise I'm doing it until Ryan speaks. "Like what you see, then?" He has such a cocky grin on his face.

"Uh huh," is all I can get out as he steps into the bath with me. The muscles in his arms bulge as he lowers himself and slides his legs along mine.

I know I'm staring at him with my mouth open, but I can't help it. When his feet hit my arse, I snap out of my daze. "Please join me, why don't you?" I say, laughing.

"Sorry, but I needed to be close to you. You have no idea how I felt when I thought you were dancing at that club." He places his hands on my shins and slowly rubs up and down.

"I'm sorry I didn't tell you. I should have." I smile at him, feeling comforted by his need to protect me. Maybe I should be pissed that he even thought I could have been a stripper, but the knowledge of how much it angered him to think of other guys looking at me pushes that away.

"Come here." He puts his arms up and slides over to one side of the bath. "I'll keep my hands to myself, I promise."

Ryan

WHY THE HELL did I say that? There's no way that will be possible if she slides her wet, naked body up against mine. This has got to be the stupidest thing I have ever done.

After looking a little reluctant, Molly slides herself next to me. The feel of her naked skin gliding against mine feels incredible. Tingles shoot around my body from the amount of skin-to-skin contact I have with her. When she throws one leg over mine and puts her arm around my waist, I have to shut my eyes and concentrate on breathing for a few seconds. I'm so worked up that if she so much as touches my dick, I'm afraid I'll go off like a rocket.

"Are you okay?" Molly asks. When I open my eyes and glance down at her, she has a confused look on her face.

"Yeah, it's just a bit much, you know? I needed a few seconds to pull myself together."

"I know what you mean. This is crazy, but I sort of like it."

"Really?"

"Yeah. A lot, actually," she says, squeezing me a little tighter against her. I can feel all the soft curves of her body against mine, and it's driving me crazy. "I know you said you'd keep your hands to yourself, but you can hold me."

She tilts her head up from where it's resting on my chest, and I see a little cheeky smile playing on her lips. I wrap my arm around her, gripping to her hip with my hand and holding her tight.

We lie like that for the longest time, silent and completely lost in our thoughts, but suddenly I feel Molly tense up next to me.

"What's wrong?"

"Something you said when you came in."

"Which bit?"

"You said I'd slept with Adam. I haven't."

"But you went home with him that night we went out with Abbi and Jax. I watched you two go at it on the dance floor, then you dragged him off like you wanted to eat him alive."

"That was only encouraged by you dancing with Holly. It was just innocent dancing until you two appeared and I had to watch her grind herself against you."

"You did that because of me."

"Yes." She looks embarrassed.

"Well, I was only dancing with Holly because I was watching you two. I was quite set on going to the bar and getting shitfaced until she stopped me and suggested I give you a show in return."

"Whoa, hang on. Holly actually suggested you dance with her? To what? Make me jealous?"

"Yeah, something like that. Apparently, she could tell how miserable I was. I can't believe I'm admitting all this; I feel like a right pussy. I didn't bring her home. She actually had to bring me home because I got so smashed after you left with Adam. All I could picture was you and him, and I needed to drown it out."

Molly slowly props herself up on her arm so she can look at me. "So, you didn't sleep with her?"

"No. What happened that night? You didn't come home."

"When we got in his flat, things did get a little heated, but it just wasn't right. We ended up just going to sleep." She lets out a deep sigh while she contemplates her words. "He wasn't who I wanted him to be. Every time he spoke, touched me, kissed me, it just wasn't right. He wasn't who was in my head."

I have to do it. I have to ask. "Who *was* in your head?"

Her eyes snap straight up to mine. "You."

My heart's beating so fast after hearing that one word, it feels like it's about to break through my chest. I pull her tight with the arm I still have around her so that she falls onto my chest, and I kiss her like she's my lifeline. Having her breasts pressed against my chest while her lips are on mine is the best feeling ever. I grab on to her arse to encourage her to straddle me. When she does, my dick lines right up with her, and I can't help but grind against her. The feeling is out of this world.

"Ry," she says into my mouth, but I can't pull away yet. I've wanted her for so long.

Eventually, she pulls her lips away from me, but I go for her neck instead, needing to have my lips on her.

"Ry, I know what I just said, but it doesn't mean it's going to be happening anytime soon."

"That's fine, as long as I can do this."

I continue kissing and sucking on her neck whilst running my hands from her knees up the backs of her thighs, over her arse, then up her back. I continue to gently rub myself against her. I know she's ready for it, because the heat coming from her is unbelievable.

She pulls herself away from me so she's sitting. Unfortunately, there are so many bubbles in here that I still don't get a look at her tits. I guess good things are worth waiting for. She puts her hands on my chest and looks down at me with heated eyes.

"I'm not going to lie, I've thought and dreamt about this so many times over the last couple of months that I've lost count, but I don't want to rush this. I've spent so long convincing myself that this, us, is a bad idea, that I want to enjoy the build-up. I don't want to jump in headfirst. Does that make any sense?"

"Yes. I'm happy, as long as I know you're mine."

Molly smiles down at me before settling back down, cuddled against my side.

We both fall silent again.

"Did you end up seeing Emma yesterday?"

"Yeah, I did. We actually spent all night chatting and catching up. It was really nice."

"What did she have to say about this?" I ask, gesturing between us.

"She said the same thing she told you in the summer, apparently."

"One day soon, Molly, I will tell you exactly what I told Emma that day, but only when it's the perfect time." She flashes me a dazzling smile and nods at me. "Shall we get out? The water's cold, and it's probably getting late. We've got the stag do tomorrow, so we're going to need our sleep."

I give her a quick kiss on the lips before jumping out and grabbing a towel. I turn back to look at her before I wrap it around my waist and see her eyes are fixed on my arse.

"Molly, if you keep looking at me like that, neither of us is going to leave this house ever again."

"Sorry," she says, shaking her head. "I can't help it. Plus, I know for a fact that if you'd just watched me jump out of the bath and walk naked to the towels, you would be looking at me in exactly the same way."

She's got me there. I would probably be worse, if I'm honest.

"Here," I say, holding open a large towel I can wrap her in. She just shakes her head at me. "What?"

"Shut your eyes."

"Are you serious?"

"Deadly. I said we were taking this slow."

"Okay, fine." I shut my eyes and hold the towel up again.

I hear the water slosh before she presses against the towel in my hands. I wrap it around her body, then open my eyes and watch as she adjusts it and tucks it in place. She looks up at me with a smile before walking out of the bathroom. I go over and let the water out, turn the music off, and grab her glass of wine, still three quarters full. I think that was forgotten when I suddenly stormed in.

When I enter her bedroom, she's propped up against her headboard, still wrapped in her fluffy towel. I walk straight over to the other side of the bed, put her glass down, and lie next to her, pulling her to me and placing my lips back where they belong: on hers.

I move away from her when things start to get heated again. What I said in the bath was true. I will wait forever, as long as I have her in my arms and against my lips. I roll onto my back and pull her so she's once again tucked into my side. She places her head on my chest, right above my heart.

Twenty-two

Molly

I wake up feeling hot and sticky. My whole body is plastered against Ryan.

I'm completely stark naked and stuck to a similarly naked Ryan. I feel myself tense, my heart rate increase, and I can't help but smile. I've dreamt of waking up like this many times, and now it's actually happening.

I feel Ryan's arm tighten around me, so I tilt my head up to look at him. His eyes are shining bright and he has a smile on his face to rival mine.

"Morning. You look happy to see me," I say, smiling at him.

"You have no idea how much. Especially since you're wrapped around me naked."

"Yeah, about that..."

"Don't look at me. As much as I wanted to rip that towel off your body, I didn't. I only just woke up myself. You must have done it in your sleep."

"What about yours?"

"It must have come undone, because I'm still lying on it."

I run my hand down his stomach and feel his muscles clench as my hand travels lower. Much to his disappointment, I move it to the side and over his hip to feel his towel.

"Oh yeah," I say with a smirk.

"You're going to be the death of me, woman," he says, scowling. I can't help but laugh at him. "Do you want tea?"

"Always."

"Okay, I'll go make it if you promise to still be naked in this bed when I get back."

I pretend to think about it for a few seconds before agreeing. I watch as Ryan drags his sexy body out of my bed, and I can't pull my gaze away from his perfect arse as he walks into my bathroom. After a couple of minutes, he returns, wearing his boxers and clearly showing me how much he loves the idea of me naked in bed.

"Hey, if I've got to be naked, so do you."

"I promise to take them off when I come back, but

you know what the woman next door is like for nosing in. The only eyes I want on my naked arse are yours, Miss Molly."

I watch him walk out, then lie back in the bed smiling, listening to him pottering around upstairs.

Before long, he's back, carrying two mugs. He places them on the bedside table before taking his boxers off as promised and slipping back into bed. He pulls the duvet over him, but only so it just covers his lap, leaving his top half uncovered for me to drool over.

He looks at me looking at him. "I love your body," I tell him. I trace my finger between his pecs and over his six pack before running it over his happy trail and off to the side. I know I'm teasing him, but I just can't help myself.

"So, you get to do that, but I have to wait to see your fit-as-fuck body. Explain to me how that's fair."

"Hey, you decided to get your kit off in front of me; I didn't make you."

"It's worth it to watch you drool over me," he says with a knowing wink.

I just shrug him off while I sit myself up against the headboard and tuck the duvet under my arms to keep me covered. I know it's irrational, but I don't want all the mystery gone after only one day.

We spend hours sat in bed, chatting. Ryan makes regular trips to the kitchen for more drinks and food. He regularly tries lifting the duvet from me while I'm not paying attention, but he only ever gets a peek at my side or my leg. Even that has him licking his lips and swallowing hard. I can only imagine how he'll react when I give in. He makes me feel more beautiful and sexy than I have in my whole life. I feel like I'm on Cloud Nine right now.

Ryan's happy and playful mood falters a little when I tell him I think we should still go to the party tonight as planned, with Adam and Holly. I also watch his face drop when I explain that I want to keep what is going on between us just between us for a while. I know people are going to judge us, and I want to make sure we're solid before we get hit with any scrutiny. Although Ryan isn't happy about either suggestion, I know he understands. Both Adam and Holly were invited to this party weeks ago, and both have outfits ready. Plus, I need to sit down with Adam and explain, and a stag do isn't the time for that.

Before we know it, it's time to get ready for the party. I usher Ryan out of my room so I can do it alone. I want to surprise him with my outfit.

I'VE JUST HEARD the taxi pull up outside five minutes early, so I do some final touch-ups to my hair and makeup before slipping my shoes on.

"Molls, the taxi's here. Are you ready?" Ryan shouts as he comes down the stairs.

"Yes, two seconds." I do one last check in the mirror

before turning around, grabbing my bag and pulling the door open.

"Oh, holy mother of God. You cannot go out like that. I'll end up punching any guy who happens to look in your general direction."

I just smile at him. "I got the right one, then?" I knew instantly that the policewoman outfit was his favourite.

It's a navy blue halter neck, cut quite low. It has a full skirt with lace petticoat making it puff out, with handcuffs hanging off the belt, a badge on my left breast, and a hat. I've paired it with a pair of black lace-topped hold ups and high black platform heels that have silver chains on the back to match my handcuffs. Even I thought I looked pretty hot when I looked in the mirror.

"Yeah, apparently so—although I'm thinking you shouldn't be allowed out wearing it. It should be banned, for use in the bedroom only."

"Oh, for goodness sake, Ry, everyone there will be dressed in something like this. No one will even look twice."

I give him a onceover. He looks truly edible in his sharp black suit. Even the chain and shiny shoes he complained about look great. I don't think he'll be the only one with some jealousy issues tonight. I just know the amount of attention he's going to receive from looking like that.

"Hmm," he says as he watches me grab my coat.

Luckily, it's long enough to cover everything so I won't look too out of place before we get to the club. Adam and Holly are meeting us there as they both live in the city.

"Come on." I grab Ryan's hand and pull him towards the front door. He does not look happy about this at all.

"I'm not going to be able to do anything I want to do to you tonight, because you're going with your 'date'." He sulks next to me in the car.

"That may be true, but you'll be the one I go home with at the end of the night and, if you're a good boy, I might even let you sleep in my bed again."

That perks him up a little. He turns his head and leans in to me. "Naked?" he whispers in my ear, his breath giving me goosebumps.

"Maybe."

I hear him groan next to me.

Before long, we're pulling up outside the club. Ryan pays the driver and we both get out. As soon as we enter the foyer, I spot Adam and Holly talking together in the corner. They must recognise each other from the night at the club.

"Here she is," Adam says as he spots me. He comes racing over to me and goes to give me a kiss, but I quickly turn my head so his lips land on my cheek. I know Ryan's watching, his eyes are burning into the back of my head. Maybe this is going to be harder than I thought. I look over to see Holly watching us, too. Has he already told her something's happened between us? From the way she's scowling at me, I'd say yes.

The four of us walk over to check our coats in. Holly removes hers first to reveal a sexy little nurse outfit. To my surprise, Adam whistles next to me. Holly looks over her shoulder and gives him a sexy little smile. He then looks at me and raises an eyebrow. I feel less confident all of a sudden about showing off the outfit I know Ryan loves so much. I take a deep breath and pull it off my shoulders.

"Fuck," Adam says, looking me up and down.

I fidget, feeling slightly uncomfortable with his perusal. I glance over to Ryan to see his jaw set, the muscle in his neck pulsing, and his fists clenched tightly at his sides. I watch as Holly strokes his arm gently, trying to get him to calm down.

Once I've handed my coat over, I see Adam's hand move like he's going to grab mine, so I quickly lift my arm and scratch my nose. The only man I want touching me from now on is Ryan, so until I can talk to Adam, I'm just going to have to avoid it. He moves his hand to the small of my back instead and guides me to the stairs to join Shane, Chris, and the rest of their guests. Ryan and Holly follow. I can only imagine the look on his face.

Not long after we arrive, they announce it's time for dinner. There are loads of round tables filling the room. Each one has red and black feathers coming out of vases in the centre. It all looks a little burlesque, sexual, and seductive. Those are the last feelings I need to be having with Ryan and my date at the same party.

We find our table and take our seats. I'm sat with Ryan to my left and Adam to my right. This should be interesting.

THE DINNER IS bearable at best. The food and wine are amazing; Shane and Chris did a good job choosing the catering. They look so happy. Every time I glance over to them, they're either staring at each other lovingly or laughing at something the other said. It's so lovely to see.

What isn't so good is Adam constantly trying to spark up a conversation with me. It would be fine, as I've always found him easy to talk to, but under the table, Ryan keeps touching me up. It makes my conversation with Adam a challenge, especially every time his hand gets high enough to touch the edge of my knickers. I gently keep slapping his hand away, but he just keeps putting it back, while his cheeky smirk stays on his lips.

Just before the dessert plates are taken away, Shane and Chris both stand up and clear their throats.

"We know it's not traditional to do speeches at a stag do—hell, it's not traditional to do a joint stag, either, so I don't know what I'm worrying about." People laugh a little. "But we just wanted to say thank you to all of you that could come out, get dressed up, and celebrate our upcoming wedding. We also just wanted to take a minute to think of those who couldn't be here tonight. Just because they aren't in the room, doesn't mean they aren't always in our hearts."

I look at Ryan and he swallows hard. We both know that Hannah would have been here with us right now. She was meant to be a groomsmaid alongside me. I lift my hand up and squeeze his shoulder. He looks over at me and quirks the corner of his mouth up.

"You okay?" I whisper. He nods gently, then looks down.

Emma was also meant to be here, but she decided against it. Even though she told me she was trying to get back to a normal life, she still isn't getting involved with much.

"Now, we know she's going to hate us for doing this without warning her, but what would be the fun in that? Before the drinking and dancing commences, we would like to invite our head groomsmaid to say a few words about how awesome we are." Everyone laughs and a handful of people look at me. *Shit.* "Molly, come on. You're not usually one to be shy!"

I stand slowly, pushing Ryan's hand off my thigh as I go. "Uh...yeah, thanks for this, guys. Um...okay...I just want to say that you two are the most perfect couple I know. From the moment you met, all either of you could see was each other. The love you share is obvious to all of us here for you tonight, and for everyone here who hasn't found that kind of love yet." I look straight into Ryan's eyes as I say this. "You're proof that real love is out there. I hope you have a wonderful night and let the celebrations continue well into your married life." I raise my glass. "To Shane and Chris."

Everyone around me does the same, and I can't help but smile as they lean into each other and go at it for a couple of minutes—too long, considering they're being watched by everyone in the room.

"Come on, it's not your wedding night yet. We've got some dancing to do first," I say, making them pull away from each other.

Shane looks up at me and mouths his thanks. "Right, everyone, let's party."

People start to get up from their tables and follow the happy couple into the bar area and the adjoining room where the music has just started up.

"I just need to go to the toilet," I say to my group. "If you go to the bar, could I have a glass of wine, please?"

"I'll come with you. Same for me, please, boys," Holly says, getting up and walking out with me.

Once we're out of view, she puts her hand on my arm to draw my attention. "Has something happened with Ryan? He is even more distracted by you than usual."

I can't help the smile that breaks out across my face.

"Oh my God, it has. Are you together? Why are you here with Adam?"

I try to work out which question to answer first.

"I guess we're together. I'm with Adam because I'd invited him and didn't want to cancel at the last minute. He's been really good to me, and I want to end it with him the right way."

"Well, you might want to be quick about it."

I start walking towards the toilets before answering. "I know, I know. I don't want anything to ruin the guys' night. I intend on doing it first thing in the morning."

"You think tonight is going to go smoothly enough that he won't know?" Holly asks skeptically.

"I hope so."

We both do what we've got to do, then go and find the boys at the bar. They're standing next to each other, but their body language shows their displeasure. "Oh God," I groan.

"It's starting already. Molly, you're going to have to just do it." I let out a big sigh before joining the boys, grabbing my wine and gulping half of it down.

"Take it easy, Molly. The night's still young," Adam says with a suggestive look on his face. Holly and Ryan snap their heads to me.

Everyone around us is starting to get a little buzzed, and they look to be having a better time than we are. We, on the other hand, are stood with an uncomfortable tension around us. Even people that come over to chat don't stay long.

"Come on, let's go and dance," Adam says with a smile.

If he's hoping for a repeat of the club, then he's going to be bitterly disappointed. I don't want to touch him, let alone grind myself against him.

I finish off my drink before getting dragged to the dance floor. Luckily, the songs are fast, and it's easy to just dance by myself in front of him. The whole time, I can feel Ryan's eyes on me from the bar. Every time I look up, I can see him getting angrier and angrier.

Eventually, the song changes to something with a slower beat. The couples around me get close and dance together. I look up to see Ryan shaking his head at me in warning. Adam reaches out and pulls my body to his, but as soon as I get close enough that he can hear me, I tell him I need to use the toilet.

I let him lead me off the dance floor before escaping to the ladies' room. I lock myself in one of the cubicles, put the lid down, and just sit there.

What the fuck am I doing?

Eventually, I get up and go wash my hands to give myself something to do to waste more time.

When I open the door to the ladies' room, Adam is waiting outside for me. He grabs my hand and pulls me around the corner, out of sight.

"What's up with you tonight? It's like you don't even want to be here. Have I done something to upset you?"

"I'm sorry, I'm just not feeling right."

"Okay. Do you want me to take you home?"

"No, I need to be here for Shane and Chris. I can't just leave."

"Well then, can you at least try to look like you're enjoying yourself?"

"I'm sorry, I jus—" I get interrupted as Adam crashes his lips to mine, taking advantage of my open mouth. I shut my eyes for a second as my slightly drunk brain tries to figure out what the hell is happening.

When I open them, Adam is still attached to my lips, but the only thing I see is Ryan stood behind him, looking mortified. I lift my hands to Adam's chest and push as hard as I can. "Adam, stop," I mumble into his mouth. I eventually manage to push him off.

"Ryan!" I shout. But when I look up, he's gone. I can't help but start to panic. "Ryan!" I shout again, moving so I can look down the hall, but it's empty. *Fuck.*

"Has it always been him, Molly?" I turn to see a very sad looking Adam. "I guess I should have seen this coming. You're always talking about him, checking up on him. I don't know why it didn't register earlier, but you've been practically eye-fucking him all night."

"Adam, I'm so sorry. It just happened. He's been my friend for so long, I didn't really expect it."

"How long?"

I stare at him, silent.

"How long has it been going on, Molly?"

"A couple of days. I was going to tell you tomorrow."

"And you thought coming with me tonight would be okay? You thought that you would be able to act normal while your 'boyfriend' watched?"

"I know it was stupid. I realised that as soon as we arrived."

"Well, it's too late now. I suggest you go find him and sort it out. I always knew I liked you more than you liked me. I just hoped I would grow on you."

"I'm so sorry, Adam." I lean forward and kiss his cheek.

"Go. Be happy. I had fun with you, Molly. Just so you know."

"I did, too. I'm sorry." With that said, I leave him in the hall and jog back to the party.

I spot Holly standing at the bar, but she's alone. "Where is he?" I half shout at her. The panic is obvious in my tone.

"He just left, Molly. He came to tell me he had to go, then he ran out of here like a bat out of Hell."

I grab my phone, find a number for a taxi firm, and put it to my ear. I turn back to wave at Holly just as Adam approaches her. He frowns at me but quickly wipes it off his face as he looks down and smiles at Holly.

The wait for my taxi feels like it takes forever. It's fucking freezing outside, and although I remembered to get my coat, it's not like I'm wearing a lot. After what seems like hours, my taxi arrives and I shout my address at the driver.

The journey takes forever. As soon as he pulls up outside our house, I throw money at him and run to the front door. I'm in such a rush, I drop my key twice before I get it in the lock.

I know he won't be in there, but I quickly check my room first, throwing my bag on the bed and ripping my shoes off my feet before dropping them on the floor. I take off running up the stairs and check the living area—also empty. He must be in his bedroom. I again run up the stairs as fast as my legs will carry me, open his bedroom door, and fly into the room. It's empty, but there's light coming from the half open ensuite. I don't think twice before heading over and walking in.

What I find stops me in my tracks as soon as I enter the room. Ryan is stood under the shower, leaning forward with his palms flat on the tiles and his head hung low between them. He looks completely lost.

I caused that. Pain rips through me at the thought.

I move closer to him and, as if he can sense me behind him, he lifts his head slightly and looks at me. My breath catches in my throat at the look in his empty eyes.

I have to go to him. I need to be close to him.

I start unbuttoning my coat and slide it off my arms, letting it hit the floor. Still, Ryan watches me. I reach behind me, unzip my dress and let it join my coat, keeping eye contact with him the whole time. I slide my holdups down my thighs and off my legs before once again reaching behind to unsnap my bra. It hits the floor next to my dress, quickly followed by my knickers.

I walk up behind him and place my hands on his chest, encouraging him to stand straight. I then walk around him so I can look into his eyes. What I see in them scares the shit out of me.

They're cold.

What if he refuses to listen to me, let alone believe what I'm about to tell him?

Find out what the future has in store for Molly and Ryan in part two, now available...

Acknowledgements

It's been over three years since I first hit publish on this, my very first book. Reading back through it now, it feels like it was a lifetime ago. So much has changed in that time, but I wouldn't want it any other way.

Not only have I learnt a huge amount about this industry, but I've made some incredible friends along the way. It's really been quite an incredible journey. I never expected to write a book, but as I sit here now, I've got over twenty with my name on them. It blows my mind that my life took this turn, but I'm so grateful that it did because not only do I get to spend my days doing something I love, I also get to be at home with my daughter and watch her grow every single day.

Molly and Ryan changed my life, and I will forever be grateful that they appeared in my dream one night. When I originally started to write their story, I didn't tell anyone—bar my husband, who thought I'd lost my mind. But it wasn't until an unexpected meeting with a carer who was looking after my mum at the time that I found the confidence to admit what I was doing. If it weren't for my mum and the long and painful journey we experienced together, I never would have met Michelle, who is still with me every step of the way today. They say everything happens for a reason, and I truly believe that. I know I wouldn't be here now if I'd never met her.

So, I need to say a huge thank you to my mum, who sadly didn't have a clue about any of this, but as I sat next to her hospital bed, typing, she gave me the strength and determination to chase my dream. I know she is up there supporting me every step of the way.

To Michelle, meeting you totally changed my life, and I can't imagine it any other way now. So, thank you for turning up that day, corrupting me, and introducing me to a world I didn't know existed.

To my husband, who allowed me to chase my crazy dream. I don't think he really expected what was to come, or how many books I would write, but he's supported me the whole way. And now my daughter, too. When I wrote this, I had no idea that I was going to be a mum fairly soon, but she's been the best thing to ever happen to me. She inspires me daily, and I hope that as she grows and sees me doing something that I love, I'll inspire her to do the same.

Evelyn, this book must almost be as big a part of

your life as it is mine. I can't thank you enough for all the hours you've put in, polishing it up and making it as perfect as possible. I'll be the first to admit that I didn't know what I was doing when I embarked on this journey with just a crazy idea in my head, and I'm sure you'll quickly agree with me after the amount of editing you've done!

And to you, for taking a chance on me, and Molly and Ryan. You've no idea how much it means to me that you've got this far. I hope you pick up many more of my books and I allow you to escape reality with some hot, sexy men and sassy women.

Until next time,

Tracy xo

About
Tracy Lorraine

Tracy Lorraine is a M/F and M/M contemporary romance author. Tracy has just turned thirty and lives in a cute Cotswold village in England with her husband, baby girl and lovable but slightly crazy dog. Having always been a bookaholic with her head stuck in her Kindle, Tracy decided to try her hand at a story idea she dreamt up and hasn't looked back since.

Be the first to find out about new releases and offers. Sign up to my newsletter here.

If you want to know what I'm up to and see teasers and snippets of what I'm working on, then you need to be in my Facebook group. Join Tracy's Angels here.

Keep up to date with Tracy's books at

www.tracylorraine.com

Falling Series

Chasing Series

Chasing Logan

Ruined Series

Ruined Plans #1

Ruined by Lies #2

Ruined Promises #3

Never Forget Series

Never Forget Him #1

Never Forget Us #2

Everywhere & Nowhere #3

The Cocktail Girls

His Manhattan

Her Kensington

The Halloween Honeys

His Sorority Sweetheart

Second Helpings

Cheeky Trifle

Santa's Coming

Santa's Naughty Elf

Resolution Pact

Resolution: Exposure

Matchmaker

Dear All Star Player

Ireland Forever

Forever Ruined (A Ruined series spin off)

Mr. Billionaire

Mr. Silver

Spring Breakers

Spring Break Secret Baby